The Ante-Room

The Ante-Room

Kate O'Brien

ARLEN
HOUSE
The Women's Press

47898

ISBN 0 905223 22 5

To Nance and Stephen O'Mara under whose kind roof
the greater part of this book was written, I dedicate it
with my love and gratitude

Design Bill Murphy

Printed by Cahill Printers Limited, Dublin 3
Published by Arlen House, The Women's Press
P.O. Box 1113, Baldoyle, Dublin 13, Ireland

Contents

Preface
by Eavan Boland

I like to think that the ante-room still exists: a small room with gracious, potent proportions in a white house like the Roseholm of this book. Those houses, those rooms are part of a poignant Irish past and that past is part of this story.

In a real sense, of course, the ante-room does exist. It is part of Kate O'Brien's world. She made of it, in this novel, an emblem of the light and the dark of a class she loved, their complacent grace, their spiritual clumsiness. This was her second novel and her own favourite. I do not believe she ever excelled it. It is a masterly study of her own origins and her attitude to those origins—which, by the way, was not an unmixed one. Therefore to understand this book it is worth trying to understand the preoccupations of the young woman who wrote it, the Kate O'Brien of 1933.

To start with we must forget the woman of the last photographs, the cropped head, the heavy face, the eyes that seem to glitter with a joke like Yeats's lapis lazuli musicians. As a young woman Kate O'Brien was beautiful, with good, strongfeatured looks. Nor was this unimportant. "The Ante-Room" is partly about beauty and the deceptions of beauty. Appearances mattered in the merchant class and they matter to Kate O'Brien. Agnes Mulqueen, the heroine of this novel, is described with care: "her profile saved from perfection by too much length of bone, by subtle irregularities of mouth and nostril". Is there a touch of self-portraiture here? In any case the young novelist of 1933 was good looking enough to write about the beauty of her characters with empathy not envy. And what else did she share with them? Well, she was bourgeois in the good French sense. Like the people in this book she felt that wine and a fire and silver and well-presented food made the world somehow a more solid place. We hear her own tones of approval coming through her description in this book of how Roseholm struck the avaricious Nurse Cunningham:

"This big and quiet house so excellently run, this spacious dining room, full of mahogany, its roaring fire, its two long windows facing a smooth green garden, its heavy silver tea-service and silver dishes filled with food which no one ate, all this was of fascinating interest".

Beauty and the bourgeoisie—they hardly seem to mix. But they do in this book as they did in Kate O'Brien's vision. This is a book about the middle-classes, not in their glory, but in their moment of travail. It is Kate O'Brien's achievement to make us love these selfish merchant souls. They are dross. We know they are dross. But by the end of the book we have spent such golden hours in their company that they look different. As Hazlitt said "we can scarcely hate anyone we know".

She achieves this out of her own love. She came from them, she understood them, she abandoned them. "The Ante-Room" is part of the process of abandonment, just as it is part of the love. So let us go back further than 1933, to the nineteenth century in fact, to look at the roots she dragged up so painfully.

The Limerick she was born in in 1896 was struggling upward. The brick houses, the squares, the fine iron railings, the wide streets and the constant bells—some said imported from Italy—were all evidence of new prosperity. Kate O'Brien's family was part of it, if only just. Fifty years before her grandfather, Tom O'Brien, had brought his family and the debris of an eviction into Limerick on an ass-cart. He settled there, bought a horse, sold it at a profit, bought another, repeated the process and was very soon an acknowledged authority on both the process and the product. It was a good thing to be. Horses were everything. The whole of a gentry-farmer class rode to hounds, harnessed their thoroughbreds and paid handsomely to have a piece of horseflesh that might make them the envy of their neighbours. By the time Tom O'Brien's late, last son was born he was building a villa to go with his stud farm.

That last son was Kate O'Brien's father. Judging by the portrait she left of him in "Presentation Parlour" here indeed is a transformation: gone is the dark of the post-famine apocalypse; in its place is an Edwardian cavalier: "He dressed well in tweed cutaways; his hands were freckled, expressive and well cared for; everything about him was of good taste and quality from cigar to boot to handkerchief". This expensive and cheerful man married Katty Thornhill and sired six daughters. With his brothers he maintained and expanded the carriage-horse business. They flourished. In their large houses—no doubt insulated by the sort of food and warmth and wine and service described in "The Ante-Room"—they shut out the cacophony of the times: the Land War, evictions, the disgrace of Parnell.

But one reality could not be excluded from their houses anymore than it can be shut out of Roseholm in this book, and that is death. In 1902 Kate O'Brien's mother died. She was six. Thereafter, for nine years—and happy years at that—she lived largely at Laurel Hill, the convent in Limerick.

And so we come back again to the year 1933, to the novelist Kate O'Brien writing a book about the world she came from. But now we can get a more rounded view: A scholar of the world she may be, but her forcing house has been the solitude of a convent; she may indeed cast an eye on the silver and the wine, but might it not be a monastic glance?

She is in her mid-thirties now and much has happened since 1902. She has gone to University, published a bestseller, contracted and dissolved a short-lived marriage. These are momentous events but as far as the writing of this book goes they might as well not have happened. For the purposes of "The Ante-Room" nothing matters but that she is looking at the world of her birth with the eyes of an exile.

That is what makes the "Ante-Room" a disturbing, not to say subversive book. But not at first sight. On a preliminary reading it seems to be an unadorned but conventional story of conflicting loves: the two Mulqueen sisters love each other and one, moreover, loves the husband of the other in a torment of regret and guilt. The dying mother, Teresa Mulqueen, loves her blubbering son, Reggie, and he reaches out in a parody of love towards the cool but shrewd Nurse Cunningham. William Curran loves Agnes from his solitude and pride and she, in hers, is blind to it.

A novel of passion then such as the post-Victorian era was almost too rich in. But look again. There is a rottenness to these loves, a corruption to these characters that has nothing to do with the era of happy endings. Another look and we see the glint of the scalpel in Kate O'Brien's hand. She cuts deep into these people, into the sickness of their self-deceptions. And who better should know them? In the winter fastness of her childhood she must have seen that the family above all was something more than a myth and something less than a morality.

Love, marriage, the family—all are investigated, all are found wanting. What is left? Not religion indeed. The cold fears and aloneness of the characters in this book are not really warmed by their rituals. Catholicism is part of their orthodoxy and orthodoxy is part of what stifles them. So, after all these questions, what answers has Kate O'Brien for us, her readers.

Well, love is one of them, surprisingly enough. Maybe it is less surprising when you consider it is not so much the love of the flawed characters for each other, but the love Kate O'Brien has for them. In all their habit, pride and panic the Mulqueens glow with the colours of a Flemish painting. As in such a painting, they are doing ordinary things but in an extraordinary light and that light can only come from the fierceness of Kate O'Brien's act of recollection. We feel rather than know that there is a possessiveness in her attitude to them that can only be self-possession: She makes them argue and reflect and live with as much urgency as if they were acting out an episode of her own life. As of course they were. They are part of what formed her. "The Ante-Room" like all true works of art, never loses the surprises and force of self-discovery.

So, to end where I began, the ante-room symbolises something, but what? I think Ben Kiely gives the best answer: "The Ante-Room of the title" he has written "is not a place where the bourgeoisie suffer before they become poets, but the dread hall of silence and pain where body and soul kiss for the last time before the final parting in death." I do not think his quotation can be improved on, but perhaps I could add something. "The Ante-Room" is also Kate O'Brien's last act of love for the world she inherited. Henceforth as a novelist she would study the solitude of the individual. Here, for one last time she looks at the individuality of the orthodoxy. The family, society, Limerick, those houses with great proportions and small minds—she will never study these matters so urgently again and she will never write of greater ones with more energy and love.

There was an Ireland between the mortgaged acres of Maria Edgeworth and the strong farms of Mary Lavin's short stories. It was an Ireland of increasing wealth and uneasy conscience, where the women wore stays and rouged their cheeks, had their clothes made by Dublin dressmakers and tried to forget the hauntings of their grandparents. This was Catholic Ireland; it was never nationalist Ireland. Its citizens were wealthy merchants and it perished overnight when the ghosts of their ancestors walked again in their hunger and their anger.

Kate O'Brien came from that Ireland. In ways she is our only link in literature with it. She wrote "The Ante-Room" as a complex study of individuals certainly, but also surely to commend to us a society I think she suspected her readers might in the end wish to overlook. It is not a place or a time or a people we can be proud of, but if we forget them we forget that what we are ashamed of is nothing other than ourselves. In "The Ante-Room" Kate O'Brien gives us the chance to remember, as she does, with love.

Eavan Boland
Dublin
June 1980

BOOK I

THE EVE OF ALL SAINTS

The First Chapter

By eight o'clock the last day of October was about as well lighted as it would be. Tenuous sunshine, swathed in river mist, outlined the blocks and spires of Mellick, but broke into no high lights on the landscape or in the sky. It was to be a muted day.

Roseholm, the white house where the Mulqueens lived, stood amid trees and lawns on the west side of the river. Viewed from the town in fine weather, it could often seem to blaze like a small sun, but it lay this morning as blurred as its surroundings. It neither received nor wanted noise or light, for its preoccupation now was to keep these two subdued. And this morning that was easy; there was no wind about to rattle doors or tear through dying leaves, but only an air that moved elegiacally and carried a shroud of mist.

Agnes Mulqueen slept with her curtains open, so that at eight o'clock, though still almost asleep, she was aware of movement and light. She turned in her bed, and the weak sun fell upon her face though her eyelids still resisted it.

One by one the Mass bells ceased to ring in Mellick, and as their last note dropped away the clock in the hall at Roseholm, always slow, boomed out its cautious strokes. Agnes stirred and sighed. Once, when every whisper in the house had seemed to aggravate her mother's suffering, she had suggested silencing that clock. But Teresa would not have it. "When I can't hear it any more," she said, "I'll know I'm at the Judgment Seat."

Agnes opened her eyes and pulled herself into a sitting posture. Bells and clock and thin autumnal light were calling her back to things she did not wish to face. They had done so every morning for a long time now.

There was a knock at the door. Old Bessie entered with hot water.

"Good mornin', Miss Agnes, good mornin' to you, child."

Agnes made a reluctant effort at response.

"Let you get up smart now, Miss. The Master'll be in from Mass in half an hour's time."

"How did Mother sleep, Bessie?"

"Ah, betther then, thanks be to God. Sister Emmanuel is after sayin' below that she had a quiet night, the creature. Ah, the poor misthress! 'Tis she's the saint if ever I seen wan! God help us all! God help us all!"

Praying and shaking her head, old Bessie waddled from the room.

God help us all. Agnes bent her head into the support of her two hands. The baby frills on the neck and cuffs of her white nightgown, and the silky dark plait of hair that lay on the curve of her long back made her seem younger than twenty-five. She stayed very still, her knees bent upwards to take the weight of her hands and head. But there was more neutrality than weariness in the attitude, as if her soul were a camel, crouched to receive the usual baggage of its day's march. And here it was assembled for her now, according to routine.

Sometimes at this hour of the morning she found herself inclined to idle and melancholy reminiscence. She wondered then if other lives had more unity than hers, which seemed to have only a circumstantial and not a spiritual consistency. Her early childhood, for instance, except for a few comic and catastrophic memories, and a suspicion that then already her sister Marie-Rose had seemed specially to decorate the scene for her, might have been from her present vantage point someone else's, uninteresting, normal, happy and unhappy. Schooldays with their violences, their ludicrous peaks and chasms, intellectual triumphs and emotional shames, their crazy, agonising spurts of fun, their priggishness, savagery and vanity, seemed again the experience of another person, neither the child of early memory, nor the young woman who remembered. Though through that time the thread of Marie-Rose indeed ran vividly. The little sister, two years older than herself, had then been for her prettiness and grace and sweet, supporting friendliness an absolute mania, an adolescent craze. Hero-worship had begun to flame, perhaps, on an evening of their first term, when she was ten and Marie-Rose just twelve. A new-made friend of Agnes's had informed her that she was, by popular vote, the plainest girl in the school. This affirmation of what she herself believed had so shattered Agnes that unwisely she yielded to Marie-Rose's commands to tell her what the matter was. The savage, ribald public vengeance which she took then, golden-headed twelve-year-old, upon the luckless insulter of her little sister, had been both shocking and delicious—and had turned her for a while, in Agnes's eyes, into a dangerous, delightful Joan of Arc. But schooldays were not particularly happy thereafter, nevertheless. The idea stayed that she was ugly and awkward, and that Marie-Rose's denial of these facts was quixotry. Her mental superiority to most of her schoolfellows, including Marie-Rose, was no real comfort, for she observed, through her sister and some other girls, that beauty carried the surest weapons. And she conceded the naturalness of this. So, jealous of every pretty face except Marie-Rose's, for the empire of which she fought many a vigorous field, she became at school priggish and shy and insolent, a gusty awkward creature, whom now, smiling at her, she could call stranger, except for the linking love for Marie-Rose, which proved her to be very Agnes.

And then there had been another Agnes—gone too, but much regretted. The home-from-school and just-out Agnes, who, encouraged by family standards to be extravagant in adornment, and encouraged and guided most exhilaratingly to that end by Marie-Rose, had discovered cautiously, had at last been unable longer to deny to the long mirror, that she was, after all her doubtings, beautiful. Ah, then the world had blossomed! Marie-Rose, two years her senior, had been a worldly and amusing foil, a merry guide, at her first ball, at her first dinner-party. Sharing this room, sharing this bed, as they had done since nursery days, sharing each other's secrets and giggles, ribbons and perfumes—the hero-worship long forgotten, they had become the very best of boon companions, and had together grown extremely frivolous. The days wore a radiant inconsequence—flirtations, conquests, *billets-doux,* and long advisings, long confidings every night in bed with Marie-Rose.

And then they met Vincent—Vincent de Courcy O'Regan—and Marie-Rose married him, and with her going, for ever now, to their beloved Dublin, loneliness settled down for its remaining inmate on the room that had hitherto been only half her own.

Then, her occupation gone, Agnes had time to observe what was happening to the other members of her father's house. This, from being a noisy place, had suddenly, it seemed to her, grown very quiet. Her eldest brother, Ignatius, who was eleven years older than her, had long been gone away, and now was in

Australia, a Redemptorist missionary. Reggie, the next brother, who lately did nothing for his living, hung about at home; Alice, Agnes's eldest sister, married to a country doctor, lived in the wilds of Galway, overwhelmed by many babies. Daniel was on the Stock Exchange in Dublin; John, a barrister, lived in London, in the Middle Temple—and Marie-Rose had married Vincent. Young Joe, still at school when Marie-Rose was married, went up to the University the following autumn to begin his medical studies.

No wonder then that Roseholm had grown quiet. And it was in that autumn too that Teresa, Agnes's mother, gave up her pretence of being perfectly well, and entered into the long illness, the chain of operations and treatments, ups and downs, hopes and fears, that was not ended yet. For two and a half years now Teresa Mulqueen had fought a losing battle with life, and as pain alternately half-strangled and then half-released, whilst never ceasing to defeat, her the quiet house grew deadly quiet. People moved creepingly now on the stairs and slid past the board that creaked on the first landing. Teresa herself lay too still and spent to make a noise; Reggie, her son, whose only stay and light she was, was too much frightened by her plight and his to let any protest break that might define it; and Danny, her husband, jealous of the lifted look that Reggie could bring to the tortured woman's face, and he could not, jealous and sick with pity, could do no more to ease things for himself than potter to and fro in false and chatty cheerfulness. It was too quiet a house, in which the only permissible noise was Reggie's Chopin-playing.

"I'll open both doors, and then you'll hear fine, Mother darling."

"Try to get to the end of it for me this time, will you?"

"I'll try."

But he never got to the end.

It was too quiet a house for Agnes, on whose courage and direction it had come to depend entirely now. And as it had no room for gaiety, neither had it place for the irrelevant griefs of the young and strong. There was no space in it where a heart might scold against a private wound, and so, though Agnes had been mortally hurt on the day when she and Marie-Rose met Vincent, in three years she had learnt to fix her eyes upon the griefs of others and, for her sanity's sake; ignore her own.

Still, in the hour of waking, she sometimes reflected coldly upon the unrelated phases of her life, through which the only unifying thread was Marie-Rose. The lives she read about in novels were not like that. There one thing always led to another, whereas what struck her about her own span of experience was that no section of it seemed to have offered preparation or warning for the next.

That was not true, however, of her present day-to-day existence. At each falling asleep she knew what she would presently wake to; at every waking her spirit went through the same dull exercise of pulling itself together for the foreseen.

Still with her head bent on her knees, she said her usual Morning Offering—the simple one that she had learnt to say at school:

"Oh, my God, I offer Thee all the thoughts, words and actions of this day, that Thou mayst make it wholly Thine." The formula both saddened and consoled her—and this double effect was, she often thought, one of the menaces of prayer, which made its ideal of purity almost unattainable. Prayer that should humble gave relief by self-inflation. Agnes often wondered how it was possible to accept and honour God and yet steer clear of heroics. Would it be more honest, more prayerful, not to pray at all? But that would be a deliberate spiritual pride, and would lead her further into the desert than she had courage to go.

Desert, indeed? She lifted her head and laughed. She must be feeling very sorry for herself this morning. She got out of bed, pulled on her dressing-gown and crossed to the further window. She had always loved the prospect that it gave, and by now it was so fully associated with memories and meditations that looking at it was an escape from the rigidity of time. To-day its furthest eastern backcloth of high, snow-capped mountains was not visible, for the sky was woolly, but the town spread along the river-bank wore its usual mood of unobtrusive dignity, varied masses of grey and brown broken here by a spire, there by the gentle tones of fading sycamores. There was a pious Sunday morning stir about it now; she could hear the discreet sound of carriage wheels, and see figures moving up and down the hilly side-streets that crossed the town from the water's edge. She remembered going to tea with her grandfather long ago—she must have been about five—in one of those hilly streets; an ugly old man who had kept tame greenfinches.

There were a good many ships in dock this week, at Vereker's Wharf, at Hennessy's and at Considine's, where her father was director. The river was full and choppy, and by the Boat Club pier deserted wags and pleasure-boats bobbed uneasily around the buoys. How many times had she and Marie-Rose set off for picnics from that pier? Far down the stream she could hear the dredger coughing, and she remembered once again her little sister's silly joke about: "Your poor husband's asthma is very bad, my dear!"—a joke so feeble that Agnes had had to forbid it in the bedroom. Nowadays she often heard the fluty, giggling voice repeat it to her memory, catching itself back on a delighted half-breath while she, Agnes, rushed to administer punishment. Foolish doings like that had seemed to be great fun. But here was her father now, turning in at the gate and coming up the drive. He must have gone to seven o'clock Mass. How old and small he looked—he was getting very fat. Through the half-stripped trees she could see him trying to roll his umbrella as he walked. But she must hurry—she was very late this morning.

The Second Chapter

TERESA MULQUEEN had also heard the Mass bells ring, the hall clock strike, the distant dredger cough, sounds to which her day had always begun for thirty-seven years. So well did she know those sounds that often now, when in pain or in a morphia half-dream, she was uncertain whether she heard or only remembered them. But this morning, after a night which she must not let herself think about, there had suddenly been some real sleep and a lull. She was awake, and the pain was vague, hardly there at all, you might say. God was merciful.

She must use the chance to think—it wasn't often she felt as clear in the head as this. But first she would say her morning prayers. That was due to God, who had granted her this hour of blessed release. The least she might do was pray to Him sometimes when she could give her mind to what she was doing, for she knew that often lately she answered prayers that Sister Emmanuel said, and said some of her own, without being able to think at all of what they meant.

She fumbled about the counterpane for her rosary beads.

"Sister Emmanuel," she croaked—she had hardly any voice nowadays—"Sister Emmanuel, where did you put my beads from me this morning?"

Nurse Cunningham came to her bedside.

She was a pretty, firm-featured woman of thirty, who had recently been sent down from Dublin as day-nurse to this case by the specialist in charge of it. Teresa would have preferred to see the holy old face of the Blue Nun who took care of her at night.

"Sister Emmanuel is gone for to-day, Mrs. Mulqueen, and you've got to put up with me, I'm afraid. But here are your beads." She put them into Teresa's hand, and straightened her pillow skilfully. "That better?" she asked, with a bright smile.

Teresa nodded. She did not resent the cheerfulness, although it exhausted her; she understood that it was trained into the young woman, but she thought of how the old nun would have given them to her in silence, or would maybe have gone on murmuring the sweet Latin of her Office while she did whatever had to be done to the pillow.

She fingered the silver cross.

"I believe in God, the Father Almighty . . ." What feast of the Church was it to-day? "Do you know whose feast it is, Nurse, by any chance?"

"It's Sunday, Mrs. Mulqueen—the 31st October—I don't know——"

"Well, now—the Eve of All Saints'. A glorious day; and to-morrow better still, and after that the Suffering Souls—I'm glad you reminded me. I'll say the Glorious Mysteries——"

She shut her eyes and let the brown beads slip through her worn-out fingers. First Glorious Mystery, the Resurrection. Our Father who art in Heaven— there had always been great fun in this house on the Eve of All Saints'. The girls used to come home from school for it and have a party; Danny used to be great at playing snap-apple with them. Well, this time there wouldn't be much fun—but only Dr. Coyle coming from Dublin to-morrow night, she supposed, if he was to see her on Tuesday. She groaned a little in anxiety. She *must* have another operation. She had the strength for it, she knew she had. She could not leave her un-protected son—not yet, not yet. Not until she could see him somehow prepared to live without her. Dr. Coyle must keep her alive—no matter how. But she must say her rosary now. Hail Mary, full of grace, the Lord is with thee . . . it was time some of them were coming in to say good morning to her, surely. Oh, Reggie, my son. But she must pray awhile, she must try to mind her prayers.

Beyond the draught-screen that guarded her bed-room door she thought she heard a movement, but her senses did not function surely now beyond the immediate region of her bed. Yes, here was someone. Agnes, tall, light-footed, came and bent to kiss her.

"Good morning, Mother."

"Good morning, child. I wondered when you were coming in to see me."

"I'm afraid I'm late. I'm sorry, Mother."

"It's to your father you should be saying that, and he waiting for his breakfast, I suppose. I don't know how this house is going at all these times."

Teresa had always had an inclination to nag her youngest daughter, and now on her better days it revisited her. Agnes smiled at the good sign.

"It's going badly," she said, with graciousness. Teresa looked pleased.

"You needn't tell me."

"You're looking well," the girl went on. She never inquired of Teresa herself about her nights, wanting to keep her mother's thoughts from them. Looking down at her now she felt the irony of the true thing she had said. Teresa did look better—but better than what? Not better than death certainly, which was the only good thing left to want for her.

"Do you know the day it is?" she queried.

"The Eve of All Saints'," said Teresa proudly.

"Clever!" said Agnes, laughing at her. "And I suppose you're thinking of getting up to play snap-apple?"

"Well, I was thinking it's a pity you'll have no fun to-night, child."

Agnes laughed, almost too much.

"Snap-apple days are over," she said. "Do you realise I'm twenty-five?"

Teresa was exhausted by her own talkativeness. She closed her eyes. Twenty-five was young, she thought. When she was twenty-five she was carrying Reggie. A hot summer it was, and she felt wretched nearly all the time. It didn't seem long ago. How old was Reggie now? But the dear name, which was now the only one that never, in her sick dreams and fantasies, moved dissociate from a face and a meaning, stabbed hard with a clear and sane reminder of present grief. Reggie was thirty-five, wasted, unhappy, dangerous—dependent for his own decency and for his whole interest in life, on his devotion to her—and she was leaving him—and God had not answered her yet or told her where he was to turn then, so that he would do no harm in his weakness, and yet might be a little happy, a little less than desolate. That was what she had to think about with whatever strength these interludes conferred—not silly nonsense about fun for Agnes. Agnes could look out for herself—but Reggie—what was to become of him when she was gone? God must hear and answer. Either He must save her life—never mind how middlingly, so that her son might have her shielding always—or He must provide another shield. And where could that be found—for a man unfit to love, unfit to marry? Oh, God must be implored, since He was merciful and died for sinners. God must let her live, like this, if necessary, for five years more, for ten years. To keep him safe, to keep him interested, to keep his misery from making misery. Teresa's eyes were closed, and Agnes, observing the passionate constriction of the withered and bitten brown mouth, knew where her thoughts were, knew the despairing prayer that that defeated frame was urging up to heaven. She saw her mother's dilemma, but, with impatience, did not see why Reggie could not be compelled to face his own.

The history of this dilemma was never mentioned in Roseholm, and to this day Agnes did not know how much or little of it her brothers and sisters understood. But during the last year it had become one of her duties to be in the house when Dr. Curran called, and to hear what he had to say about her mother's condition and occasionally about her brother's. This general practitioner had been appointed to routine charge of Teresa by her specialist, Dr. Coyle, of Merrion Square, Dublin—and recently he had taken charge of Reggie. It followed that in his professional conversations with Agnes he had had to mention many things about which no member of her family could have been explicit. At last, briefly but with exactitude, he had explained her brother's medical history to her.

Reggie was now thirty-five. Ten years ago, in 1870, he had been infected with syphilis, and for three years had spent long periods in nursing homes, until sufficiently cured to live uninterruptedly at home. But marriage and love were forbidden him henceforward and seasonal doses of mercury, increased and decreased as considered necessary, and doing their specific work, also did harm. But a greater harm was wrought upon mind and spirit by the sustained humiliations and fears of his state of health, so that a native invalidism became a justified habit, until he gave up all pretence of doing any work, or leading the life of a normal man. But he was a shareholder in the rich firm from which his father's wealth was drawn, and had more than enough money for his pitifully restricted attempts at self-indulgence. The life which as a young man he had always coveted—of slippered, pottering *laissez-faire*—had become his ironically soon. He had always been good-natured, sentimental, sensual and coarsely amusing—but these attributes were of little purpose now. He had always been vain of his loose and swarthy good looks, and these were puffed and bloated now. He had always half-desired to play the piano well—but now his thickened hands were more tentative than ever as he fooled at his eternal Chopin. As the years had deepened a misery which his lazy mind would no more than half confront, and then only that he might use it as a weapon in self-pity, he had found one good thing—the love which his mother Teresa had flung like a shield before him. This love, which in the first terrified months of his illness had given understanding and patience to a woman as prudish as she was holy, had been his courage and his hope. In his invalid years, when she was still well, she had devoted herself to his consolation and amusement, thereby compelling him to keep his wits bright for her, to keep his shrewdness on the move, to keep his piano open. Firmly, ruthlessly, without a word of pity or sentiment, she had built for her wasted son a life that was safe from life. She had built it with a concentration of purpose which had almost cost her the love of her other children, and had certainly caused the withdrawal of their confidence, since it was plain to them, who did not know its reason, where her true attention was. She had concentrated on Reggie almost to the extent of forgetting the existence of her husband, who understood, in part at least, her fierce devotion, and made no complaint. Then disease had spread its dark wing over her, and for all her resistance, its shadow dimmed and shortened her view ahead from month to month. In her pain, in weary recoveries and distressed relapses, in delirium and half-dream, the bread which she had cast on the waters came back to her, for her son, for all he was worth, endeavoured to give her the courage and forgetfulness which she had resolutely found for him. He loved her now with an active anxiety which was both delight and anguish to her. He read to her, he gossiped and joked for hours by her fire, he played his bits of Chopin over and over, he sang in his weak, true tenor voice.

His love was almost heroism in its surrender of laziness to perpetual small exactions. But Reggie was not heroic enough to look beyond it. Though often terrified by the spectacle of his dying mother, he would not think of her as dead, and himself deprived of her in a world which she had both withheld from him and made endurable. For ten years there had been no future, but only this sheltered ambling from day to day. Nothing else was now imaginable—and that depended solely on his mother. Therefore such things as agony and delirium and near-death fantasies were only fantasies. She would live, since his life lived in her. She would live, because nothing else was bearable.

To Agnes. this situation of her brother, its long chain of small unselfishnesses founded on a mighty selfishness, was hideous. To her it seemed that the only way to love this tortured woman, her mother, was to set her free by making her feel, however wrongfully, that her work was done, that the strength she had put out had built something, and that the charge which she left reluctantly behind, would be safe henceforward, because of her ten years of bulwarking. She was young, and could not bear to see the eyes of a human being filmed against the consequences of himself. She could not bear the vast exactions of the sentimental. She wanted a quiet mind and a happy death for her mother—and only her brother barred them off.

"Where's Reggie?" Teresa asked, without opening her eyes. "He's very long about coming in to say good morning to me."

Agnes moved her head in the direction of the screen. "Here he is," she said.

Teresa's eyes opened and grew bright as her son approached her. He was a large wreck of a man, and although he had the habit of moving with caution, a non-adjustment between his big. virile bones and his increasing flaccidity kept him clumsy. ·His flesh, uni-

formly red, was dry and flaky about his mouth and
bulging neck, and sweaty on his forehead and hands.
His hair, which Teresa remembered thick and dark
and wavy, had receded completely from his temples
and the top of his head, and was only a dusty straggle
about his ears and the back of his skull. His eyes, well
set, and once quite fine with a spark of impudent
virility, were lashless and bloodshot, and the black
brows above them thinned away to untidy tufts. His
teeth were discoloured and broken; his hands thick,
hot and beautifully cared for. His whole appearance
had an exaggerated, antiseptic immaculacy. He was a
wreck, but still, in the tilt of his shoulders, and in the
smile that now lit his face for Teresa, there were revealed the tatters of a commonplace charm, a departed
power to please women.

He took his mother's hand and her rosary beads.

"Good morning, Mother darling. You're looking
grand to-day."

"I'm feeling grand, my son."

Agnes observed now, as often before, the change
which came over her mother when Reggie was in the
room, a change which was obviously a mighty and
painful piece of acting. Teresa raised her voice almost
to normal tone and energy for him; spoke in longer
sentences when he was there, and attempted little
jokes; really put up the appearance of a woman who
was not so very desperately ill.

Reggie jingled the rosary beads up and down in his

hand, and laid them on her bedside table.

"Well, then, give Heaven a rest for a while, let you. Enjoy yourself, woman—there's plenty of time for praying."

Teresa kept on smiling at him. Nurse Cunningham stepped up to the other side of the bed.

"Now, now, Mr. Mulqueen—my patient isn't well enough to be bullied, you know," she said good-temperedly.

There was a quality in this woman's voice which Agnes could not stand. With a smile to her mother she left the room.

"We've got to keep our patient especially well to-day, you know," the nurse went on, "with Dr. Coyle coming to-night."

Reggie's face clouded. Facts were things which he ignored as much as possible, and he had managed to wake and dress this morning without confronting this one of the specialist's coming. He could not bear her doctors, because they insisted that she was seriously ill.

"I can't see why *he* wants to come here plaguing you," he said.

Teresa took her cue.

"I'm glad he is coming, if you want to know. Because, with the help of God, I'll be so well for him that he'll be able to put new heart into all of you."

"Oh, Mother—is that true?"

"What'd be the good of saying it if it was a lie?"

He stared at her, loving the spurious conviction of

her words. But it was too much comfort; it brought weak tears streaming down his face.

"Tch, tch," said Teresa. "There, there—you mustn't cry." She tried to move a hand towards him and he dropped on his knees and pressed his heavy head against the counterpane. She stroked his bald temple, where once the hair had been like heavy silk. "There, there, don't cry. I'll be better soon. You'll see."

Teresa knew that she was at the end of her long bluff, and that very soon even Reggie would not be deceived by these lies which, because of the actress effort they exacted, were nearly impossible to her now. Often, therefore, she played with the idea of telling him the truth—that her death was only a very little distant and that the interim must be, so far as her value to him was concerned, as increasingly like death as would make no matter. But again and again she funked such conversation. In her day she had been used to bully his weakness jocosely, or even firmly— and the method had served. But now such dregs of vigour as she had were always split in pity. And soon there would not be even that poor virtue with which to cosset him. The dark stretch was coming—when on flux and reflux, pain and morphia, she would be borne, stupefied and fantasia-maddened, into death. She would not even know him soon when he came whimpering; she would not hear his broken Chopin any more, or recognise the sad shuffle of his slippers.

Now, stroking his head faithfully, though the little

movement roused up pain that had been sluggish, stroking his unhappy head, she pondered him. Amazing how he still drank up the nonsense that she talked about getting better! Amazing that he never caught a hint of her effort to assume a normally pitched voice for him, never dreamt that it was now almost impossible for her to stroke his head like that! He seemed to have no understanding at all of her disease and its relentless movement, or rather refused to understand it. As at first he had refused the realities of his own affliction. Coward! Ostrich! Yet she had no reproof to add to life's long vengeance on him. She only reproved herself in his regard. For she saw that her method of making his spoilt life liveable had been a mistake. But no other had presented itself—she did not see how another could, or what was to become of him when she had wrung the very last possible allowance of days and nights from life? Oh, God! Oh, God! She groaned very softly in spite of herself.

Nurse Cunningham came to the bed-side again.

"Really, Mr. Mulqueen, this is too bad of you. Your mother was splendid until you came in upsetting her."

Reggie stood up at once, both ashamed and reassured. Splendid was she, except for his stupidity?

"Oh, I'm sorry, Mother darling." He dried his eyes.

"But I'm all right, son," said Teresa.

He beamed at her.

"You see, Nurse, she isn't as upset as you make out."

Nurse Cunningham smiled humouringly.

Reggie bent and kissed Teresa.

"Have a good rest this morning," he said, "and then we'll have a grand read of Miss Braddon in the afternoon."

He tapped the book which lay on the little table.

"We will, my son," said Teresa, smiling at him.

The Third Chapter

AGNES found her father alone by the dining-room fire, reading a letter. She recognised Marie-Rose's writing on the sheet of paper.

Danny Mulqueen removed his spectacles and lifted his round, worried face to receive a kiss from his tall daughter.

"Sorry I kept you waiting, Father."

"That's all right, my dear. That's all right. Been to see your mother?"

"Yes. She seems much easier this morning."

"Thank God. I looked in before I went to Mass, and she was sleeping. Sister Emmanuel said that after one o'clock she got some rest, thanks be to God."

He fidgeted the letter in his hand. Agnes moved to the head of the breakfast-table.

"Come and sit down, Father. What news has Marie-Rose?"

"Well, I don't know whether you'll think it inconvenient, child, but she says she's coming here to-day."

Agnes's head had been bent over the tea-tray. Now it flashed upward involuntarily, a light of excitement in her eyes.

"Oh!" she said, and seemed as if she had many things in her mind to say. But she was smiling and Danny looked relieved. As head of the house, he was always treated with meticulous respect by his daughters, who wrote to him of their proposed arrangements, and asked his permission about matters small and large, entirely as a gesture of politeness in which they were trained. These informations and requests, however, always worried him, since they required a reaction, which until it had been indicated for him by Teresa, or nowadays by Agnes, he was unable to produce. There was nothing remarkable in Marie-Rose's announcement that she was coming to stay—but the onus of declaration had been thrown on him, and he simply could not decide whether, with the specialist expected to stay in the house on the following night, it was convenient or inconvenient news. However, Agnes was smiling, and the matter now being in her hands, it seemed quite pleasant and usual.

"Mother will be delighted," Agnes said.

"That's right, that's so," said Danny, and helped himself to butter. "And one more visitor in the house won't be disturbing for her, I suppose. Here's the letter, child, here's the letter."

Agnes stretched her hand for it. These simple notes from Marie-Rose generally meant more than they expressed.

My dearest Father,
I have been worrying about Mother as your letters have not been very cheerful lately, and I have decided

to go down to Mellick by the afternoon train tomorrow (Sunday). I would like to see her for myself and stay at Roseholm for a day or two. I hope that this will be quite convenient. Vincent is very well and sends love to you all. If he were not so busy at present he would like to come with me, but that is impossible. Please give my love to Mother and Reggie, but you can tell Agnes that it is a fortnight since she wrote to me, and so we are not on speaking terms.

With much love to you also, dearest Father.

Your affectionate daughter,

Marie-Rose.

Agnes read this twice, keeping on her face the expression of light affection and pleasure which her father might expect to see. But her deductions and feelings were complicated.

To begin with, a letter from Marie-Rose was always a shaft of light in her present loneliness, for, until they both met Vincent, the little elder sister had been the most precious person in the world. And now, in spite of him, because of him, Marie-Rose was still of terrible importance. Therefore Agnes's primary feeling was not of light, sisterly pleasure—but of relief, a relief as difficult to bear as when the blood creeps back into a limb that has been frozen. Marie-Rose was coming home. That, whatever it meant and whatever pain it might carry, was an unlooked-for radiance on the morning.

But it flung its own shadows, as Agnes knew. And deducing them with sympathy, she could spare a smile for her sister's ruthless use of her mother as a pretext. Little hypocrite! Not that she did not worry and grieve over Teresa—they all did—but any excuse could be made to serve the imperious moods of Marie-Rose. This sudden activity of worry meant, Agnes knew, another crisis of self-will and temper between Vincent O'Regan and his wife. It was only a repetition of a trick of escape which had been used at least a dozen times in their three years of married life—the only trick open to the conventionally bounded pair, and, for Marie-Rose, a useful one. For when hatred stood, almost declaring itself, between her and her husband, she who must be loved or wither remembered all the years of Agnes's love—and fled to it, imperiously, undoubtingly—and finding it, bathing her bruised, vain, charming spirit in its tenderness, its flattery, its indulgence for three, four, five, six days, was able to return, her petals dewy and refreshed, to subjugate again the perverse and irritable stranger who was her husband.

But, ironically, in the last year, her trick had somewhat failed her. Four times in that period she had, as this morning, with one pretext or another, written to her father to announce her immediate arrival in Mellick alone—and each time Vincent had come, too. With no explanation beyond an abrupt "I felt I'd like to," he had arrived—and everyone had smiled at his lover-like devotion to his wife, and even Marie-Rose, soothed from the instant that Agnes's eyes fell on her, had seemed to find a forgivable flattery in his tiresomeness.

"You seem to be getting very fond of Mellick," she teased him on the last occasion.

"Yes, I like Mellick," he replied.

"It's the shooting he comes for really," she said once, and he, a crack shot, had not contradicted her. He usually did arrange to go out after whatever sport was available.

All these brief visits of Marie-Rose were memorable to Agnes, but the last three had been very painful. In girlhood, as the younger sister had grown to seem the wiser of the two, it had become Marie-Rose's habit to turn over all her griefs and difficulties to her; that the habit still lived and asserted itself in adult life had been both natural and consoling and, in gratitude, Agnes had done everything she dared to help a situation which appeared to her to be far beyond external aid. Now, however, Vincent, in his dumb and sulky fits of misery, was learning to turn for help to that source which had always been his wife's—and when they were at Roseholm his eyes followed Agnes with an entreaty which, at his every coming, grew more imperative and angry. He got no answer, and no help, save from staring at her and listening to her voice. But his presence unsteadied her, his insolent misery thrust itself like a sword into her, and after a day spent in alternately soothing and shaping Marie-Rose's proud, shallow spirit to meet his, and in observing him, deteriorated and unhappy, she went to bed in a state of mingled torture, pity and desire that made sleep impossible.

Now, though Marie-Rose's letter said he was not coming, Agnes knew that he would be in this house, at this table, with her to-night.

She glanced at the place at her right hand, at the empty chair which he would fill—and saw him in it, more clearly than to-night she would allow herself to do.

Three and a half years ago when, affianced to Marie-Rose, he had sat in that chair by the right hand of Teresa, Agnes, looking diagonally up the table to him from the unimportant place she occupied then—had sometimes thought she saw a demigod, a creature destined for unchanging gaiety and triumph and success, one from whom life, for a whim, had withheld nothing, and on whom even the commonplace of being in love lay like a celestial illumination. He had seemed remote, Hellenic, in his perfect balance of gaiety, intelligence and beauty. Now, his hostess and his sister-in-law, receiving him frequently into a house of stillness and shadow, whence all the nuptial brightness and the young crowds that had assisted in it were scattered, she saw no demigod at her right hand, but only a man who, for all his power and comeliness, resembled other men in seeming older than his years and, at the roots of his heart, much disappointed. If now she found—in the furrowed shapely brow over which the brown hair still fell silkily, in the powerful shoulders, the smouldering grey-blue eyes, the strong and fidgety hands, any reminiscence of her old, school-girl deification, it probably sprang from his imperiousness, from the silence with which he countered the humdrum life of normal men in which he had to share, but which he could hardly bother to perceive. From gay he had grown sulky, from intelligent bored, from heavenly beautiful to mortally, so that time and pain could scar him.

Agnes stared at the empty chair and saw its ghost with pity, so that involuntarily her hand ran along the edge of the table as if to touch his lying there. Then chilled with fear by such an odd impulsion, she drew it back and shivered. Her mind took covert in prayer, and she turned back to Marie-Rose's letter—which was no more than a cry of help to her.

She must prepare herself to give that help—for what it might be worth. But for honesty and safety in attempting it she knew that, even at this short notice, she must face and overcome that which against all her will had in the last three months begun again to luxuriate and flower in her spirit. For some reason of fatigue and recklessness, she had allowed her rigorous conscience a little sleep of late, and her forbidden love a space, though small, to move and turn and hurt her. A paradoxical indulgence which she had shirked examining, but which had, nevertheless, with-held her, for she was honest, from those practices of the Church which are the routine of a good Catholic. It was ten weeks now since she had gone to Confession, whose habit from childhood it had been to confess each Saturday. For three months, since the last visit of Vincent and Marie-Rose, in fact, she had not received Communion, although for two years until then she had done so twice a week. To her strong and honest faith this state of things was very startling, and yet, though she knew it could not, must not, continue, she had not found the will to end it. She could not under-stand this sluggishness, which even resisted, though un-easily, a growing sense of guilt against her mother, for whose health and peace the rest of the family were now leaving no effort untried of prayer and self-denial. At Mass and in her prayers Agnes sought to face her moral problem—but kept ashamedly turning back from its categorical demands. "I'm doing no harm to anyone, and I have nothing else of my own to think about." She hated this casuistry, and went on using it. But she knew that she could not temporise forever with the ninth commandment. And now this ges-ture, this seeking of a ghostly hand, betrayed how far her laxity was bearing her. She was frightened by her need to touch that hand; she was terrified to think that to-night, in its flesh, it would lie within her reach.

She folded up the letter.

"Really, Father—you must try to eat more breakfast. You're eating nothing lately."

"Nonsense, child, nonsense, I eat plenty. 'Eat at pleasure, drink by measure.'"

Danny Mulqueen was full of parrot talk and proverbs. Agnes thought, as she smiled by habit at his too familiar saw, that it was unlucky to look as smooth and plentifully nourished as he did, and yet be the lonely, desolate, fretting figure of ineffectualness which his wife's long illness had made of him. A little chubby, rosy man, always bleating and chatting to keep the gloss of cheerfulness on life—for her, as he thought, and for his wife and son—and hiding himself when he had to weep and bathe his little sore eyes. In these days Agnes could not make up her mind whether she would have liked her father to be intelligent and to distract her with good talk and with his authority, or whether this was best—this feeble kindliness which exacted no more than her absent-minded courtesy. Sometimes she found herself wondering—and with faint shock—what his relationship with her mother had been, and how, and through what phases it had moved to this last stage of dragging, stupid sorrow.

"Another kidney? Do please, Father."

He did not want another kidney, but strong persuasion always flustered him. He helped himself to one, and handed his cup to his daughter for more tea.

The door opened, and Nurse Cunningham came into the room, followed by Reggie. Although Agnes had arranged a small sitting-room for her upstairs, she seemed to like to have a cup of tea in the dining-room at this hour, when Bessie was tidying her patient's room. She was a sociable woman. She was smiling now, no doubt at some pleasantry of Reggie's.

Agnes made a vague gesture of hospitality towards a vacant chair at some distance from herself, and rang the little silver bell.

"I must ask for some fresh tea for you, Nurse."

"Oh, please don't trouble, Miss Mulqueen."

"But it's no trouble at all."

Danny had stood up and was making vague, fussy sounds and movements.

"Sit down, Nurse, sit down. Is the room warm enough for you?"

Reggie pushed in her chair, and Nurse Cunningham acknowledged the action with an amiable glance over her shoulder, while responding suitably to his father. Agnes addressed her attention to Peter Robinson's winter catalogue. A maid came in with a replenished silver kettle and placed it on the spirit-lamp.

Nurse Cunningham looked with interest round the quiet, heavily furnished room. From her seventeenth year her life had been hard and insecure. The only child of an unsuccessful, tippling doctor, she had found herself at his death both friendless and penniless. The matron of an obscure small hospital in South Dublin, having been in love with Dr. Cunningham, gave his raw young daughter work of an indefinite but strenuous kind in her inefficient establishment. The girl was energetic and level-headed. She saw that, in her circumstances, the life in which this work gave her a foothold had, such as it was, more hope in it than any others open to her. As a companion-help she might, with luck, earn more money and have more comfort, but there would be few changes of scene and probably no random chances of any kind of personal enjoyment or success. As a governess—but she had been most sketchily educated and could not endure the society of children. She would be a nurse then, for without blinking the uncertainties, vague status and small rewards of such a career, she was stimulated by its promise of perpetually changing scenes and contacts, its shocks and crudities, its many chances of association with men.

She had only remained in that hospital six months. Thereafter each of her many changes had been an advance in professional experience and even, within narrow limits, materially. Now, after thirteen years of slaving by sick beds and flirting carefully with doctors, she was known as one of the best nurses in Ireland. This pleased her, but it was not what she had really planned for. Security was her goal. Comfort and social standing were more worth conniving at than a success which would wane with age, and leave her faced with lonely poverty. For the pay of a nurse made saving impossible, and though many patients had given her presents of money, she had generally allowed herself to spend these on her own adornment, for she was pretty and liked pretty things. Therefore, excellently though she had tackled life, and gallantly though she had played for marriage—finding in that game that though almost any doctor would kiss a pretty nurse, none could be trapped into marrying a fortuneless person of no social standing—the years ahead loomed bleak and insecure.

This big and quiet house, so excellently run, this spacious dining-room, full of mahogany, its roaring fire, its two long windows facing a smooth green garden, its heavy silver tea-service and silver dishes filled with food which no one ate, all this was of fascinating interest to Nurse Cunningham. She considered it with respect this morning, as she sipped her tea and buttered a piece of toast—then turned to observe its present châtelaine.

If Agnes did not like Nurse Cunningham, there was no love lost, because the latter took no interest at all in her, or rather, had not done so until this morning, when for some reason she thought it might be as well to size her up.

I must admit she's good-looking, the nurse told herself now. Indeed, I suppose some people would call her a beauty. I wouldn't though. Too severe—and lanky. Men don't like that. Too white in the face, too. Anæmia. The cold-blooded kind. Grey-eyed women are always supposed to be cold. But I must say I think her hair is lovely. You don't often see black hair that looks as soft and young as that. I wonder what her real age is—heard her saying something about being twenty-five to her mother this morning, but she sometimes looks older than that. It'd be hard to tell her age.— "Yes, thank you, Mr. Mulqueen. I will have a little more toast." She knows how to spend money on clothes, anyway. That dark red merino must have cost a nice penny. The bodice fits like a glove. A lovely cut. I wonder what she's thinking about? Not that catalogue, you can be sure.

"What time do you think you'll be wanting the carriage to take you to Mass, Nurse?" said Reggie.

"Yes, yes," chimed in Danny. "I must send word to the stables. And for you, too, my dear. Of course."

Agnes lifted her head.

"I shall go to twelve o'clock Mass, Father," she said.

"As for me," said Nurse Cunningham, "my movements depend entirely on Dr. Curran."

"Fortunate chap, Curran," said Reggie, with a sudden swagger.

Nurse Cunningham's face was playfully responsive.

"He doesn't think so," she twinkled.

Agnes resented the bad taste of this badinage. So she's the kind of woman who cannot ignore that sort of remark, even from Reggie, she thought, and shot a cold look down the table, flustering her brother, but causing faint amusement in the woman, who returned to her interrupted consideration of her.

Oh, hands off Dr. Curran. I see. I thought that was

how the land lay. Well, God knows she's welcome to
him—for of all the conceited young bullies in the profession! Just the sort she'd take a fancy to. No fun in
her. Time she was getting married, I'd say. And she
must have a good fortune. But, of course, if she did
marry—it'd be hard on these two. The mother hasn't
long to live—and then——

Nurse Cunningham's attention returned from Agnes
to the room she sat in and the life of ease it repre-
sented. They were more interesting than any young
woman.

"Did Father tell you that Marie-Rose is coming here
to-day, Reggie?" said Agnes.

"No." He looked good-naturedly pleased. "That'll
be nice. Do Mother good to see her, too."

Nurse Cunningham looked interested, and Reggie
turned to her.

"Marie-Rose is my sister, my second sister. Mrs. de
Courcy O'Regan, of Dublin."

"Oh, the de Courcy O'Regans!" This hospital nurse
knew her Dublin genealogies, and was impressed. "I
think I've sometimes seen her driving with her
husband in the Park. A very handsome couple."

"Yes; Vincent's a fine-looking chap. All the
O'Regans are."

"And so are all the Mulqueens," said Nurse Cunningham, with a laugh.

Agnes could hardly believe the evidence of her own
ears that anything so cruelly idiotic had been said, but

Reggie was leaning across the table, with a foolish glitter of pleasure in his bloodshot eyes. His aspect was pitiful to his sister, who knew that even nowadays the most obvious and flat-footed quips of femininity had a distressing power to stimulate him. All his mother's strength had been directed in deflecting him from just such banal excitations.

Agnes's mouth curved in disgust.

Really, she thought, for an experienced nurse, who must guess something of his history, she's curiously irresponsible.

A maid came in, followed by a tall and grey-haired priest.

"Canon Considine," the girl announced, and Agnes rose, in some surprise, to greet Uncle Tom, her mother's favourite brother.

The Fourth Chapter

ALTHOUGH the magenta buttons which indicated his ecclesiastical status had only adorned Canon Considine's black silk stock for seven months, their wearer had the look of a man born to a higher office than they allowed, one whom the gaiters and purple of a bishopric would well become, and who, though for intellectual reasons unlikely to be elected Cardinal, would in physique have adorned the Sacred College. A big, blond man of fifty-eight, with fair hair turning silver white, and pink skin spread neither too richly nor too sparingly across his bones, he looked a virtuous and comely priest. By reason of his great devotion to his sister, Teresa, he was of four maternal uncles the one whom Agnes saw most frequently, but familiarity had not established any special ease or sympathy between them.

"Good morning, Uncle Tom."

"Good morning, Agnes. Good morning, Danny."

"Good morning, Tom, good morning to you. This is an early call—and on Sunday and all——"

"Where will you sit, Uncle Tom?"

The priest walked over to the fireplace.

"Yes, I'm early, but it was my turn to say seven o'clock Mass, and I have a visiting preacher for twelve o'clock. That's why I was able to drive in at this hour. How is Teresa?" His face was anxious, and his eyes moved from his relatives to Nurse Cunningham. "What sort of a night did your patient have, Nurse?"

"A great deal of pain and restlessness until after one o'clock, Sister Emmanuel reported, and then some really good sleep. She is fairly comfortable this morning, Father."

"Ah! I'm glad. I'll go up and see her presently. But here's what brought me in in such a hurry. As you all know Dr. Coyle is coming down from Dublin to-morrow night and will see her on Tuesday. According to Dr. Curran, the visit will be of great importance, because it will have to settle how much longer they can hope to fight her disease with human means. And we all know how set she is on the fight, and her great desire to live."

Danny nodded and blinked. Nurse Cunningham looked professionally attentive. Reggie had got up and was moving uneasily about the room in his queer, shaky way. His breath came hissingly. This facing of facts was intolerable to him, Agnes knew.

Father Tom put a hand into his coat pocket and produced a letter.

"I had this," he said, "by the evening post last night. It is from Dr. Coyle, and he wishes me to ask you, Danny, if he may bring another doctor with him. Sir Godfrey Bartlett-Crowe, of Harley Street, happens to be in Dublin as consultant in another case, and according to Dr. Coyle, he is to be regarded as one of the greatest authorities on cancer now living. Dr. Coyle thinks his presence in Ireland very opportune."

"Of course, of course—whatever Dr. Coyle thinks." Danny clasped and unclasped his chubby hands. "By all means, he must come—by all means——"

"Very well then; we will wire to-day. No doubt Dr. Curran will also have heard from Coyle about it."

A silence that was almost lethargic filled the room, and was only broken by Reggie's hissing breath, as he went lumbering between the windows. "Oh, God!" he whispered as he moved. "Oh, God!"

Canon Considine looked at him with compassion. "But that is not all that brought me," he began again. "These doctors, like the rest of us, are in God's hands, and whatever they know is only an infinitesimal fraction of His knowledge." Danny looked up with a happier face. When men talked of God he saw light. Doctors were mysteries. God was a household word.

"He is merciful," the Canon went on, "and her perplexities and sufferings are known to Him, as well as all her goodness. He knows how necessary she has become to—to all of us, and that her great desire to live has nothing but unselfishness in it."

Reggie paused by the table and wiped his shining forehead. His flaccid flesh was trembling. Nurse Cunningham handed him his still full tea-cup.

"Drink this," she said professionally, but softly. He took the cup and drank.

"And when I was praying for her at Mass this morning it struck me that we have not prayed for her enough. No matter how much we are praying, perhaps it is not enough. We must renew our efforts in these three days—three great days of triumph and intercession in the Church—we must make a special Triduum of them—all of us, everyone. We will entreat God for her with special prayers and acts of self-denial to-day, to-morrow and Tuesday, so that on that day He may guide these men—and if it is His Will, permit them to lengthen her dear life, as she desires—and ease her pain, and make clear His Will to her about her many anxieties——"

Agnes moved a very little in her chair.

"And if that is not possible?" she asked softly.

"All things are possible to Him, child—and all we ask in this Triduum is that His Will should be made clear to us. We will intercede with all the strength and faith we have. I will have special prayers said for her on each of the three days in my own parish and at Priory Lane convent, where your Aunt Mary must ask the community to join in her intercessions."

"Yes, yes. I'll go and see Mary to-day, Tom. A Triduum. A Triduum of prayer—oh yes. We'll pray."

"I will myself arrange to say Mass here in the house to-morrow, to bring God's special blessing on our efforts—and everyone will offer up Holy Communion for her, and do everything they can in devotion and self-denial. We will place this great intention in the keeping of the Communion of Saints. To-morrow is the feast of the Church Triumphant, and Tuesday of the Church Suffering—they could not be better days for united faith and intercession—I'm glad I thought of it in time—it will give her courage for Tuesday."

Agnes looked with gentleness at the priest, her uncle. His faith, more florid than her own, though not more natural, had power to move her, and constantly he touched her deeply by the tender, unceasing fret that he carried in his heart for his dying sister. An unimaginative man, imagination came to life in him before the spectacle of her suffering, just as, a prudish man, he had mastered his prudishness in relation to Reggie, for Reggie's mother's sake. He alone probably, for she had always talked to him with confidence, knew from Teresa's own lips why the approach of death was so unbearable to her if it must leave her helpless son unshielded, and, search life's probabilities as he might, he could, like her, find no solution that could bring her ease and resignation save in some miraculous extension of her tortured life. She wanted her martyrdom indefinitely prolonged—that was the miracle she wanted. And nature, the doctors said, could not grant it. Perhaps God, who could do all things, would see fit to change the course of nature, or would quiet her troubled heart and compose it for death by revealing some scheme of safety and non-desolation for her son. And that would indeed be a miracle. Agnes, guessing these thoughts in the priest's head, felt an impulse of affection for him, and at the same time wondered at the fundamental failure of that feeling between him and her. "You must tell Mother, Uncle Tom. It will indeed give her courage."

He looked at her with gratitude. This girl did not often speak to him in such a tone of sympathy.

Nurse Cunningham stood up.

"Bessie will have finished," she said, "and Mrs. Mulqueen may be wanting me."

She moved towards the door, and Reggie stumbled after her to open it.

"Oh, please don't trouble," she said. But he plunged on.

"I hope, Nurse," said Canon Considine, "that you will be so good as to join with us in this Triduum? I want every possible prayer."

The nurse bowed her head.

"Of course, Canon."

"Thank you. And will you send me word presently, if Mrs. Mulqueen is well enough to see me?"

She nodded and went out. Reggie closed the door and shambled back in vagueness across the room.

"Is she satisfactory, that nurse?" the Canon asked Agnes.

"Oh, quite. Mother prefers the Blue Nuns, though."

"Still, she seems a nice, bright creature."

"She's very good to Mother," Reggie said.

"We're all forgetting about Marie-Rose," said

Danny, waving her letter. "Fancy our forgetting like that. Tch, tch!"

"What about Marie-Rose?" asked the Canon.

"Only that she's coming to see Mother to-day," said Agnes, who had not forgotten.

"I must run up and tell your mother. I must read the letter to her." Danny moved towards the door. "You want the carriage for twelve o'clock Mass, Agnes, is that right?"

"Yes, Father."

He went out, leaving the door open.

Reggie turned from the window, wiping his forehead.

"Those doctors on Tuesday—oh, I wish they'd leave her alone," he muttered. "It's hot in here. Oh, God! They ought to leave her alone."

He followed his father, closing the door.

"Poor Reggie!" said Canon Considine.

Agnes said nothing. Words could never measure what she felt before the wretched spectacle of her brother, who went to pieces always in this manner when an ordeal of reality could not be circumvented.

"I am glad that Marie-Rose will be here to join the Triduum," the Canon said. "Is Vincent coming with her?"

"She says that he's too busy."

"Ah! Well, it will be nice for your mother to see the child. And it will cheer you up, too, I expect. You're looking a bit pulled down, you know. You really oughtn't to go to second Mass to-day."

Agnes looked surprised.

"Second Mass?"

"But you ordered the carriage? Oh, I see, you haven't been to early Mass."

"No."

The Canon looked grave.

"I should have thought that in these sad days you would try to go as often as your Confessor permits to Holy Communion."

For her uncle's sake, not for her own, Agnes offered an excuse, which happened to be a true one.

"I sleep very badly in the small hours, Uncle Tom, and then I do not wake easily later on."

"I know, my child. These are not easy times for you. However, as you go to Confession every Saturday, you will be able to receive Communion at my Mass to-morrow morning—for our special intention."

Agnes said nothing, but some shadow flitting across her eyes caught her uncle's attention.

"You were at Confession yesterday, Agnes?"

"No, Uncle," she said, keeping her voice light.

He cleared his throat. It was very terrible to him, very cruel that any child of Teresa's should be neglectful of the routine of religion at this time when there was so much need of prayer and strength.

"Well, of course, I am not your spiritual director, but I thought it was your good habit to go to Confession every Saturday. Naturally, you will be able to join in the Triduum, but it would have been more complete, more pleasing to God, if you had made that little effort which every good Catholic makes against a mood of laziness. However, as I say, it is not my business."

She saw that he was deeply disturbed, that he wanted a passionate rigour of effort and self-denial to carry these three days of intercession to the feet of God. Again she was touched; again her strong faith sympathised with his. God must be stormed. He was omnipotent and omniscient, but He had arranged human things so that they should work upwards only by guess and faith, by intuitions almost entirely blind. This ill they wanted to put to rights was human and their own, and they could only bring to it their human means, of which one very certainly was prayer. No use in folding hands before the problem of God's Will and His incomprehensible attitude to suffering. So long as the soul knew God to acknowledge Him, then she must intercede, against all her own questionings and waitings. If prayer came naturally—and nothing was more natural to Agnes—now was its special time. No point in guessing at its value, its immediacy—only pray, if that seemed the true thing to do. Pray, and forget or forsake those little petty secrets of the selfish heart that made prayer difficult. Words of Saint Matthew flashed across her. "He saved others. Himself He could not save." But the saving of others was the thing that had had to be done. And if it couldn't be done? But that was not the point. She had just worked out that that was not the point. The blind effort, the passion was what must not be grudged.

"I will ring for a priest to hear my Confession after Benediction this evening, Uncle," she said.

His face cleared.

"Do, child—and God bless you."

Old Bessie came into the room.

"The mistress will be delighted to see Canon Considine now, Miss Agnes."

"Thank you, Bessie," said the priest, and moved to the door. "I'll see you again, Agnes. We must talk about the arrangements for Mass here in the morning."

Old Bessie's face was irradiated.

"Oh, glory be to God, your Reverence, are we to have that holy, blessed privilege? Oh, praise and glory to the Holy Name!"

Her canticle sounded back to Agnes after the door had closed behind her and the priest. Praise and glory. Praise and glory. She threw back her head and gave a little laugh. Were devils then so easy to exorcise? For courage suddenly was coursing through her. How easy! To ring the sacristy bell when Benediction was over and in a few minutes to destroy the unclean and sentimental selfishness of these three months. Be clean and free of it, and filled with prayer, before she saw his dreaded face again. Dreaded—no, no. A human face. A face as weak and selfish as her own; a face on which little sensual troubles were making a disproportionate, a silly mark. As no doubt they were upon

hers, too—while round her here a sea of pain was lapping. She would pray for its tide to drop, even if her
prayer were as vain as Knut's command. If she could
not save others, she would go those ways towards saving
them which instinct told her had some virtue. She
would seal her ears to sophistry and to self-pity. Oh, it
was easy, this sudden plunge.

The first bars of that study in E major that Reggie
was forever playing came shambling to her ears from
the drawing-room as uncertainly as the player's footsteps would have done—but she winced a little, for the
wearisomely familiar music was now a part of the illicit
pain that recently had dogged her. She smiled again,
however. Such onslaught was a bagatelle compared
with that against which she must be armed to-night.

She stood up and ran her hands across her eyes and
temples, as if to clear some film from the front of her
brain. The Chopin study crept along, gaining steadi-
ness. Humming it, she took her key basket and crossed
the room, but as she passed down the hall the piano
ceased, and through the open drawing-room door she
saw her brother lean his elbows on the music-rest and
cover his face with his hands. She paused a second,
pitiful; then, shy and fatalistic about his invalid misery,
she went her way. She had much to see to. All her
days were busy ones, and this, though Sunday, would
be busy, too.

The Fifth Chapter

DR. WILLIAM CURRAN came down the stairs of Roseholm as the hall clock announced half-past ten.

"Tell Miss Mulqueen that I'd like to see her,
please," he said to a maid, and went into the dining-
room.

Agnes was some time in coming to him there, and as
he waited for her he paced the length of the room with
quick, uneven steps.

Aged thirty-one, he had returned from abroad to
Mellick three years ago to take up the almost non-
existent medical practice of a stupid, muddle-headed
father who could afford him no better jumping-off-
ground into his profession, and to whom, in any case,
his prolonged and expensive studies in Europe had
seemed an absurdity. But Dr. Curran, junior, was as
unlike Dr. Curran, senior, as it is possible for any
man's son to be. The old doctor was soft, plausible
and, in spite of a reputation for stupidity, well enough
liked. The young man was dynamic, direct and, in
spite of a reputation for brilliance, unpopular. But he
had plenty of self-confidence and did not seem to be
aware of his unpopularity. Scrupulous, quick and
given to calling a spade a spade, he was said by many
of his patients to be unsympathetic; Teresa Mulqueen

had never found him so, however.

The six months which had passed since, instructed by Coyle, of Merrion Square, he had taken charge of Mrs. Mulqueen's illness, had been significant for him. For one thing, they had wrought a gradual change in the size and quality of his practice. The Mulqueen household stood high in the prestige of the Mellick bourgeoisie, and the doctor who attended them could safely be considered good enough to minister at other genteel bedsides. Young Doctor Curran had recently received many professional calls which had surprised and stimulated him. But more stimulating had been the relationship which had sprung up of necessity between him and Agnes Mulqueen. One visit to the house, of which hitherto he had known nothing, had been enough to show where now its intelligence and authority lay. The poor old husband, he decided, was incapable of following anything he had to say, or seeing any instructions carried through; the son—well, after five minutes' observation he could have rattled off that dreary medical story with far more accuracy than Reggie later used when he brought it to him for advice; the daughter was the person he must talk with and rely on.

At first his conversations with her were perfunctory. There were trained nurses in the house, and she had only to know in outline how things seemed from week to week. But as he searched deeper into Teresa's mind and found at last the reason for her resistance of disease, after Reggie had, by her request, sought his professional advice, and as he realised that Agnes was perplexed about her brother's ill-health without knowing anything definite of it, he decided that for everybody's sake she had better know the facts. Briefly and accurately, then, he gave them to her; but he was a conventional and puritanical young man, she was a young unmarried lady, and the year was 1880. They did not get through the conversation without some embarrassed pauses. At their next meeting, however, they both found that a sense of release and naturalness had crept under their decorum, and henceforward though their friendship remained formal, its terms of ease and confidence might have surprised their world of Mellick.

William Curran had always been clear in his views about women. Every inch a doctor, he deplored the mischief which the amorous instinct had done and continued to do to the human race. It would always have to be reckoned with, he knew, but he did not see that it was worth its own high and often hysterical claims. The sane thing was to despise, since you could never kill it. For his own part, women so far had been hardly more important to him than so many decorative toys. He had enjoyed himself abroad, and kept his head. Here at home he was continent, because he believed in continency and found it practicable. One day, and before he was much older, he would perhaps want someone to keep his house and bear him children. If he found a wife who fulfilled those functions pleasantly he had no doubt that he would grow very much attached to her; should she fulfil them less than pleasantly, he thought that he could probably manage to be kind, and keep his side of the social and religious contract. But life, he thought, the central impetus of life was in oneself and the work one did. Emotional attachments, after first youth, were only added things, graftings—of value to some men, but necessary to none. He did not know if he would indeed avoid it, but it was his hope that when he came to choose a wife, neither he nor she would be immediately in love. For that reason, though he would like his children to be straight and comely, he did not intend to woo a beauty. Beauties, he told himself, looking at Agnes Mulqueen, beauties are troublesome things about a house. They hold the eye, they need a setting. It would be distressing to see them wrongly dressed, or fading, or outshone by other beauties. Childbirth can be hard on beauty, especially it can hurt the narrow, slender kind of woman. So, looking at Agnes Mulqueen, he confirmed himself in his wisdom. And talking with her, had it the more endorsed. For intelligence, allied with beauty, made just such exactions on the spirit, he observed, as only the romantic is prepared to face indefinitely, exactions which, taken too seriously, taken for life, bring down on a man all the clumsiness and inefficiency of suffering.

So, for four months and more of his acquaintance with the Mulqueens, he had stroked and steadied his soul, until at last one night unaccountably he let passion have its head. In something as superb as ecstasy then he realised that this girl with whom he held sad and friendly conversation on four or five mornings of each week, had become the unique and mighty hunger of his life.

At first that was enough. Delighted, he let the flood of his new knowledge take him. How fine, how heavenly satisfying, to be all shot to bits like this! How glorious to be transformed, alight and mad, with no one knowing it, not even, in a sense, one's outer self! How exquisite a game, to match one's everyday control and skill against this inner frenzy! What power it gave to look upon her face with absolute appreciation, to hear her voice with ears tuned as no other ears could be! He was on fire, and for a space could do no more than suffer the unexpected flames.

But he was not a poet. He was a Victorian bourgeois, rationalist in the idiom of his mind, Catholic in tradition and practice, a man eager to harness feeling into usefulness. This unlooked-for love once quick in him, he must examine his chance to satisfy and domesticate it, since it seemed now to be an essential to his future ability and peace. What hope had he that Agnes Mulqueen would marry him?

Socially, though he would not be regarded as a triumph, he believed that he would pass. His family was poor, but it had been sinking in the social scale while the Considines and the Mulqueens were rising—

which always is an advantage. Financially, he was making a livelihood, and his prospects, with his energy and ambition behind them, were excellent. Naturally, in proposing to a wealthy young woman, he would be called a fortune-hunter, but he did not give a snap for that. Personally—well, he was young, healthy, muscular and intelligent—and when he bothered to try had no particular difficulty in pleasing women. But now these commonplace assets made him shiver with apprehension. Love, much larger in him than his rationalising powers, told him that he had no hope at all, that it was hopeless. Love told him that he was nothing more than a bumptious, everyday conceited man, no better than a million others.

But where were the million others? She had only a simple notion of herself and in her folly would almost certainly marry someone. At present in that quiet house no suitors came and went or would have been encouraged. Probably she would not consider marriage while her mother lived—but such a bar had now a sharp definition to it. Some day she would marry someone, and William Curran was not disposed to believe that here in Mellick she would find a man more likely to be good enough for her than he was. He gathered that in the days before her sister married she had been gay, and had enjoyed the attachment of admirers. She had indeed the ways of a woman used to male attention; she liked flattery, too. Once in the early days of their acquaintance he had said to her, without particular reflection: "You are like your mother." For half a second, before she accepted the tribute with demureness, he had caught a flash of surprised exasperation in her eye—for had not her mother always been considered plain? He had meant no more than a vague, the vaguest, physical likeness, and that their natures had a similarity which commanded something of the same quality of respect. But the quickly covered look of irritation had delighted him.

Summing up these normal things, he could assure himself that, on their plane, he had an honest chance. But beyond them, in the dark regions of her essential self, he had no light by which to grope. Her reserve was, he knew, an armour for more than a characteristic fastidiousness and sensibility. These, since they were in any case her nature, he would be prepared to face and understand, for he had in himself much sensitiveness with which to answer them, and to be admitted into conflict with them, though a perilous delight, would be delight enhanced. He was no more than decently afraid of the general exactions of her purely tempered nature. But she seemed to him to stand on guard over something more specific than just these—something circumstantial. He thought he found within the clarity of her grey eyes an anxious darkness, a shadow carefully laid across a secret. "There's something there," he told himself, "that she's afraid of, that no one must lay hands on."

This made him miserably uncertain, not merely because, since it existed, it might eclipse his hope, but lest, in the clumsiness which his desire for her might put upon him, he should hurt her through its means, and so lose that confidence of hers which he knew he had, and which he had taken care to build.

On this Sunday morning, having seen her mother, he waited for his customary interview with Agnes in a mood which had become uniform to all these waitings since he had revealed his own passion to himself. Outwardly he appeared at ease, decorous and friendly, a man of detachment and intelligence, sufficiently sustained by self-conceit. Inwardly he burnt in the usual hell of human longing which it had been his studied intention to escape; inwardly he did not know how he was going to endure the brilliant moment when the dining-room door would open and Agnes would come towards him across the threshold; he did not know whether it would be then that formality would grow insupportable and his heart insist on delivering its load—then or ever. He did not know for how many years or seconds the words of worship would refuse their cue, or when they would break from him in crisis of his malady. In regard to her he had left his rules and certainties behind, and lived from hand to mouth without direction, so that when she stood before him, though he steered with credit through automatic talk and gestures, his only true awareness was of her starry beauty and of the pounding of his blood.

He paused in his swinging walk by one of the windows, and stared at the pleasant orderly garden, now damp and flowerless, which Agnes's mother was so fond of, and into which, for her distraction, he had had her carried as often as possible during the vanished summer. "She'll never see rose-trees in flower again," he had told himself compassionately.

Now he gave his eyes to the contemplation of stripped trees and sodden lawn, and the upper reaches of his mind to the condition of his patient. But he was in a passion of alertness for one voice, one foot-fall.

Sunday morning was always quiet, except for Mass bells, in Mellick, and as still as death in this secluded suburb. The bell of St. Anthony's; the slow clop-clop of hoofs, from where, beyond the short drive, his gig was being paced along the empty road; a stamp, a jingle from the Mulqueen carriage-horses drawn up at the hall door; a rifle-shot to announce that some garden fanatic had potted a rabbit or a rook; in spite of his rational nature, in spite of his tenseness of expectancy, the sounds, isolated in quiet, brought in on Dr. Curran a cold sense of the futility of life, its brevity and sadness. "We are helpless," he thought coldly, "ignorant and helpless. And it isn't the final impassivity of heaven that matters, though that's like a cawl enclosing the world. That's unavoidable. But our worst helplessness has only to do with the affairs of this immediate life—and we'll never correct it, because we'll never find a way to learn the workings of each other. This uniqueness, this isolation—oh, God, it makes the simplest day unbearable! If I could know her as, say, God knows her—or if I could even for one minute see her with her own eyes—but exactly—then I might know what to do with life, for her and me. Then I might find a way to clean out sadness. If I could know her spirit even as little as I know her poor brother's body, or her mother's, I might see how to escape this love, or manage it. If there were accuracy anywhere—if one knew anything——"

But Saint Anthony's bell nagged on to proclaim the vagueness and immortality of the soul; his mare's hoofs clopped with patience to remind him that he was chained to a little human round; the Mulqueen coachman murmured to his horses. Nurse Cunningham, in outdoor dress, appeared on the hall door-steps, with Reggie shuffling after her in slippers, to open the carriage door.

Dr. Curran smiled indulgently. He had had some brisk passages with this pretty woman before she grasped that he declined to flirt with her. She was a good nurse, however—he would say that for her. Poor old Reggie! Always the chivalrous gentleman, even though he hated movement or standing about in the cold. But no doubt these posturings of mock manliness towards the female, grim as they were, were as good for him in their way, though not as safe, as potassium of iodide.

"Saint Anthony's, Paddy," he heard Reggie say to the coachman.

"I can walk back," said Nurse Cunningham.

"You cannot," said Reggie. "He'll call for you."

"Well, if you're sure he'll have time before Miss Mulqueen wants him——" Nurse Cunningham smiled and stepped into the carriage.

"He'll have to make time," said Reggie gallantly, waving his puffy hand before he turned to shuffle back into the warm house. The carriage moved away.

Dr. Curran, watching it idly, did not hear the door open and shut, but he wheeled with a start in response to Agnes's light footfall near him on the carpet.

How well she looked, almost gay, with her head so gallantly tilted and a half-smile flickering round her eyes and mouth. They shook hands formally, as they always did, and William Curran, hurled now into all the deep excitations which her presence roused in him, lost his cold sense of futility.

"I beg your pardon, Miss Mulqueen. I was watching the departure of la belle dame from Dublin."

"That's natural," said Agnes lightly.

"She's very 'coquette,' isn't she?" He raised his eyebrows in amused enquiry.

"I think so." Agnes's thin eyebrows drew together. "No harm in that, is there?"

He often encouraged indolent talk like this, for the sheer pleasure of watching the quick movements of her face and also because the light tone steadied him, and gave him time, as he told himself—without exactly knowing what he meant.

"No," she said, and then more softly: "Only, there's Reggie . . ."

William Curran laughed.

"Yes, I've just seen him waving her off with a flourish."

"So have I. He's very attentive."

"Does him no harm."

"Perhaps not. At any rate," her voice changed, "no one could encourage him *much*, poor fellow."

"That's true." He responded to her serious tone with seriousness. "And in any case, though la Cunningham flirts with everything, I should think, out of sheer habit, what she wants is a husband."

"Yes. Almost any husband."

"You don't like her?"

"No; do you?"

"No. But she's a first-rate nurse. She knows her work."

Agnes looked thoughtful.

"Then—you'd think that, from all the signs, and with her experience, she might guess about—about Reggie?"

"But of course. She'll have put two and two together days ago."

"Oh, well—if that is so——" Agnes's face cleared—"she, she won't be too irresponsible with him."

"Not she. Her amiable prinkings are just a habit.

But the only men she'd bother to encourage must be definitely in the market!"

Agnes laughed, and in her relief grew audacious.

"You, for instance," she challenged.

"Yes, me—by all means."

He twinkled at her, swaggering to cover the panic he felt whenever she focused on him, even as lightly as now. Agnes acknowledged the swagger with a quick look of amusement, then waived the airy nonsense with a circumspect swerve to their usual business.

"I kept you waiting just now, I'm afraid. I'm sorry, but my uncle, Canon Considine, is here and I had to confer with him about things. He's in the drawing-room, and would like to see you for a minute before you go."

"Yes, your mother told me. There is to be a Triduum, I hear, so that the great men may be guided aright on Tuesday."

Agnes cocked a grave and questioning eye at him.

"No, I am *not* being ironical. Why should I be? And the idea has made your mother very happy. But you see, I'm vexed with Coyle for bringing this fellow on Tuesday."

"You think it will do no good?"

"Bartlett-Crowe knows as much as any other consultant about cancer. That is to say, for the purpose of cure, or even of control, he knows nothing. The ordeal of this solemn examination, with the atmosphere of suspense which it is impossible to keep out of these things, is going to use up your mother's small reserve of vitality and is bound to curtail this interval of comparative ease which I find has set in this morning. It's going to cost your father a pretty penny, and will mean enormous emotional strain for all of you."

Agnes moved past him towards the fire, her face set in sadness.

"Ah, now I've depressed you!" said William Curran.

"Mother *wants* another operation."

"I know. But Coyle shouldn't encourage her. I can't bear to see her hoping and insisting like this."

"Well, at least it will console Father to know that nothing is left undone—and they might find that——"

"A fourth operation?"

"It would lengthen her life?"

He did not answer.

Agnes, standing in front of the fire with an elbow on the mantelpiece and her head resting on her hand, stared down at the point of her shoe that peeped out from under her dark red skirt. William Curran fed his eyes with a greed which he thought a life of staring would not satisfy. The long, narrow lines of her body, the girlish thinness of her arms, the sweet young breast, the soft dark fall of hair, her profile, saved from perfection by too much length of bone, by subtle irregularities of mouth and nostril and upslanting eyebrow, above all by its exquisite mobility of expression—all these beauties raised in him such a conflict of senses and spirit as made victory and defeat alike unbearable. For if he won her, what skill or right had he in such possession, and if he lost——

He thought of the Triduum she was about to make, and of the mystery of prayer. An hereditary Catholic, he took prayer as a matter of course, a natural human impulse which it was not his business, or perhaps anyone's, to explain. As a doctor he observed it to be the most salutary of medicines. The pros and cons of religion never stayed his thought, life as he found it being the field of his concern. And in that field it seemed to him that the Catholic Church provided as good a system as might be found for keeping the human animal in order—a necessity which he emphatically accepted. A good system because, through thick and thin, it exacted a soul of every man and instilled in the very lowest of its creatures an innocent familiarity with things not apprehended of the flesh. Mysticism and its chance to ennoble, or at least to alleviate, granted, Doctor Curran would be rationalistic, as indeed he observed the Church to be, in his manipulation and acceptance of the religious impulse. So he viewed this fervent Triduum with a saddish satisfaction. Emphatically it would help his patient towards and through a day he dreaded for her; it would lift up the sapless hearts of her husband and son by reminding their weakness of an almighty force that they might lean upon; and, it seemed to him, though he was only guessing, that it might provide a temporary escape for this too much hemmed-in girl from some unspoken personal trouble.

"It's peace of mind that you must ask for her in your Triduum," he said gently.

"I know. And that's the sort of thing you'd think He'd grant."

"Your prayers might accomplish anything, I think," said Doctor Curran in a voice that he found unfamiliar.

"My prayers?"

Agnes lifted her head and turned to him, her grey eyes open wide in sad astonishment. The glance distressed him, hinting again as it did at a trouble that was not his business. He smiled to help her.

"You say prayers, don't you?"

"Oh yes—I say them."

The emphasis was distributed for self-contempt. She took a step nearer to him.

"When you came into the room just now," he said, "your spirits were high. You were full of fight and courage."

She smiled.

"That's right," she said, seeking for lightness in her manner. "I thought I had broken a spell."

"What spell?"

"Oh, nothing. But moods change—mine do. And just this minute I don't feel full of fight, as you say."

"I have discouraged you?"

"Your medical knowledge has. I'm superstitious,

you see—and I suppose I thought I had driven a bargain with God."

"You had something to offer Him?"

"No, really. One's bare duty as a Christian is hardly a thing to haggle over."

"I imagine that you generally do more than your bare duty."

Agnes shrugged evasively.

"Tell me how you found Mother," she said.

Stung and relieved at her jibbing, he took a deep breath and a professional manner.

"Quiescent," he said; "she's entering a comparative lull. We must try to protract it, and keep her soothed and gently distracted. I have instructed Nurse Cunningham. The great thing is to keep her calm and help her through the strain of Tuesday. She said to me just now that she's going to live a long time yet, in spite of me!"

They laughed gently.

"That's a sign she's feeling a great deal better."

"Of course she is. Release from pain is deceptively like a renewal of life. Do you know that she has asked me to dinner to-night?"

"Asked you to dinner? Why?"

"How hospitable you are!"

So the only eyes whose acuteness she need fear would be upon her! Well, so be it. That would give added strength. Her courage rose again to the shock, and she laughed at her bad manners.

"Forgive me! But no one ever comes to dinner nowadays—and we have to be so quiet."

"I'll try not to throw things about or stamp my feet."

"Vincent and Marie-Rose are coming to-day."

"Oh! I didn't think *he* was—your mother said only your sister."

Agnes would have given much to stop the hot blood from creeping up her neck. She knelt to poke the blazing fire, in the hope that its heat might excuse her change of colour.

"Yes, Marie-Rose. Did I say Vincent? We always speak of them together, so I suppose the names get stuck from habit."

"I see. How are they, do you know?"

"Oh, very well, I imagine."

"When I met them here last August they did not strike me as happy people—and they ought to be."

She tried to feel angry at this intrusive comment on the private affairs of strangers.

"I'm sure you're wrong," she said detachedly.

"You are devoted to that sister, aren't you?"

"We were always great friends. It's a silly thing, but I still miss her very much."

"This life you lead is unnatural."

"What could be more natural than keeping house?"

"Oh, that!" He waved assent. "But you were

shocked at my being asked to dinner. That's a sign of what I mean."

She smiled.

"I don't know that I was shocked. And having to live very quietly is not a tragedy, you know."

"And yet," he spoke musingly, and more to himself than to her, "you're tragic, somehow."

She threw back her head and laughed, to cover a great embarrassment.

"How unlike you to say that," she said.

He was nettled by his own sentimentality and her amusement.

"I could be even more unlike myself, since it amuses you," he snapped.

She turned to him, all gravity now, with eyes that were kind and startled.

"Why, what's the matter?"

In her voice, in her kindness, with an intuition which he despised he saw his own inability to woo and reach her. The moment became both hideous and farcical; he hated it, hated its setting, and himself and her, its centre. How ludicrous, in black frock-coat, in healthy, sweating flesh that covered healthy bones, surrounded by the reassuring decencies of mahogany and mantelpiece and ticking clock, to be unable to ask a decorous and personable young lady to do him the honour of becoming his wife! To do him the honour of ministering to a common desire of the flesh, and to a hunger of nerves and spirit, a state of pain, distraction and uncertainty which she who had brought it about must in mercy bring to peace. What a grimly mixed request! And how to voice it to the sisterly enquiry of those eyes? How to hope? How to abandon hope?

He was cold and he trembled. The moment slid from its hideous liveliness to still despair. Despair—that was it. That was her gift to him—despair, the romantic slimy thing that made men unsure and useless.

"It was no part of my plan," he heard himself saying, and recognised an insane anger in his tones, "it was no part of my plan to fall in love with a *femme fatale!* I am a plain man of sense, a man with work to do, and I have always insisted that love should keep its place. However great it is or seems, you know, it comes to the same old mess of misery or dullness in the end. No man worth his salt should pay the price of his own intelligence and self-confidence for it. Because, after all, one can get its essential comforts cheaply."

Agnes was staring at her own reflection in the mirror over the mantelpiece.

"This is a strange declaration," she said icily, slowly.

"It's not a declaration at all. I'm not asking for anything, mind you. Not even that you should tell me what the barrier is that you have raised between us."

"I'm glad you're not asking for anything. If you

were, it might have occurred to me to cheat you."

Since he was indeed in the pitiful see-saw state which he despised, his anger fell under those words to let hope rise.

"What do you mean?" he almost whispered.

But she moved away, walking towards the window, then turned unexpectedly and flung her hands apart.

"Is no one happy, then?" she asked him fiercely. "Mother, Reggie, Father, Marie-Rose——" there was a pause—"now you as well! Is no one happy anywhere?"

"Are you?"

"How could I be?" Her gesture indicated the lives surrounding hers.

"You're dodging me again. I'm not exactly a complacent fellow, or a savage of cruelty either, but I could be happy underneath, I imagine, before the most awful spectacles of misery."

"Ah! But one is so much involved——"

"Not finally. Don't think you are. In the last analysis we are isolated—in spite of ourselves, and by that a bit protected. Why, if we weren't we'd all go mad!"

"And people do go mad."

"Yes. But not vaguely. They go mad from their own causes." He took two slow, unself-confident steps in her direction. "When you said just now that you might have been tempted to swindle me, what did you mean?"

"I shouldn't have said it. It was a feeble thing to say."

"Oh, God! This pose of strength!"

"I know. But I have to do it."

"Why?"

"Please! Because there are such things as right and wrong. Don't pester me!"

"I wish I needn't. I often wish I'd never seen you."

"I'm sorry."

The simple beauty of her as she spoke, the look of friendly sorrow in her face made easy for him those words which a while ago he had found unpronounce-able.

"I love you, Agnes," he said. "I had hoped that some day you might be my wife."

He spoke with circumspection now, as she did.

"I don't know when it would be possible for me to marry anyone," she said.

"Your mother's days are numbered."

"Someone will always have to stay with Father and Reggie. In any case——"

"Yes."

"You'd want a lot from a wife."

"Love is a lot—and I'd want it."

Agnes began to pace between him and the window.

"Oh, believe me, I'd be glad enough to give it to you!" Her voice was sharp with sincerity. "I've always wanted to be happy—and now, if it were only to show myself that someone can be! But by a fluke——!"

She stopped by the window and looked out across the garden. He came to her side.

"What is this fluke?"

She turned and lifted her face to him. It was deathly white. He noticed, with detached precision, the young and delicate perfection of the skin, the baby-fine eyebrows, the sanity of the grey eyes.

"The worst of it is that it's nothing," she said. "It's only a maggot in my brain."

He was wounded then, in that second, by a bright, scorching pity such as he had never felt before and could not explain, but he took it to be of the very seed and potency of love. He felt a thrill of resignation too. Her face, quite near him, transcended every common thought of beauty. He smiled at the mortal anxiety that shadowed its immortality.

"A maggot in your brain," he said dreamily. There was such a sudden music in his voice, such a fall of tenderness, that involuntarily she, who was distressed and afraid, came nearer. "We'll cure that, Agnes; we'll find a way to cure it."

In silence, still able to smile, he watched the tears flood into her grey eyes.

The dining-room door opened, and Canon Considine came in.

The Sixth Chapter

SUNDAY afternoon devotions began at half-past four in the Jesuit church in Mellick, and on this Sunday, which combined the last of the month of the Rosary with the Vigil of All Saints, they were long and ceremonious.

As Agnes entered the dark porch of the church she could hear the high voice of a young priest giving out from the pulpit the First Glorious Mystery of the Rosary. "Our Father Who art in Heaven, Hallowed be Thy Name, Thy Kingdom come, Thy Will be done on earth as it is in Heaven——" and sweeping in passionate depth and incoherency against him, the great voice of the congregation in response. "Give us this day our daily bread."

"Hail, Mary, full of grace!"

The priest's voice was dramatically distinct.

"Holy Mary, Mother of God——" the massed voice of the people was wordless and passionate, like the voice of the sea.

Agnes slipped into the shadowy end of a long bench. When, as a child of eight, she had first heard this tremendous-sounding form of prayer she had burst into sobbing for which she could offer no explanation to her exasperated mother. Was she frightened? Was she sick? Was there a pin sticking into her? No. Would she like to go home? Oh no! Teresa, unwilling to slap her before the Tabernacle, had looked a great many slaps, and then rejoined her calm contralto to the prayer-thunder which was crushing her little daughter's heart.

Agnes was reminded of that now, and smiled as she settled in her place. Nearer the communion rails, in the more chic benches of the centre aisle, she recognised the bonnets and back views of certain aunts and cousins, and was thankful that she was well placed for the strategy of avoiding them at the conclusion of Benediction. Normally she would not have minded a cousinly word with some of them, or even a lift home in one of their carriages, but it would be embarrassing to have to explain that one tarried this evening to go to Confession. Respectable young ladies did not ring the emergency Confession bell; to have to do so proclaimed either religious morbidity or, God forbid, a state of sin. And though it was often done on the quiet by ladies, young or old, as unimpeachable as Cæsar's wife—still it was done on the quiet.

"Second Glorious Mystery—The Ascension of Our Lord into Heaven. Our Father Who art in Heaven——" Agnes, who wished to be at the slow and difficult business of examining her conscience, held her breath nevertheless to await the startling rush of the antistrophe—"Give us this day——" that it might lift, as it could hardly fail to, her flattened, springless heart to God. But having felt the prayer-surge of the congregation catch her, she pulled back, jibbing, as always, against the easy way. She had not come here to gush at God, having so long dodged Him. She had come to examine her sin and purpose amendment.

How long since she had last confessed?

Vincent and Marie-Rose—she winced at the immediacy with which they plunged into her affair—had last left Roseholm on August 7th—she remembered Vincent's saying at breakfast: "Saturday, no luck at all," and that she had made the flurries of their afternoon departure an excuse to herself for avoiding her weekly confession. However, still refusing to think of the thing that was hurting her, and therefore, as she had insisted to herself, still innocent of sin, she made her usual confession on the following Saturday, the 14th, but had, to her own alarm, been unable to go to Communion all the same for the Feast of the Assumption.

August 14th. But that was ten weeks ago. And since then, quite apart from the central trouble, oh, how, over all that time, was she to recall and marshal her million sins against God, her neighbour and herself?

Against God—she must accuse herself, though she supposed no theologian would be dogmatic here, of what seemed to her the offence of lip-service, the cautious adherence to routine. She had said her usual prayers and attended Sunday Mass, had paused in her household affairs to say the Angelus when its bell came over the river to her. In such submission to her training she did not find herself all guilty, for she knew that if she could only bring herself to face these prayers with vigour, they would help her—and she hoped from day to day for that. But she also knew that human respect and a deeper kind of cowardice were elements of her conventional devotions. Against God, then, there were ten weeks of hypocritical tepidity.

Against her neighbour. Much pride and detachment always. A critical rather than a sympathetic front to the world. Some gestures of impatience, which she hated to remember, against her kindly old father. No words, but many inexcusably impatient thoughts against her brother Reggie, and from those thoughts the occasional withholding of impulses of kindliness, half out of shyness, but half out of contempt. Against her mother—oh, a million small sins of omission, moods of despair and weariness, slackness in prayer for her, slackness in hope. Against Doctor Curran—she smiled. In spite of his rage of this morning, she could not find much guilt in herself against him. She had not flirted, and she had quite honestly come to like and trust him. That he loved her was no surprise, but secretly, rather distressingly, a comfort. And in that, no doubt, she must admit unscrupulousness that she should take comfort in receiving that for which she could offer no adequate return. And in

accusing herself she had to smile again for thinking
how well met they two would have been as man and
wife. Ah well! Where was she in this long examination? Against Vincent? She took a long breath, then
bent her head still deeper into her covering hands.
She listened awhile to the torrential rise and fall of
prayer about her— ". . . Blessed is the fruit of thy
womb, Jesus. . . . Holy Mary, Mother of God. . . ."
Vincent. No sin against him. Oh, God, there is no
sin. Love happens—out of the simple fact that one's
eyes can see, that's all—and in itself it is pure, it has
no evil in it. Sins ring it round at once—ah, yes, because we are so weak and sensual that we cannot love
and let be. But against the thing we love, how can we
sin, however we offend against the world that parts us
from it? Passionately, as if afraid of finding out its
casuistry, she hurled this faith of hers to heaven—but
without pausing in it was swept on to where, in human
terms, her great guilt lay. Against Marie-Rose. Yes
—against the beloved, pretty sister whom she had
once loved above all living things, whom still in
essence she loved like that, or even, in her torment,
more than that, against Marie-Rose, the flippant and
untrusting, who would trust her soul to her, her sin,
long hidden even from herself, had grown in these
ten weeks into an offence which the shoddiest morality
could tilt at. The common sin against the ninth commandment, enhanced by all the pitiful complications
of sister love.

That brought her to the last section of the examination of conscience. Against herself.

She was sitting upright now, for the sermon had started. The Rector of the Jesuits was preaching. He had a quiet, holy voice, and after the swinging tide of prayer its unbroken flow was tranquillising. Agnes did not bother to take in the words, which seemed to be such as she had heard a hundred times, but she let herself assent contentedly to their tone of steady faith. Thus she might legitimately postpone the real business of this preparation for Confession. There was plenty of time yet before she need ring the bell and ask for a priest. Really, she might rest and listen to these blessed platitudes about the Queen of Saints.

For her final fear was of words. When she was a schoolgirl once or twice she had had to accuse herself of vague curiosities and stirrings of her sensual imagination—matters which she had not understood, but which she knew to wear the look of sins against the sixth commandment. The problem of how to frame these shapeless things for Confession so as neither to exaggerate nor minimise them had been an agony—but to her great peace the chaplain had accepted her half-breathed phrase, "immodest thoughts," with an incurious calm. From then until now the sins of the senses had not over-troubled her confessions. And whereas in relation to her neighbour, her sister, Marie-Rose, her sin could be described as an abstraction, an idea, against herself, in its recurrent visions, its suggestions, its seductive day-and-night dreams, it took on a particularity and harmfulness which could not be shirked.

The voice of the preacher thinned away from her, and she leant an elbow on her knee, bending her face to the shelter of her hand.

Must she then say that since she had last seen him her defences had grown less and less against definite adulterous longing? Must she tell of nights when sleep would not come, however she sought it, because of his mad haunting—or of other nights when she would hold sleep off, the longer to delight in him? What words were there that would be honest and yet utterable, in which to describe fool-fantasies of being his wife, or even, in secret, in treachery, his mistress? Oh, God! Must she say even that? Must all her hoard of misery be sloughed away?

It was too much, this shame, this pitiless exaction. She had fought her dark imaginings, and if they had defeated her, were they not only dreams, and senseless, hers alone, safe in the shame of her heart? Safe maybe—her disciplined spirit answered—except from God. It is for what He accounts your sin against yourself that you are searching now, and here it is. You answer to Him for your own soul as for every other. And as to shame—you have merited it. Without it, what would confession be?

She surrendered to the training that was at least half

herself. Surrendered into a sudden prayer for contrition and honesty.

The preacher left the pulpit. Young acolytes, moving softly about the sanctuary, had lighted more than a hundred candles. The atmosphere of the church was hot and still. There was a breath of incense and the soft clink of a thurible, then as the organ emitted a familiar chord of music, a procession of boys poured out from the sacristy and led a gold-coped priest to the altar steps.

"O salutaris hostia——"

Contrition, which for her characteristically was self-contempt, in the relation of personal pomposity to a ritual and a mystery which overwhelmed, contrition flooded her, cooling her shame as effectively as it did her heart-ache. Desires of the flesh, it told her, were not only as unimportant and transient as gnat-bites in summer, but quite as common, so that a confessor must be sick to death of little dreary tales of them—and hardly able to listen to another. To stage one's miserable narration in terms of distress and tragic uniqueness was nothing short of idiotic, a school-girl conceit so green and silly as to insult the whole purpose of the soul. Surely one must ask God to forgive that sort of idiocy as much as the idiocy of specific sin? Our absurdity must be more of a wound to the Eternal, Agnes thought, than our guilt. To have sinned was only too nauseatingly ordinary; not to see that and to make a self-inflating drama of sin was not so ordinary, but more despicable.

That was her contrition—to deny her own awareness of the agony which this confession was to be. Her contrition and her safeguard.

So, resolutely cold and still, resolutely contemplating, for its effect of levelling the ego, the beautiful pattern of Benediction, she took her place in that pattern, and refused herself to agitation. She was not herself. She was, much more fortunately, part of a formula. What was required of her was to be accurate in moving with that formula. Accurate, regular and cold. So conforming she would reach her own small objective, which was a part of the whole, and thus important.

They sang the Litany of Our Lady, and Agnes listened, concurring in the list of glories. They sang the "Tantum Ergo," and a little alarmed by the assault which the great words made on that personal anguish which she was here to kill with coldness, she snatched at two lines: "Praestet fides supplementum, Sensuum defectui—" and roughly adapting them to her own need, she took their message that faith was her supply, her sufficiency, the senses yielding nothing. Faith a cold thing, a fact—that was what she must use to destroy fantasy.

The monstrance was raised. God's blessing spread above bowed heads, and Agnes, feeling it, was afraid, as now she was afraid of everything she felt. She only wanted to know even this—that God blessed her. Not to feel it. Feelings, amorphous things, pressed on each other, merged, disturbed—and were of their very nature stained by human life.

But—"Blessed be God, blessed be His Holy Name—" the divine praises were pure, and to be raised up without anxiety. Agnes's voice joined in them, coolly triumphant. Blessed be God, who exacted self-forget-fulness. Blessed be God, who made so absurd a thing of human love.

". . . Laudate Dominum omnes gentes . . . sicut erat in principio. . . ."

Benediction was over.

The crowd surged down the aisles, bearing on it those cousinly hats and bonnets which Agnes had marked down to be avoided. Her corner was dark and it sheltered her. One by one the candles were extinguished in the sanctuary; quickly, once doors were opened, the atmosphere of heat and incense thinned.

She rose and walked to a door in a shadowy part of the centre aisle. She pulled the bell beside it. Far away she heard it jangle coldly. The aftermath of silence seemed very long before it was broken by the shuffling of old feet on tiles. Brother Fahy opened the door and peered into the shades. She made her request, which he took in silence. Then, dropping into a bench she waited, kneeling.

She must keep herself cold and quiet. This was a matter-of-fact and necessary transaction. an excellent means to an excellent end. In ten minutes it would be over, and she would be loosed from sin. How good an expression, cool and invigorating! "Since my last confession I accuse myself of—oh, Vincent!" Her heart contracted in pain, and simultaneously she thought that this calm which she was enforcing upon agitation was probably very like the calm a murderer would assume. She was going to murder the only thing which could be said to live in her heart.

She twisted about, her body unable to keep still. There was a curious twitching in her fingertips. "Oh, I wish he'd be quick," she whispered into her hands, almost sobbing suddenly; "I can't bear this waiting. Oh God, make him be quick!"

She heard the door open, and lifting her head saw a priest advance across the aisle to a confessional box. His Jesuit "wings" flapped as he moved; he carried his stole in his hands. Something both familiar and mystical in his aspect steadied her. She rose and followed him.

"Bless me, Father, for I have sinned."

Beyond the lattice, as she grew accustomed to the darkness, she could trace the grave, averted outline of his profile, could see his hand move slowly in the blessing as he spoke it.

"It is ten weeks since my last confession." She paused on that, but the confessor did not move, holding himself detachedly in listening attitude.

"Since then. . . ." The tale of venial sins came out

accurately and simply. Sometimes when she paused, the priest inclined his head to indicate attention. At last there was a longer silence.

"Is that everything, my child?"

"No, Father. The chief thing I have to confess— the chief thing——"

"Yes, my child?"

Steady, steady. Remember how cheap and commonplace the whole thing is. Hysteria and self-indulgence. Remember that it is God who hears us in confession— God, to whom time is not, and who knows the end as the beginning of this triviality.

"For three years, Father, I have—I have cared more than I should for someone—who is married. Married to a near relation of mine—a sister. At first it was all right. I could control myself, and didn't think about it. But lately it has been more in my head, and in the last ten weeks—it has been an occasion of sin. I have committed sins."

"You have spoken to him of it, do you mean? He to you?"

"No, Father."

"There has been no expression of feeling between you—no indication?"

"Oh, no. I have only sinned in my thoughts."

"How often?"

"These last weeks I have thought of very little else."

"You have prayed against it?"

"Not enough. I have said my routine prayers.

G

But I have not really prayed—I couldn't—and I didn't want to."

"You were afraid of the power of prayer—that it might kill this thing?"

"Yes."

"You have faith."

"I haven't used it. I took a middle way. I accuse myself of having been mean and cautious in my prayers—half afraid to give them up, in case all decency would leave me, but afraid to use them honestly too."

"At least you do not deceive yourself."

"I pity myself—isn't that the same thing? I have often pretended there is something tragic in my case."

"That is a human thing to do."

"Oh, human—yes!"

The priest moved a little, then resumed his immobility.

"After ten weeks of more or less surrender to yourself, this decision to confess and repent is impulsive?"

"Yes. Two things made me come to confession to-day. There is a special family intention for which I want to pray particularly—and for the sake of which I felt I must make this effort. And—and I shall be seeing him again this evening. I want help, Father. Oh, I want courage."

She bowed her head.

"God will assuredly grant you both, my child. It is your honest intention to give this thing no further licence in your mind—to keep it out of your imaginings at any cost?"

"Yes, Father."

"Since that is so, and if, with prayer, real prayer, you stick to it—have no fear. It will die."

"Yes. It will die."

Her voice was desolate.

"That is in any case the fate of earthly love, my child. Whereas in the search for God, in the idea of God, there is matter for eternity."

"Ah—for saints, or philosophers."

"Why should you not be either or both?"

Agnes smiled in the darkness.

"I am a frivolous kind of person, Father."

He seemed to smile a little at that.

"That would not have struck me," he said. "But these imaginings then, these illicit thoughts—were they only frivolous perhaps?"

"No." She paused and when she spoke again her voice was less distinct. "They were serious and—and wicked. I can't explain them."

"There is no need to. I only feared that you were perhaps making a mountain out of a mole-hill—though it did not seem as if you would. Do not distress yourself. I repeat that with prayer and courage you can kill this thing. You are disciplined in your mind and you do not deceive yourself. Have courage. What you want to do cannot be done without struggle, and perhaps frequent failure, but God will by no means refuse you the help you are striving for. For your penance you will say the Litany of the Saints once a day for three days. And I advise you to return to what was probably your former practice of frequent confession. Now compose yourself, child, to make a fervent act of contrition—and God will absolve you."

She saw him, still sitting in profile, lift his head and hand as his voice dropped mystically into the Latin absolution. Then she bent her own head into her hands and began her act of contrition. How simple! How formal and civilised was the method of the Church in its exactions. As she prayed and allowed the priest's words to flow into her mind, she was aware of coolness in herself, that her heart was only beating normally now, that the tiny twitchings had ceased under the flesh of her fingertips. She had done that which her belief exacted, and here, without fuss or probing, was the immediate reward—the cold comfort which assured her with gentle contempt that everything dies except the idea of God—even sin itself, being more mortal than the sinner. No need to distress herself. Self would thin away if one pursued the idea of God. Oh, blessed absolution, which can absolve us not only of our sin, but of its occasions, by making out of its own tranquillity nothing of them and of our confusion in them. She felt, most blessedly, of no importance to herself now, and Vincent of still less. It was strange, her mind asserted, to be able to say that without a quiver, and without a suspicion of hypocrisy, but her body gave her none. She was cold all through, and coldness, she was now aware, was the perfect state. Good-bye to vagueness, pain and restlessness, good-bye to heat and fidgeting and to fear of Marie-Rose's eyes. God had absolved her from all that. She was loosed from sin. What was that nonsense she had talked with Dr. Curran this morning? A maggot in her brain? And he had said he'd cure it. Well, she had found a quicker doctor. "Oh God," she prayed with gaiety, "Oh God, that folly's over. And with all I am I thank you. With all my strength I thank you for this strange thing you have done. Lamb of God that takest away the sins of the world——"

"Go in peace, my child—and pray for me."

The Seventh Chapter

"I DO think she might have stayed away from Benediction the evening I was arriving," said Marie-Rose.

She turned from the drawing-room window and gave the curtains a little pull into place.

"I'm sorry, my dear, I'm sorry—but she won't be long now," said Danny. "She doesn't like to miss her evening devotions, you know. She won't be long."

"As a matter of fact, she hasn't gone to them for weeks past," said Reggie.

"Well, she used not to be so madly religious. I hope it's not growing on her." Marie-Rose, pouting, came and sat near the fire. "I'm hungry too. Aren't you, Vincent?"

"It's very nice that you were able to come down after all, my boy," said Danny to his son-in-law. "Very nice indeed I call it."

"And very devoted," said Reggie. "Husbands are unaccountable fellows, aren't they, Marie-Rose?"

Reggie had spent the earlier part of the afternoon with his mother, draining from her spirit that reassurance of permanence for the existing state of affairs which it was essential to him to have. Having then had a drink or two while he refreshed the traveller,

Vincent, he felt his world secure now under his feet, and could strew it with his affabilities.

"Oh, I'm cross with Agnes!" Marie-Rose went on, tapping her toe in irritation against the fender.

"You'll have to look a more convincing Fury if you want to frighten her, Mrs. O'Regan," said William Curran, who was studying this pretty woman with interest. She was in his eyes as completely unlike Agnes as it was possible for another female creature to be. Fair, small and most delicately made, she might nevertheless have been almost commonplace in her extreme prettiness were it not for the dazzling accuracy of her 'chic' and a certain sweet imperiousness that accompanied it, an arrogance which could be both gay and pettish, but counted on victory from either method, a charm which could not help knowing that it had gained its ends before ever it went into action. The classic feminine of polite literature, William Curran thought, the sort of heroine whom lady novelists visualise as holding the hero in the hollow of her little hand. Not quite the happiest resting-place, the doctor surmised, for the particular hero she had married. Withal, though he did not think she had much mind—and there lay the spiritual complement of her faint physical resemblance to her father—he sensed that her intuitions would no more seriously mislead her about herself than about other people. Her own weaknesses she would not blench at, for she found so much compensatory strength in her strengths.

Moreover, though she might not be able to say it, she had probably found out by now that the rulings of tradition were, when in doubt, the best possible substitute for intelligence.

A spiteful summing-up, he mused. And why am I feeling spiteful? She is a delicious sight. But it's odd that in her different way she is probably just as difficult a woman as her sister! Poor old Mulqueen! William Curran let his eyes rest on his host, and took a flash of amusement from the idea of his fuddled begetting of enigmas.

"I am sure that you haven't many more minutes in which to endure our efforts to amuse you," he went on, smiling at Marie-Rose.

She liked the smile, which flattered. She looked him up and down with benevolent curiosity.

"You are very much *persona grata* here, aren't you?" she questioned amusedly.

Vincent was fidgeting with glass lustres on the mantelpiece, running his finger along them to make them tinkle. On this question he paused and half turned. The silence, and the sudden stillness of the man had an irritant effect on William Curran which he did not bother to examine.

"If I say 'no' to that, I am ungracious," he said, "but if I say 'yes', I'm a fool. As a matter of fact I believe that your mother *has* some confidence in me."

"Indeed she has," said Marie-Rose. "You should

have heard her singing your praises a few minutes ago."

"She is very brave," he said gravely and softly. "It is terrible to be of so little use to her."

The young woman's face saddened.

"Ah, poor mother!" she said under her breath, so that he felt no spite, and thought he saw a reason beyond her charms why Agnes loved her. She is a realist and she has feeling, he told himself. But why am I always pondering on failings and qualities? Surely I'm used to the old mixture as before by now?

The hall-door bell rang.

"That's Agnes," said Marie-Rose, jumping up as delightedly as a child. "I'd know her ring anywhere!"

She ran across the room, but a maid had reached the hall-door first and the sisters met just beyond the drawing-room threshold and, kissing, stood as if caught in a frame for their spectators.

"Agnes! You disgusting sneak! Oh, Agnes, I'm glad to see you!"

"I'm sorry, pet. I had to go to Benediction."

"Walked back, too—as if there were nothing to hurry for."

"It was a lovely walk."

They advanced towards the brighter lamplight of the room, their eyes still smiling on each other, and Marie-Rose hanging on to her tall sister's arm.

The four men, standing up, looked towards them,

two of them, Vincent and Dr. Curran, near the fire together, very still. Indeed, for a full second now, the whole atmosphere of the room suffered a strange hush, an almost violent expectancy, against which Agnes moved without concern, crossing the threshold. What was this triumph that she brought in out of the night— some of her watchers wondered; why did she enter her own drawing-room almost as if she were some gay, self-confident stranger, lifting its mood into excitement as she came? And yet there was nothing unusual in her manner or her words, which were simply and affectionately directed on Marie-Rose.

"Did you have a nice journey?"

"Oh, a cold old train. Vincent came too, you see, after all."

Casually she jerked her head towards where her husband stood, and Agnes looked at him, smiling.

"I thought he probably would. It's very nice that you were able to, Vincent."

Her voice was happy and gracious.

Vincent inclined his head and murmured: "Thank you very much."

Curious fellow, thought William Curran. You couldn't call him awkward, but I've never seen anyone take less trouble with his manners. He overdoes the "god in marble" pose. But the doctor was in a race after more important thoughts than of a sulky-seeming stranger. A maggot in her brain! he was thinking. My God, the moody nonsense with which women torture us! There's no maggot behind that triumphant face! And yet when she said it it was credible. Oh Agnes, Agnes!

"Doctor Curran!" She was greeting him now with the same easy grace she had bestowed on her unresponsive brother-in-law. "How dreadful of me to make dinner late the first time that you dine here!"

"I'm starving," said Marie-Rose. "It's long after half-past six, you wicked girl!"

These sisters made together as glorious a picture of vitality and promise, Dr. Curran thought, as their father and brother were a depressing one of hopelessness. Their complementary beauties were now accidentally in total contrast, for Marie-Rose's elaborate silk gown, its skirt all frilled and flounced in tones of pink, gave her in her delicacy the shameless and flirting seduction of an opening rose, whereas Agnes's outdoor dress—dark skirt, dark, tight-fitting sealskin jacket and little forward-tilted hunter's hat, dark-feathered, seemed rather to suggest offhandedly that beauty can hold aloof as well as challenge. For all that, Dr. Curran thought, her eyes had life and attack in them to-night instead of quietude, and her walk home against the small chilling wind from the river had whipped a faint sweet colour into her face which made a man dream she was eighteen and happy. She can look centuries older than this sister two years her senior, he said to himself, smiling at how such imformation would annoy her, but then she can look younger too. I have seen childhood and adolescence in her face.

"Oh, I know. I'm hungry too. Come up with me, while I change, will you? I won't be ten minutes, Father—I promise."

Danny took out his watch and wagged his finger playfully.

"Now, Father, no proverbs, please!" said Marie-Rose, and the young women moved to the door almost as one person, a gay feminine sympathy harmonising them even in their attitudes. Their mood of reunion, had William Curran but known—and he observed it now astonished—had always this merry flow in it, for it deceived them with the notion that they returned to the lost familiar, to their shared girlhood, its soft, uncornered happiness. Forgotten silliness reviving in these two when they met, made them move lightly together, in time to an echoing tune—and lookers-on, hearing nothing, seeing no ghosts, were chilled by a sense of being forgotten and shut out.

"Come on—I must fly."

The door opened and closed, and to the swish of silk they were gone.

Vincent O'Regan turned back to the fireplace and tinkled the lustres.

"They won't be long now, they won't be long," said Danny, blowing out his cheeks in an effort at brightness. Reggie dropped on to the piano-stool, and Dr. William Curran, sitting down, decided that he might as well take a look at the profile and long limbs of the sulky god in marble.

Being a good doctor, he saw more in his brief, veiled examination than most men could, enough at least to make him arrive at only negative and hesitant conclusions. This was a man, he told himself, about whom one could scarcely decide more than that he was unusual, and not to be measured by rule of thumb.

The admission irritated Dr. Curran, and he turned away from the god in marble.

It might however have pleased him to be told that his diagnosis was sufficiently to the point. Vincent was unusual. Born into an age not so much of feeling as of disseminated attachments and sentiments, he lacked the disposition to experience them. He felt neither good nor ill will towards men, and that it was the habit of his fellows to react towards and from each other did not engage his attention. He was observant, but he saw mankind, as he believed it to see him, remotely, detachedly, figures in a play. This made his views, when he did in rare fact express any, seem cool and unsympathetic—and people disliked with justification his neutrality, which they believed to be a pose. It was, however, so natural in him that he was not aware of it. And indeed it was not immediately to be discovered—even nowadays when unhappiness made him more exposed to diagnosis. But as a schoolboy, as a student, as a young man infatuated, good manners, adding the grace of tact to beauty and liveliness, had made him seem, though more victoriously armoured than his fellows, yet as vulnerable, as gullible, as easily moved as they. And he was in a sense more vulnerable, though his intimate friends, his brothers, the girls he toyed with, the women who took him to bed, all had to discover, however slowly, that he was immune from little scratches. He really was not, never had been, in the ordinary sense, involved with life. Until he was nineteen the only human creature who could rouse the discomfort of great feeling in him was his mother— and she, by her beauty and its poignant fading, by her benevolent detachment from life and her especial adoration of him, could always only too easily exult or wring his heart. She died before he was twenty and mourning her he suffered a storm of love and sorrow that left him more than ever neutral towards the rest of life. When he came of age and entered his father's shipping business, he assumed with grace the rôle marked out for him as one of Dublin's important eligibles. He sowed wild oats with an air. His good looks made him remarkable everywhere, his riches made him welcome. It was discovered that besides being a shot and a dancer he had intellectual powers as well, and a high commercial integrity. Some had cause to discover that he was kind, but in spite of the evidence of their senses most men continued to doubt that virtue in him, for it was revealed unemotionally, as if its dispenser mistook it for mere justice. There was no unction in him certainly, but still he used the balanced gracefulness of his body and spirit in order to conceal from society his dreaming coldness.

For he was a dreamer. If he was detached from the immediate world that was because he knew of others better adapted to his inclinations. He knew that life could have, and sometimes in fact had had, an exciting grace, an energy or a clarity, an intellectual significance, or a poetic—of which its partakers must have been somewhat conscious, and which must have made them complete, if not happy men. He did not exactly visualise himself as one of Pericles' young men when the Parthenon was rising, or of Alexander's in Persia, or with Pompey in Rome; he did not literally sigh to have been a poet with Ronsard, a statesman with Burke or a soldier with Napoleon—but he had a lasting nostalgia for his own conception of such days and personages. And he remained detached from actuality. He was always said to be more of a man's than a woman's man. He got this reputation not through any special affection of his own sex—for he troubled no one with great friendship—but because of athletic prowess and ability in affairs. Also, because, though only subtly, he betrayed that he found women more comic and pitiable than men. In his bachelor days it had been said in Dublin that no one could make him fall in love, and certainly none of the girls he kissed in his gay years could have sworn that she made him feel anything but amused.

And then he had met Marie-Rose Mulqueen, who, though very lovely, was no more so, many Dublin people thought, than a score of their own beauties, and perhaps not as good-looking as the tall young sister who accompanied her everywhere.

But Vincent saw no star but one from the hour he met her. His wooing was as frenzied as it might have been expected to be leisurely; from being cold, he became overnight a creature of flurry and uneasiness. It was as if her acceptance of him were to be life, her refusal death. And actually there was some analogous notion in his head. For, when he had long abandoned crying for the moon, here it seemed to be dangling near him. He thought that her beauty, her astonishing effect on him, gave an unsought chance to give reality to dreams of a civilised and gracious life. He thought that at her fire he would grow warm and confident enough to be himself, as he had been with his mother —only now in a richer, more developed way, and with the passion of his body to enforce expression.

He thought in fact what every young man thinks of marriage—only he came to it out of a habit of great loneliness, and with no experience of the traps and intricacies of feeling. He came to it too with a great deal of conceit. He brought to the relationship all that nervous attention and exacting self-consciousness which he had withheld from the rest of life, since his mother's death. Worst of all he came furnishing it with his own dreams, and leaving no room for another's.

Marriage, however it fails, marks and changes its participants. Vincent's marriage was a failure. A son had been born of it after ten months and had died very quickly of some sudden ailment; early in their second year Marie-Rose, overwrought no doubt by their reciprocal difficulties, had had a miscarriage and been seriously ill. They were thus still childless, and inclined to an unspoken superstition that that was only a symptom of the predestined misfortune of their union, which, beneath its decent worldly gloss of peace, was unstable and unhappy. For some time now both were aware that their original power to drown mutual offences in passion, and build again on the oblivion that passion gives—that this power was going, if not gone. And one of them knew that the will to seek such periodic mending was now gone out of him. But, having been infatuated with Marie-Rose and having failed in that infatuation, he was no longer the man he had been before he saw her. She had taught him much, and taken much away. There was no regaining his old imperviousness to feeling; there was no going back to contented isolation. She had taught him to sulk at the world on which he had been used to smile. Having led him much further than any other woman into the maze of passion, she had somehow with him missed the way to a central and explanatory love so that he was left guessing at the measure of her disappointment, but ruthlessly and bitterly aware, out of his accomplished knowledge of her, that it

H

could never be as deep and dark as his. And yet, though he knew her lightness, and made to himself both a grievance and a consolation of it, pride nagged at him in her presence. For she was exquisitely tempered for those urbane pleasures he had dreamt to find with her, but had ironically made false and bitter for them both. This was a failure of the artist in him, of the dreamer—and an additional soreness. His predicament was the worse because his habit of mind left him without a friend to turn to, and, sceptical of contemporary life, he had no ideal or enthusiasm to distract him. He had staked everything first on his mother, then on a life of amused detachment and last on a frenzied love which had overthrown that life. Now love, since he had failed it, had come back to play a devil's trick on him—had changed its face and, taking on impossibility, had settled down to mock. And he was young and had no friend or dream or child whereby to escape love's plaguing.

It was the nemesis of his temperament. Because he knew nothing of the little fads, attachments and day-to-day sentimentalities that keep men too fidgety to notice pain, he was now immensely more vulnerable and defenceless than he need have been. A convicted, practised dreamer, he was shut in now with one quite impossible dream. He felt the irony of his predicament in all his nerves, and they were growing merciless in expression of his resentment, so that there was hardly any trace left of a once famous grace and gaiety.

He relied unconsciously on his proud bearing and on the automatics of good manners to carry him through a life he barely noticed. But his wife had to suffer the hysterical reactions from this outward insolence, as well as the deeper and more cruel vengeance which he had no will to practise on her but which decreasing self-control released in spite of him. And he had to take on his unready shield the swift and shattering rallies which Marie-Rose's lively spirit, however bewildered, never could forgo.

A desperate situation to have to conceal from the sharp and prudish eyes of Irish society in 1880. No wonder Dr. Curran refused the rules of thumb. No wonder that even as he talked now with his host his brain, in spite of him, returned uneasily to the sulky god who tinkled idly on the lustres.

The Eighth Chapter

"MOTHER may be asleep now, so look out for the creaky board," said Agnes softly.

"Yes, I remember," whispered Marie-Rose. "You ought to have it mended."

"Well, the workmen would make such a row, and take so long."

"That's true."

" 'Sh—her door is half open."

They tiptoed along the dim and carpeted corridor.

If it were for no more than such interchange on household matters, thought Agnes, long used to debating them in silence, how delicious to have this sister here again! And now, with heart cleaned of offence against her, now cooled by the antiseptic of confession, to be able to turn to her, with the old, deep, unstained affection—it was glorious! To have been able, after ten weeks of miserable dreaming and self-pity, to enter a room where he was and look at him and feel no fear or heat or tenderness—oh God, that was bliss, that was a miracle!

She opened the door of her own room. Marie-Rose, with an arm round her waist, was hugging her excitedly.

"The dear old hole! You keep it much too tidy now!"

Agnes raised the flame of a lamp.

"I often wish you were back, to muddle it up!"

"God knows, so do I!"

Lightness had gone from Marie-Rose's voice. She stood apart from Agnes and her eyes searched over the well-known objects of the room.

" 'Sh, silly—you don't mean that."

"I do. Oh, isn't it just like him to pester me by coming here, when he knows that all I want is peace."

Agnes had got out of her hunter's hat and jacket and was rummaging in the wardrobe.

"When did he decide to come?" she asked, listening to herself with suspicious attention.

"I don't know. He announced it half an hour before I left for the train. Anyone would think he cared about me, the way he goes on sometimes."

"But he does," she said. "Don't look, pet. I really must wash."

Marie-Rose stared absent-mindedly at her back view as she stood at the wash-stand in silk petticoat, with arms and shoulders bare.

"You're very thin, Nag," she said, using an old pet name of her own invention. "But I must say you look young. Though you're getting on, like myself. Oh Nag, it's awful to be twenty-seven!"

Agnes, splashing the hot water about herself, did

not answer. Marie-Rose sat on the bed and examined the sealskin jacket lying there.

"Lovely coat. Glad to see you're not dowdy yet, anyway. All this praying and going to Benediction scares me!"

Agnes crossed the room slowly, holding a towel against her throat and breast. She stood near the bed, smiling down on the lovely creature perched on it. Her own face, just washed, was flushed and shiny like a child's.

"Little heathen!" she said gaily. "Perhaps if *you* did some praying for a change, it might be no harm!"

Marie-Rose shrank away.

"Are you going to lecture me?"

"Do I ever?"

"I'm not doing anything wrong. How could praying help me?"

Agnes was in a dangerous condition of feeling invincible against the elements of her life. A condition touched with insanity, which visits the sane. A condition of pride which made her humble and tender. She sat on the bed and began to brush her hair.

"It's amazing what it can do," she boasted vigorously, then pulled herself up. "What do you want anyway?" she said.

"Just not to lead a cat-and-dog life forever."

Fatuous, Agnes thought, to suggest that such achievement depended on oneself, since oneself depended on unpredictable tides and movements. A reflection so contradictory of her own self-reliant mood that she smiled very broadly, even while she admitted that her sudden return to self-control and effort was due to some heavenly accident rather than to any virgin movement of her will. We are as the day's necessities impel us to be, she thought, and life with him is starving her of something, and she is starving him of something too. Accidentally, without plan, they are destroying each other. A cat-and-dog life and I don't see how they can help it.

Youthfully in love, Vincent and Marie-Rose had entered married life, each unconsciously on guard against a passion which might submerge the beloved and familiar self, which might ask arrogance to die. And quick emotional antennæ had not been long to find for each this hidden hardness, this antagonism in the other. Delight made little enough of it at first—indeed exulted sometimes in its stimulation—and found no trouble in subduing it to natural rapture. But the aftermath was always bitter—neither could see why; neither could bear to have it so. Resentment, always quicker in both than tenderness, spread itself, evolving a game for them to play, so that if Marie-Rose, in temper to punish her own softness as well as her husband's, ignored or jibbed from his moods of amorousness, he had his vengeance when in her turn she played the lover. While this state of things established itself with only very infrequent lapses into mutual pleasure, they never spoke of their disharmony, or of such a grave thing as unhappiness, but acted their marital comedy at speed for what they saw it to be worth, each more and more for self and for the good theatre of a moment—he refusing the tones and attitudes of yielding flattery which he knew were meat and drink to her, she tiring him with inconsequence and mockery. A cat-and-dog life, the only real escape from which for Marie-Rose was return to this sister who had always rejoiced to take her as she found her, who, if she knew her for a bargainer, accounted her a fairly generous one who in return for light acceptance could lavish many kinds of faith and soft indulgence. And Vincent, weary and contemptuous, grown jealous of this shelter Marie-Rose could seek, had fallen into dreaming of it for himself with hopelessness.

A cat-and-dog life. How hateful! How absurd! An anger that was quite impartial swept over Agnes, but turned to partisanship as she looked again at her lovely sister. Then the light of pride, the look which perhaps was all that Marie-Rose had come for, was unmistakable—saying the things of blood-love and remembrance and sheer pleasure which Agnes never said in full, though sometimes hinted.

"It'll get better, little Rose. Oh, I promise you it must get better!"

"How?" asked Marie-Rose, with that innocent hope which must be answered.

"You'll come to understand each other."

"Ah! That's our trouble now. Understanding people is sheer madness."

"Maybe. But you and I—in a way we understand each other."

"That's true. Oh, Nag, if only I were here with you still! If only I had never seen him!"

Agnes's life-long tenderness responded to these cries, and her body moved towards her sister on an impulse of consolation—but meanwhile memory searched for what life had actually been before Marie-Rose, before they both, saw Vincent—the movement hurt her, as a sensitive nerve in a tooth quiescent and forgotten can unexpectedly stab. She was startled. Was love not dead after all? But the voice of the confessional came back—"That is in any case the fate of earthly love." Oh, good, oh, splendid!

She flourished her hair-brush and jumped off the bed, singing softly.

"What's come over you, Nag? I thought I'd find you terribly depressed, with Mother so ill and everything——"

"I know. Am I shocking you?"

"No, only what's the matter? You're so lively. Are you in love?"

Agnes was pulling herself into a rustling, flouncy, tight-waisted dress of oyster-coloured silk.

"Lord! Who's there to be in love with?"

"That doctor—perhaps."

"Oh—silly." She was struggling with hooks and

eyes. "You might help me with this, lazy-bones."

Marie-Rose came to the rescue.

"This the dress they made you at Switzer's lately?"

"Yes."

"I think it's perfectly lovely. The colour makes your skin look like milk."

"Well, I can't let you have it all your own way, my little beauty." She was staring at herself in the mirror, smoothing her silky black hair, and running quick, vain fingers over her narrow eyebrows. "Washing does make you shine," she said bitterly. "Do you think they'd notice if I powdered, Rosie?"

"Not they. I'm powdered, as a matter of fact—but men are stone-blind. I'll do it for you. You're in such a fuss you might easily overdo it. Sit down."

Agnes sat down, and submitted herself patiently to her sister's skill with the powder-puff. She closed her eyes.

"You look quite saintly that way," said Marie-Rose.

"Nice kind of saint, powdering my face! That reminds me. I have my penance to say to-night."

"Penance? But this is Sunday. You weren't at Confession to-day?"

"Yes. Thought I'd better—for the Triduum. And I hadn't time to say it just now."

"What did he give you?"

"Litany of the Saints," said Agnes evasively.

"The whole Litany of the Saints!" Marie-Rose stared. "But I've never heard of such a penance. He must be a terribly cross priest!"

Agnes laughed, but Marie-Rose was still staring at her with curiosity.

"I can't make you out, Nag! What are you up to?"

"Only trying to save my soul—which is more than you're doing, my lady."

"I like your impudence. No one's ever had to give me such a scandalous penance yet. And by the look in your face, I—well, I'd swear you're in love!"

"If there's any 'look in my face,' as you call it, it's for the exact opposite reason."

"Rubbish!"

"Here—I must be like a mill hand by now!"

"Wait—it's showing a bit on your cheek. There! Now you're lovely."

Agnes laughed at her.

"And so are you. A pair of raving beauties. Come and see Mother for a second."

Rustling their silks and laces, they hurried out of the room and along the corridor. They paused by the half-open door and whispered through the draught-screen. "Sister Emmanuel!"

The old Blue Nun peeped round it.

"Come in, children—come in. The sight of you in your grandeur would do anyone good, glory be to God!" She turned back into the room. "Here are two fashion plates from Paris calling to see you, no less!"

Teresa's pillows had been lowered for the night, but

her eyes were wide open and in the half-light of the
room she looked fairly well. She flickered her fingers
in mocking recognition of her daughters' splendour.

"Great goings-on to-night, seemingly," she murmured.

"Well, Marie-Rose is so grand nowadays," said
Agnes.

"That we have to show what poor old Mellick can
do. That's right."

"It'd be hard to pick between the two of them, God
bless them!" said Sister Emmanuel.

"True for you," said Teresa, though probably her
instinct veered towards Marie-Rose, the antithesis of
herself. "Have great fun now, let you, for a change—
it's All Hallows'—and don't be thinking that you're
disturbing me, because I'm wide awake, and I'll be
glad to hear something going on in the house. We
have enough quietness."

"Maybe you'll come down and join us, you're so
lively," said Marie-Rose.

"I wouldn't put it past her," said Sister Emmanuel.

"Is Nurse Cunningham having dinner with you to-
night?" Teresa asked.

"No, Mother." Agnes seemed surprised. "She
always has dinner in her own sitting-room. She's
generally tired, you know."

"Well, on Hallows' Eve it'd be more friendly——"

"Oh no, Mother," said Marie-Rose. "Let's have a
little peace. I hate all nurses anyway, except Blue

Nuns." She smiled brilliantly at Sister Emmanuel.

"But Nurse Cunningham is a nice girl, Rosie. And we ought to be kind to her."

"I don't see why," said Agnes, deliberately softening her comment with a mischievous smile at her mother.

"You ought to be ashamed of yourself, miss," said Teresa, half severely. "Ask her down to the drawing-room afterwards, anyway, let you."

Agnes was obstinate.

"She goes to bed early, Mother."

"So will you all to-night—with Mass in the house to-morrow. Be nice about it, child, to please me."

"Oh, well——"

The hall clock struck the quarter-past seven. Teresa looked startled.

"Good gracious me! That's three-quarters of an hour you're keeping them waiting for their dinner! I never heard of such a thing!"

"Poor starving gentlemen!" said Marie-Rose amusedly. "Aren't you glad you never got married, Sister Emmanuel?"

"Delighted, child, delighted—thanks be to the good God."

"The nonsense they talk," Teresa whispered tolerantly, "and that girl has the best and handsomest husband in all Ireland, God bless him!"

Agnes bent over and kissed the broad, grooved forehead.

"Good-bye, Mother. We'll look in later on if you're awake."

"That's right, child." She closed her eyes. "Don't forget about Nurse Cunningham!"

Agnes pulled an unwilling face. Marie-Rose laid her white hand lightly against Teresa's cheek, and together they rustled away beyond the screen and down the corridor. They were silent until half-way down the stairs, each recovering from and thinking about the sick-room.

"Poor darling Mother," said Marie-Rose very softly at last, and then: "This nurse—is she a dreadful creature?"

"Everyone tells me she's very pretty."

"Puss! Puss! Why don't you like her?"

"I don't see why I need."

"Is she after your doctor, do you think?"

"Oh—but of course."

"Ah! I see. What fun!"

Agnes laughed.

"You've got it all wrong, little silly."

The Ninth Chapter

AGNES and Marie-Rose, crossing the hall together at the end of dinner, having left the gentlemen to their wine, remembered their mother's admonition, and sent a message to Nurse Cunningham, inviting her to join them in the drawing-room, if she were not too tired.

Presently, with coffee, the maid brought Nurse Cunningham's cordial thanks and promise to descend very shortly.

"*Maintenant ça va commencer,*" said Marie-Rose.

But for Agnes, dinner had set so many things in train that she could only be absently amused at her sister's flippant curiosity about this other woman. No doubt it would be fun to watch her making hay while the sun of a social occasion shone. The pity was that her harvest could only be of nothing—for with Vincent and William Curran in embattled, concentrated, dangerous mood, it was unlikely that the fascinating nurse would be required to use anything more exacting than the coarse gambits which pleased Reggie, and in which she got ample practice every day at breakfast.

Agnes moved to draw back curtains and open a window.

"Can you bear it, Rosie?" she asked as the icy wind whipped in.

"Well, for a minute. I must say, although it is a cold night, I feel hot. Excited or something. As for you, you're looking feverish, Nag!"

Agnes felt a little feverish. This pause, with all the males shut off, was blessed.

"Lovely dinner," said Marie-Rose. "I must drag that sole recipe out of old Maggie somehow." She sat down at the piano and began to strum. "Oh, it's nice being back again, Nag!"

"Enjoying yourself?"

"Well, in a way. At any rate, I feel alive for a change. But Vincent's driving me mad this evening!"

"Why?"

"Making a fool of himself!"

"Rosie—he isn't."

"Well—could you tell me when you've last heard him talk and laugh like this—and hold the centre of the stage?"

"Actually, not since your wedding-day."

"And it's nearly as long since I saw it happen."

"But what's the harm in his being happy?"

"He isn't happy. He's showing off—and I can't stand it."

"Why is he showing off—here?"

"That's what's so silly. Pretending to Father—and you, I suppose—to be the glorious and charming husband!"

"He's never troubled to do that before, though."

"With him, that's nothing at all against his doing it now." She rippled a fierce arpeggio up and down the keyboard, then swung round on the stool and faced her sister.

Certainly, Agnes thought, she looked, as others were by magic looking to-night—alive, and even a little feverish.

"You know, Nag," she said, "if that doctor man weren't obviously your property, I'd take my revenge on Vin by scalping him to-night!"

"What revenge? Why shouldn't Vincent be lively?"

"Why only when he chooses? And after months of sulking!"

Her face was baffled, angry.

"Rosie, my pet," said Agnes sorrowfully.

"Of course, it's really Dr. Curran's fault. Vin's jealous of him."

"Jealous?" Agnes was startled.

"Yes. You see, he never admits that anyone has any brains except himself, or any personality—and if they really have, he either ignores them absolutely or behaves like to-night—decides to outshine them at all costs!"

"I think those two are getting on amazingly well."

"But they hate each other. Couldn't you see it?"

Agnes didn't answer.

"And Vin is talking and posing so much, that I'm

I

sure Dr. Curran thinks he's a fool. And really, that's infuriating!"

"If he thought it, he'd be a fool—and he isn't."

"Vin is drinking a lot to-night."

"I thought that. Does he often?"

"No. Not when I'm about, anyway. This is very queer. But what do I care?" She swung back to the piano and began to strum. "Do you remember our duets, Nag? Do you remember this one?" She gave an amusing parody of herself, aged about eleven, playing "Paul et Virginie."

Agnes smiled.

"Come and play your bass," said Marie-Rose.

"I don't remember it, Rosie."

How quick she was, thought Agnes—quick, but mercifully not deep or ruthless enough—or perhaps only still too innocent to reach the true meaning of her observations. To have seen that those two men, so suave and yielding to each other, so appreciative and gracious, had become already, before they had eaten their soup, conscious and excited enemies; to have seen that William Curran, though far from thinking him a fool, did in some special sense despise this sudden foe; to have seen that Vincent, to-night the personification of what we call happiness, was, in fact, not happy at all—well, a wife might see that last, even a stupid wife, which Marie-Rose was not, or a contemptuous, which she appeared to be.

Dinner had not been at all what Agnes had at breakfast visualised it—a saddish family meal, conducted in monotone, with Vincent sulkily non-contributory, and Reggie concentrating on his food and wine, while she and Marie-Rose supported each other in effortful passages of brightness designed to cheer their father.

Three things had changed its character. Her own decision at self-conquest, with the sense of triumph, control and contempt for emotion which that had brought; the alert and effective presence of William Curran; Vincent's mood of radiance, alarmingly put on as he ate his soup, and carried with triumphant ease through the whole meal.

Alarmingly put on. Agnes could not, search his eyes as she might, decide what his game or impulse was. Only she could swear that it sprang from some particular and sudden seizure of unhappiness, from some hidden accident of a moment which had provided the last straw. Thereafter, with a touch of madness in it, Agnes thought, as if it must be this or murder, he brought his lost youth spinning back, to dizzy himself and them. He was delightful—to his father-in-law, to his wife, to Reggie, to William Curran, and to her, at whose right hand he sat.

It was a curious onslaught. Agnes thought as she watched him that Heaven, doubting perhaps her denial of love, her resolve on coldness, had sent this theatrical test to try her out. An idea with some irony in it which she applauded. To show you, grown older and conceited, inflated by the heroics of renunciation, just what young love had been, and why it had been scorching enough to wither up girlhood. But even Heaven, it seemed, could not quite do that, could not quite bring back the demigod of that far time. Her memory was a better re-creator, and this charmer who was carrying off his part so well was no more than a tired, unhappy man, impelled to give a superb impersonation of the dead.

Well, one does not fall in love with the dead, or with a figure in a play. Heaven's irony would not defeat her this time. Had she not said before the Blessed Sacrament that she was done with love's illicit laziness, and did he not belong to Marie-Rose? This teasing and surprising of her was no good. She had meant what she said in confession. Besides, he was silly. Surely by twenty-nine the sane had grown an extra skin? Ah, but if they hadn't? said pity suddenly, and Agnes, frightened, had turned her eyes to the left side of the table, to William Curran.

Here was a man not very much older than this playboy, a man with just as much right to what he wanted, a man of brains and charm, who yet would consider it indecent not to carry his own load without making scenes, a man who refused the tantrums of romanticism. And yet—"It was no part of my plan to fall in love with a *femme fatale!*" How angry his voice had been! Sane he might be and adult and all the rest of it, but he was fool enough to make a *femme fatale* of her. How long ago it seemed since he had said it—that almost irresistible phrase! Her eyes softened as they rested on him.

"But, Agnes," Vincent's voice had broken in, imperiously swooping, "don't you please admit that Catherine is utterly uncharming?" They had been talking of "Washington Square," which everyone was reading in the *Cornhill*. "Unless there's charm in a kitchen dresser, say, or a set of fire-irons?"

"The poor, unfortunate girl!" said Marie-Rose in real amusement.

"Couldn't fire-irons ever be charming?" Agnes wondered.

"No, no," said William Curran. "You see, they simply can't be frivolous."

"That's depressing," Agnes mused, "because neither can I, I think."

"Oh, what a story!" said Marie-Rose. And she turned to Dr. Curran. "It's appalling the way this girl is going on lately. She used to be so nice and disedifying. What's the matter with her?"

"Nothing more than a frivolous affectation, I imagine, Mrs. O'Regan."

"Oh, Agnes!" Vincent said, and his smile had a strange radiance. "I assure you frivolity is the only wear!"

William Curran, observing the two, wished that in receiving that smile from her brother-in-law, Agnes had not turned her face at such an obtuse angle from himself. And yet was half glad she did. For if the quick drop of her eyelids was really as suggestive of disturbance as from where he sat it hinted, he would not know how to endure the revelation.

Holding his place quite steadily in the conversation, he knew that a fear which had inexplicably visited him when he turned to survey Vincent O'Regan in the drawing-room, was growing and growing now in his breast. Fantasy, he told himself, the mad illusions that always turn a man in love into a fool.

"Oh yes, I expect it's comfortable," Agnes answered Vincent.

"Oho, how disillusioned she sounds!" said Marie-Rose.

"What else would you have her be?" Vincent asked.

"Happy, perhaps." Marie-Rose kept her tone delightfully light.

"'Happy is he who serves the happy,'" Danny murmured to himself.

"It's news to me that you're all so miserable," said Reggie mockingly.

"Well, now you know," Marie-Rose had laughed across to him.

And now she twirled on the piano-stool and looked uncertain whether to be vexed or happy.

"I hate this interval before the men come back," she said.

Agnes laughed at her.

"And I thought you had really come down to see *me*," she said.

"Oh, Nag, I did! And if we were having the evening in peace together—I'd adore it. But this kind of thing!"

Agnes mused. Marie-Rose might say what she liked about the exasperations of marriage, but male society was bread and wine to her. She ought to be happy in what was visibly her natural state.

"Nurse Cunningham is a long time coming down."

"I bet you a pair of gloves," said Marie-Rose, "that she enters this room exactly five minutes after she has heard the gentlemen cross the hall."

"You seem to know her?"

"I only know what any female would do."

The drawing-room door opened.

"If only they'd leave it to Mr. Gladstone," Danny was saying worriedly.

"They've been leaving it to Mr. Gladstone, or his equivalent, for quite some time," said Vincent, laughing, and drawing Agnes into the talk with a quick, appealing smile.

"Worried about the Land Leaguers, Father?" she asked.

"This business with that unfortunate Captain Boycott now," Danny went on, "what's the idea in that, will you tell me?"

"Actually," said William Curran, "there is a good and natural idea in it."

"It'll lead to trouble—that's what it'll lead to."

"Probably," said Vincent. "Most good and natural ideas do."

"Oho!" said Marie-Rose. "My husband among the hot-headed idealists! What sort of wine have you been giving him, Reggie?"

"Port, just now."

"The wine that made the *status quo*," said William Curran.

Vincent came and sat by Agnes near the fire.

"There's no such thing as a *status quo*," he said.

"Oh yes, there is," said William Curran.

"What do you think, Agnes?"

"For ordinary purposes I think there is, in spite of everything."

William Curran drew nearer.

"What a lot of qualifications!" he said.

"But naturally!" said Vincent. "Nothing is fixed. Nothing is what it appeared a moment ago to be."

"Then if I assume at this moment," said William Curran, "that you are a Catholic, an Irishman, a ship-owner, a householder and a husband—am I wrong?"

He bent on Vincent a measured smile of ingenuousness which the younger man gave back with exactitude.

"Take X," he said, "and stick those labels on him which you say you can read all over me——"

"They're not labels," said the doctor, "they're you. They're X."

"Poor X! Since he assumed some of these things

of his own choice, and by thinking he'd perhaps like
to, and since he can detach himself from those others
he was born with, to think about them either with
approval or dislike—how can they be he?"

"So X is only himself in so far as he doesn't think?"
asked Agnes.

"Very likely."

"All the easier to find a *status quo*," said William
Curran, "since no one thinks."

"But I, for instance, think I think," said Marie-Rose,
"and isn't that a kind of thinking?"

"Not the kind, I hope, Mrs. O'Regan, that could
prove to your husband that you aren't you."

Marie-Rose clasped her forehead with her two white
hands.

"Have you become a 'blue', Agnes?" she asked, "and
is this your salon?"

The question set another light to Vincent's rising
mood. Not that he gave a snap for blues or salons,
but his sudden quarry to-night was non-reality, and
any window opened, even this, to suggest an escape
through time or space, let in an air that maddened
him. A blue with a salon, and he that salon's leader—
ah, an absurdity indeed, but the idea's virtue was that
it could not be this, could not be family life in a
family drawing-room. It would be a place, a chance—
though he could imagine better—in which he and she
could speak and be their real selves. Bring such speech
what it would, it was now the first necessity in life.

With a laugh so soft and inward that Agnes, catching it, half thought it was her own, he got up from where he sat beside her and went to lean upon the mantelpiece, tinkling the lustres.

He had come to Mellick in a leaden mood of selfishness, deciding on a journey which he knew would have none but bitter fruit for him mainly in order to exasperate his wife, and by his presence thwart her full enjoyment of her sister. He saw no reason why he should be left in his large house while Marie-Rose fluttered off to rest from their perpetual discord. If he knew of anywhere to go alone for reassurance, he supposed that he would not be so dog-in-the-manger as to deny himself—but he did not. He wanted nothing in these days but what was here in Roseholm, and on which his wife made such exacting, maddening claim. He wanted nothing but that which no illusion ever told him he could have. And so, though he came to this house with Marie-Rose, he came in perversity and cruelty, as much to plague her peace as to suck up misery for himself by looking on the face in which he believed he saw, without illusion at last, his personal heaven.

But all that mood, the familiar of many visits here, was departed from him now. A glance into another man's face had swept it clean away—a glance of which he could not now remember whether it had been entirely accidental or that he had lain in wait to take it. Had he known, outside his brain, when they stood up in the drawing-room to meet her, that this doctor was in love with Agnes, and had that blinding moment at the dinner-table been only the surrender of his body's knowledge to his mind? It mattered nothing now. All that did matter was that in the time which it takes a man to lift a sherry-glass from the table to his lips, looking at Curran, whose eyes then happened to be on Agnes, he had understood that this man desired and was in good trim to fight for her.

The moment, immense and bright with many passions, hatred, egotism, pride and love, was the best because the most remote from everyday life that he had ever known. As there are spaces of experience, generally induced by great physical pain, which have a brightness of agony never to be either recalled or forgotten, so Vincent knew that he would never be able to remember or forget that second. All that he could clearly know of it was that it had changed him, spiritually, chemically, so as to give him back, as a spectator might have thought, his youth—but within the alteration was into a light, mobile, edged and arrogant condition for which the most embracing word might be insanity, a buoyant tide lapping so high in him, he knew, as almost to escape in his words and in the light of his eyes. And, though it brought cunning and subtlety, he hardly cared if it did escape.

He drank to it, and to secure it. In Moselle and Burgundy he drank to his release and all its consequences. And keeping his eyes on Agnes, repeating

her name, shaping all that was said so that it curved
about her, paused for her, he beckoned to those
consequences.

So men presumed to her, did they? And she even
a little maybe to them—while his life rotted in want
of her? She would be married then, and flung on the
marriage-heap to waste, as he and Marie-Rose had
been? There would be a wedding, there would be a
wedding night. As he looked at William Curran his
eyes had an impure glitter, so that Agnes, catching it,
had known that this was not her demigod reborn, but
only a man in torment.

She, seated opposite her father at one end of the
dining-table, with Vincent at her right side and
William Curran at her left, with Marie-Rose glitter-
ing and curvetting on the young doctor's other side,
and Reggie, next to Vincent, brooding happily, almost
dreamily above his Burgundy-glass—contemplating detachedly this softly lighted group, had felt a cold
amazement stir in her that a house ostensibly
surrendered to one sorrow should all at once give
roof to so many unmentionable intense and contradictory emotions. Her mother lay upstairs, waiting for
God to reprieve a sentence which He would not reprieve—and because of her and her approaching death
this scene—so exciting, so reviving, so passionately
alive—was set. She gave Marie-Rose a pretext to be
here, and so gave Vincent one. She was the reason,
too, of William Curran. And she would die, but the

maze they were treading to-night—in her honour, one might say, and because she had bidden them celebrate the Eve of All Saints'—when would they who were caught in it have learnt and forgotten, forsaken its intricacies?

Agnes shivered once during dinner at these reflections, and William Curran had noticed it and raised his brows.

"There's no excuse for that. Your brother-in-law is being very amusing, and this glorious Chambertin——"

"A goose walking over her grave," said Marie-Rose, who liked mixing up her father's sayings. Danny had begun to put her right, but the word "grave" had a heavy echo and disheartened him.

"One can never be quite sure how much one is amusing Agnes," Vincent had gone on. "To-night, until this humiliating shudder, I thought that I was passing muster, but when I first met her—oh, what a stern young judge!"

She had laughed at that straight into his eyes—but a laugh of amazement. So that was what he had thought of her in those dreadful days, when she had not known how to cover her indecent heart!

"I imagine," William Curran had been tentative, "that she can still be something of a Daniel."

"Ah yes," Vincent had lifted his glass and studied the light-shot colour of the wine, "but now she must have done with sitting in judgment."

What game was he playing, Agnes wondered?

"Anyone who had wanted to marry Marie-Rose would have found me critical," she had answered, speeding a smile to her sister.

Now she was glad he had got up from the settee on which she sat, not because his nearness had troubled her senses—for she would not pause to examine such a novelettish remnant of folly, easy to reject—but because his demonstrative singling out of her, his gay and privileged flirtation, was entirely new and must, sooner or later, provoke comment, which, however innocent, she felt she could not face before William Curran.

"Father," she said, standing up, "won't you have your own chair?" And she pulled an arm-chair nearer to the fire, and made a little gentle fuss of Danny while he settled himself. "Here are the London papers," she said, placing them on a small table near him. "You're dying to look at them, I know, and we'll all excuse you."

She patted his arm and smiled down at him, but as she returned to her settee she caught the pseudo-cheerful expression on his face which always smote her.

"Ah, to know that someone's happy!" her heart cried angrily, and turning to William Curran she made him plunge into talk with her father of how well his patient seemed, and of his hopes for the specialists' visit. The doctor jibbed a minute, hating pointless optimism, but her eyes compelled him to see a sentimental point, and

ashamedly he talked then as if to imply to Danny that
his wife, and so he, had life to look to.

She's making use of me, he told himself resentfully,
she has no respect for anything but manipulation of
the moment in hand. But he knew that this was not
exactly what he meant.

"Tinkle, tinkle," sang Marie-Rose, mocking her
husband's performance on the lustres. "You ought to
buy a dulcimer, Vincent."

He did not seem to hear her. He was staring into
the mirror; vaguely she noticed, who knew him well,
a relaxed, contented, unfamiliar look about his careless attitude. She wondered what he was thinking of.
In fact, he was hardly thinking. He was looking at
Agnes, reflected in greenish mirror light, a remove
which assisted him cloudily to see her, not as his wife
did, admirable, dear and comforting; not as William
Curran did, a glorious creature, half myth, half Cæsar's
wife; but simply as his love, his heart's unsought
and absolute delight. In deep content he looked at
her.

The drawing-room door opened and Nurse Cunningham came in, looking charming. The men stood
up, and Reggie lumbered towards her. Agnes intro-
duced her to the de Courcy O'Regans. Vincent turned
with reluctance from the lustres and the mirror to
make his bow, but Marie-Rose was gracious, her quick
eyes dancing over the new arrival to sum her up. Then
as the nurse moved away to answer her employer's

courtesies, Marie-Rose whispered to Agnes:

"Sixes, Nag—pearl-grey."

William Curran twinkled, overhearing.

"What was it, Mrs. O'Regan?"

"A purely feminine matter."

Danny wanted to play a hand of whist. So did Marie-Rose. So, it seemed, did Nurse Cunningham.

Vincent was asked to make a fourth. Glancing at the table where the three players waited, he said very politely that he was sorry, but that he had given up whist, had almost forgotten it. Everyone laughed at this—he was known as a hard and eager card-player— everyone except Marie-Rose, who shrugged at his urbane perversity. But if Vincent was tired of card games, Reggie, who never before had seemed able to endure them, was willing now to take a hand, and presented himself at the table as partner to Nurse Cunningham.

The cards were cut and dealt. Silence, which this ceremony invokes, dropped softly.

"Diamonds are trumps," said Reggie.

Marie-Rose, picking up her cards, looked slowly about the room, and towards her sister, seated by the fire with head bent over an embroidery frame. The scene, she thought amusedly, whist-table, fireplace, Agnes at her stitchery, Vincent and Dr. Curran hover-ing about, would make a pretty moment in a play. But what a deadly play in which nothing ever was allowed to happen! Though change was indeed very busily at work now upon the changelessness for which this room had stood. Their mother would die, their father, and, differently, their brother were already half dead. Nag would marry and take herself off with her needles to sit in some unguessable setting with a stranger—as she had done. But for Nag, as then for her, there would never be this place of roots to hurry back to. It would be gone, like the dead who had made it. Such as it was, it was so far the only place she knew where she was taken, with the ease of love, for granted. This house, with Agnes now the kindler of its warmth for her, was her one safety—and it was dying. Her mother would leave it, Agnes would leave it, and then its memories would never stir again. It would have served its turn. How shocking a thing transience was, which sounded gradual and gentle! In a passion of love, which it was not like her to feel for inanimate things, she felt herself agonised for a second by this room and its once so solid life. Oh, Nag! she cried in her heart, as always when over-troubled, and as if the cry were uttered, Agnes looked up and smiled at her.

William Curran sat by Agnes. "You're happy to-night?" he said.

She took the gambit for what it was worth—an obvious and not too exacting approach to intimacy.

"I generally am when Marie-Rose is here. But this is a very dull way for you two," she flicked a glance upwards at Vincent, "to pass the evening. Wouldn't you like to have a cigar, or to drink something, in Reggie's little smoke-room?"

The idea of being banished together rendered both men's faces so blank that Agnes feared she might laugh outright.

"Just as you please," she said reassuringly. "I am going up to see Mother for a few minutes—so do find some means of amusing yourselves."

She laid down her embroidery. Vincent's eyes glittered on her. William Curran stood up and crossed the room. He opened the door.

"I think I'll smoke in the garden, if I may," he said to her. "But don't stay upstairs too long."

The Tenth Chapter

AGNES went to her own room before visiting her mother. She wanted to be alone a minute. The courage and coldness which Confession had seemed to bestow were growing less; sadness was taking hold of her again, and she had felt unsteadied by a strange, appealing look which Marie-Rose had sent to her from the whist-table. It was all very well, she told herself as she raised a lamp and moved uneasily about her room, it was all very well to acknowledge that your sister was unsatisfactorily married, that she and her husband, each fairly selfish, had themselves to blame, and that there was nothing for it now but to muddle through to the spoilt prime and the bitter end of life. It was all very well to fold hands before the spectacle of character working out its fate—but was there no help anywhere? If two were beautiful and very young and had the seeds of gaiety and rapture in them—must all be squandered still by that indefinable silliness called incompatibility? When Marie-Rose was snappy, unjust, arrogant—Agnes could bear these things in her and defeat her own sadness with irritability—but when, once in a blue moon, her sister's eyes revealed—to her alone, she thought—their misery, their loss, their fear of the years—that was unbearable save by letting loose in oneself, to however little purpose, a mania to heal, rearrange, revive, restore. Little lovely sister, light, impudent, imperious—how could so cumbersome a thing as pure unhappiness be allowed to crush her down? "Oh, Rosey, Baby Rose, I'll take all this away from you!" she cried, and paced about her room.

She would find a way. Her mood of confidence in herself returned and extended beyond the exactions of negation. She would not merely withhold, she would remake. Impulsively she went down on her knees beside her bed. She said the "Memorare," glorious prayer that seems to bring an answer with it in the swift rush of its own intercession—"Oh, Mother of the Word Incarnate, despise not my petitions, but in thy mercy hear——" she offered it for Marie-Rose, for Vincent, for her mother, father, brother—for all the troubled souls under the roof. And feeling the positive force of prayer, she was comforted. She would find a way. Life would move truly and justly again for some of them, and death would come in peace to those who must receive it. God and His Mother were merciful and saw the honesty of hearts. If she could feel with such vigour the inevitability of justice and order, how much more would not her Maker feel it?

She rose, making the Sign of the Cross. She smoothed her hair, lowered the lamp and went into the corridor. Vincent was standing there, not six feet from her door, under a dimly burning light. He was very quiet and at ease, and his eyes shone dreamily on her. In spite of herself she stood still, unable at once to ignore the beauty and significance of him, waiting there. He moved to her, hardly seeming to move.

He laid a hand on her shoulder. The gentleness of it, lying on her, was a vast surprise at first, and then subsided into nothing more difficult to understand than peace. The hand she had loved so long was touching her in love. That was all. That was suddenly all that her wits could hold or trouble about. It seemed a natural thing—an unexciting, sleepy thing— to stand quite still, so near him at last that to see his face she would have to bend her head backwards, to stand and suffer the love of his hand on her shoulder.

"Agnes," he said, and his voice was as natural as his touch, "Agnes, dear love."

"Dear love?" she repeated the words questioningly, and much more softly than he had said them.

His hand moved whisperingly, but without urgency along the silk of her arm.

"I love you. You love me," he said. His tone was as low as hers now, but it had a trouble in it that betrayed his quiet hand. She thought, though they stood apart, that she could feel the stormy life of his breast. His breath stirred over her hair. Still, though the peace his hand had brought was lifting, she did not move. Her nature was as if hypnotised by a revelation of its own weakness, even when tested in an hour of special strength. But how could she have known that his hand had such a power in it?

Far off, it seemed, she heard in her mother's room the patient little cough of Sister Emmanuel. A sound almost holy in its repression. It brought back the idea of holiness, the idea of pain. It brought back prayer and duty and the memory of her own confession. Dazedly her spirit moved from its moment of rightness under his loved hand to its outer, older knowledge of another rectitude. Dazedly she raised her head and looked into blue eyes which now for the first time really near her, seemed so curiously well known. Dazedly she raised her hand and took his from her arm. Far away Sister Emmanuel coughed once more.

"Never again," Agnes heard herself saying.

"Agnes, I love you."

"Oh, never again!"

"Then what am I to do?"

As the love of his touch had surprised her, so now did the desolation of his voice. These were things she had not known before. These were things which in God's name she must not know, must forget. She found she could not speak again to those emptied eyes. She could only close her own and shake her head. Then she found that she had left him and was walking down the corridor alone. She knocked at her mother's door. She had no thoughts. Her lips were repeating: "Oh, Mother of the Word Incarnate, despise not my petitions——"

Teresa's room was dim and orderly. Sister Emmanuel sat by the fire and read her Office. Agnes tiptoed to the bedside. Her mother's eyes, wide open, flickered greeting to her.

"Well, Mother darling——"

Her voice shook under its casual gentleness. A nerve was trembling through her, and she did not know whether the sensation it gave her was terrible or glorious or merely sickening. Her brain was empty, words trailing through it at random: "Mother darling; never again; oh, Mother of the Word Incarnate."—Ah, God, how faint she felt, how terrible the disinfected air!

"What's the matter, child?" said Teresa.

"Nothing. Why?"

"You're looking very white."

"Have you ever seen me look red?"

"No, faith. Sit down awhile. How are you enjoying yourselves downstairs?"

Agnes sat down. That was better. Miraculously she found herself talking in the light vein she kept for this bedside, describing what they ate and drank at dinner, reporting the whist game, and that Reggie was actually playing a hand. This pleased Teresa.

"I'm glad to hear that. I'm always wanting him to do things like that and not be moping. Is Nurse Cunningham below?"

"Yes; looking very pretty." She chattered on, and self-control returned with the effort she made.

"But what are poor Vincent and Dr. Curran doing, child?"

"I don't know."

"Ah, you'd better run down and entertain them."

"I'm all right here, Mother. It's quiet."

"Nonsense. It's too much quiet you have. Run down, let you—and tell them all when they're done with their whist that I'd like to hear some music. Maybe Reggie or Marie-Rose would sing a song for me——"

Agnes looked towards Sister Emmanuel. who peered benevolently over her silver spectacles.

"Wouldn't it be too much noise, Sister?"

The old nun shook her head.

"No, child. There's nothing does her so much good as to hear music going on below. Let you go down now and make them all sing for her, and yourself along with them."

Go down. And make them sing.

Agnes stood up. What was one to make of a day, an hour which at one minute seemed child's play, and at the next became fantastic in its painfulness?

"All right," she said, smiling. "I suppose you want the doors left open?"

"I do. And will you tell Reggie to have a try at the 'Snowy-Breasted Pearl' for me?"

"But Uncle Tom will be arriving any minute—he's sleeping here to-night, you know, on account of to-morrow's Mass—and if he finds us having a concert instead of saying our prayers——"

"There's no better prayer than a song, child," said Sister Emmanuel.

Agnes ran her hand over her mother's forehead. Then she left the room and went downstairs.

She met William Curran in the hall. He looked wind-blown and he shivered a little.

"Surely not a night for smoking in the garden," she said.

"I like being cold."

He stood to block her way, his eyes searching her face unmercifully.

"Have you had a shock of any kind?" he asked.

What a watch-dog, thought Agnes impatiently. She shook her head and seemed amused at him.

"Then why are you looking so shaken?" he persisted. "You hadn't that look ten minutes ago."

"Well, I was ten minutes younger then," she flicked evasively, and he let her go.

The whist game was languishing, thanks to Reggie's inadequacy. He rose with relief at the suggestion of music.

"I think I'll have a smoke first," he said, meaning a drink. And he shuffled to the door.

"Where's Vin?" said Marie-Rose, but nobody knew.

Nurse Cunningham was fond of music, she said. While Danny fussed at fixing the drawing-room door open, she seated herself at the piano and began to play and half sing the Barcarolle from "Les Contes d'Hoffmann." A tune which always affected Agnes with a sensation of nausea.

Reggie shambled back, wiping his lips.

"How prettily you play," he said, and beamed on the pretty nurse.

She stopped at once. "No one else can play when you're around." And insistently she made way for him on the piano-stool.

"But you'll sing for us—if I play your accompaniment," he begged. "What do you sing? There are masses of songs in the house."

She got through a ballad after some pressing. Her performance was neither good nor bad, and it delighted Reggie, who afterwards in his decayed tenor, but with a painful search after the truth of singing, sang the "Snowy-Breasted Pearl." " 'There's a colleen fair as May——' " Not one of his thin notes failed to reach his mother, who gathered them to her drowsed heart as if they were pearls, and got them mixed with her half-conscious prayers. " 'But if 'tis Heaven's decree That mine she may not be, May the Son of Mary me in mercy save!' "

Dr. Curran stared at Agnes.

"Marie-Rose," Danny was saying, "won't you sing now for us, child? It's a long time since we heard you!"

"Or since I heard myself, Father," she said, shaking her head.

But Agnes was seized with a desire for her sister's singing.

"Please, Rosie," she begged.

"Oh, Nag—really?"

"Really."

Long ago, before all this pain had started, it had been a delight to listen to Marie-Rose's songs, a delight to Marie-Rose to sing for her.

"What'll I sing?"

"Any of the things we used to like."

Obediently, but pulling a face at Agnes, Marie-Rose crossed to the piano. She paused with her hands on the keyboard to fix her eyes gravely on her sister. Then she began Schumann's "Widmung."

Her amateurish voice was high and pure. She loved the song, and after the first quiver of shyness was at ease in it, singing it swiftly, hungrily, and giving to the German a confident pronunciation which to everyone but Dr. Curran seemed perfection.

Why that of all songs, Agnes marvelled in fury at the first bar, and almost rose to stop her. But though she knew it well and should have guessed why her sister had unconsciously, in a mood of acute nostalgia for the free and happy past, selected it, its memories were no more than an uneasy blur. Twenty minutes ago they would have been its dominant value, but now, since his hand and voice had touched her in love's avowal, she heard it with new ears, a new song.

Marie-Rose, singing, wondered at herself with faint irony, and yet knew that out of some crazy loneliness she was singing to her sister, in denial of her own present life of contempt and irritation, and to praise that which could never be again, that harmony of innocence and irresponsibility in which Agnes and she had flowered, their spirits nurturing each other. She was not singing to Agnes that she was her soul, her peace and quiet, but that the years they had shared were, now she saw with fear, her earthly portion of those things. She had not been hard then—there was no one to be hard against. She had not been contemptuous. Oh, God, how the world and she had changed! Only Nag remained as people should remain—for no better purpose than to tease her with false resuscitations of the old contentment. But gratitude became an anguish to defeat her irony. " 'Du bist die Ruh;' " she sang to her sister: " 'Du bist der Friede.' "

Agnes, who often knew what Marie-Rose was feeling, knew now. And the knowledge was only an added load, an insult. No use in these appeals against time. They had been happy and had grown up to be less happy in a world in which the latter state was obviously the rule. Now, for her own and his unhappiness, Marie-Rose had in her keeping for ever the man who from her first sight of him had been able to explain to Agnes all the follies and extremities of human passion. And to-night—"Dear love, dear love" he had called her!

She sat very still, her eyes on the fire. The room was hushed for the singer as if she alone occupied it, but Agnes was as oppressively aware of all the breathing souls it held as of its essential emptiness. " 'Du meine Seele, du mein Herz . . .' " where was he?

When and how was she to look on him again? Not during this—not with this voice crying to her, crying for her. God was merciful to have kept him away.

Nurse Cunningham was not quite sure what language Mrs. O'Regan sang, but she listened with attention. A nice accomplishment, to be able to sing and play like that. Resentment against her own lack of youthful opportunity stirred and hurt her. She beat it down. This was a pleasant evening, not to be spoilt. A pleasant evening in a very comfortable house. There were many such houses. Comfort was not an impossible thing for a sensible woman to achieve. Queer, dashing sort of song—ah, it was going slower now. Must be German. Wouldn't do to let on she didn't know. Her eyes fell on Reggie, flopped in a chair, his mouth open, as he listened in deep pleasure. Her eyes stayed on him, and their gaze was calm and hard, although she retained her attitude of music-drugged attentiveness.

Dr. William Curran stood in shadow, disputing to himself every step of the song's movement. An excellently constructed expression of a mighty feeling, yes—and for the man who had made it the making was the thing—justifying the pains and confusions that it came from. But if one would never have anything to say, what point in standing thus to listen? If there were no end, no way of outlet, no given means of saying in our own terms this that Schumann said—oh, God, the young man raged, if I am too commonplace for what

she makes me feel, if I am neither to have her nor
let her be, if having her I am forever afraid of my
mad luck, or losing her, my life is turned to deadli-
ness—— His eyes feasted themselves on her bent head,
on her heavenly slenderness. I love her, love her, he
told himself in torture. A maggot in her brain—and
now, indeed, she looked not ill or startled as she had
appeared to him in the hall, but simply, intolerably
sad. But that could only be an accident of her beauty.
What could she know of sadness such as his? What
could her poor little maggot be? His love growing
heavier with tenderness, he stared at her—and the
tenderness gave him ease, gave him hope and sentimentality. My darling, he thought, I could cure that
maggot. " 'Hätt'st du mir Lieb' " . . . ay, there's the
rub. He closed his eyes and let the song wound him.
It was over soon. Marie-Rose's voice dropped clearly
into silence, and no one stirred in the room while the
accompaniment fulfilled its last curves. But beyond
the room, beyond the open door, there was a heavy
footstep, and then a man's voice singing: " 'Mein
Himmel du, darin ich lebe——' "

Dr. Curran, who was looking at Agnes, saw her eyes
turn swiftly towards these sounds, whither he let his
glance follow. Vincent O'Regan was standing in the
hall under the chandelier. He was drunk, the doctor
noticed. He looked immensely tall, and wild, and
pale. He swayed as he stood and hesitated, his eyes on
Agnes, in some curiously touching entreaty. They did

not deviate from her until he turned away as if commanded. He disappeared in the direction of the garden, singing softly: " 'Mein Himmel du.' " William Curran turned again to Agnes, and was frightened by her frightened face. He had to acknowledge now that there was a maggot in her brain.

"What's that, what's that?" said Danny, coming to.

"Nothing, Father," said Marie-Rose.

"Sounded like Vincent singing," said Reggie, turning his head towards the door.

"It was—he's gone into the garden."

Marie-Rose got up from the piano-stool and received Nurse Cunningham's congratulations on her talent with much graciousness. A moment later Canon Considine was announced, and while he greeted his Dublin niece, and the mood of the room toned itself down for night prayers, Dr. Curran took leave of the household and departed.

He almost ran through the hall and into the garden. Now that he had the obvious fact, it screamed its authenticity from so many moments of this night and of the immediate past that he could hardly believe he had not known it always. It was a truth which now her eyes, her face and every word and attitude of Vincent's seemed most shamelessly and recklessly to advertise. How could he have been blind so long?

She loves him, they're in love. The words became a chant, and he tore down the dark drive in tune to them. She loves him, they're in love. It seemed if he could only hurry enough he might outstrip the realisation, it seemed that if he could only fly he would find means to stop the diabolical waste. Only let him get outside her house, beyond her father's gate—away from her and the madness she put on him, and he would see it all and get control of it. It wasn't true. The heaven she prayed to wasn't quite so irresponsible—it wasn't true. Oh yes, it was.

On the last curve of the drive, where moonlight broke in a stream of coldness, a tall man stood with his head uplifted to the sky. An absurd, theatrical figure not perfectly in command of itself, yet looking far more glorious than any sane man cares to do. Looking like a myth, a god in marble. William Curran shuddered, striding past, and clanged the gate behind him. It clanged on his momentary notion of denial and escape, and his foolish hurry fell from him. He crossed the road to the river wall and leant on it, looking eastward at the town.

Nothing was too silly or wasteful to be a fact. Nothing was too destructive to be true. In relation to himself this would not matter so very much, he thought, when he got used to it. To have dreamt commonplace dreams of her had been, indeed, to tickle the gods; to have wanted her at home, in his arms, in his bed, to have wanted her children to be his—oh, Heaven would admit he had been superstitious and discreet with such ideas. In time, with patience, he could shed them. The proudest man on earth would always have known, with her, that that might have to happen.

He shivered. The night was very cold. For himself, then, he did not mind; he had not hoped so madly. But for her—oh, would life never weary of its monotonous ironies, would it never have done with its idiotic crime of waste? Let her love anyone, his heart cried, so long as that anyone can take her love and keep it in fidelity and fruitfulness. Let her love whom she likes, so long as he is free to love her honestly—a king in his happiness, in his power to make her happy. Let her only be happy in her loving—or was that too much to ask for her incomparableness?

But his eloquence did not deceive or anæsthetise him for very long. Windily he might rave and inflate himself, but the hard knot stayed unmoving in his breast. He wanted her and she wanted someone else.

The parapet was icy cold under his arms, but he did not heed it. He doubled up, burying his face in his sleeve. "I want you, I love you," he said. "Dearest, I want you, oh, dearest, darling girl!"

The Eleventh Chapter

MARIE-ROSE sat at her dressing-table in dim lamp-light and brushed her silky gold hair, which curled and lolled very prettily against her shoulder. In spite of weary lines about her eyes, she was looking—she could not but admit—delicious. She ran her hand affectionately along her smooth young cheek, and mused with an impartial pleasure upon the whiteness of her throat. The white frills of her night-dress, the flounces and ruches of her white silk wrap, foamed delicately, and made a dramatic darkness of the shadows in which she sat.

She gazed and meditated—and pleasure grew less impartial and more tender. With pity at last she studied herself, remembering the life of clash and re-sistance in which her beauty was compelled to wither. And there was no escape, not even here in her own home! Oh, if only he hadn't come to-day! If only she could have had this interval of peace with Nag! Tears filled her eyes, and she let them fall, leaning her cheek on her hand, and staring into the glass.

She was childish and spoilt, and had been irritated by her husband's behaviour through the evening, and very much disgusted by the apparition of him, drunk and wild, at the drawing-room door, when her song ended. But she had, too, her own kind of strength, a self-control which sometimes took the form of frivolity, and sometimes was an exaggerated gentleness with this self-loving and self-blessing mood at the end of it, for safety-valve. So to-night, Dr. Curran gone, the Rosary said and their father having locked the house and left the hall door on the latch for wandering Vincent, she and Agnes had sat a few minutes together by the drawing-room fire and talked a little, desultorily, sadly, not of Vincent or directly personal things, but of their mother. Marie-Rose knew that Agnes had seen Vincent at the drawing-room door and had seen that he was drunk—but even to Nag just then he seemed an unsafe, unbroachable topic, though her heart burned for outlet of her anger. Let him be, said pride. And she listened to what Agnes was saying of their mother, and saluted with all that was good in her such courage and such woe. She would pray, indeed she would, with all her strength that God might lessen the long torture, bring quiet to the sick heart, if not to the ruined body. Thus sadly she had escaped from her own bad temper. Thus with Nag and in the grief of her father's house she had found alleviation from littleness. Men made fools of themselves and wives were fools enough to care, and sometimes disgraceful hints leapt out of troubles on which the light of the world should never fall—but at the worst, in relation to life's real sorrows, what did all that amount to? And, anyhow, one could always sit for a while with

Agnes and let things slide.

The hall clock, striking midnight, had warned them of early rising to-morrow for Mass in the house. Still with no mention of Vincent and yawning affectedly to cover her panic at turning away to face herself in solitude, Marie-Rose had kissed her sister good night very casually on the first landing, and climbed alone to her room on the second floor. But even here sad, trailing thoughts of her mother seemed to have banked down her state of personal irritation, which remained only in vague physical oppression about her, a weight, an awkwardness.

And the sight of her charming reflection had dissipated much of that. Now tears bore off its vestiges, the easy tears that beauty sheds upon itself, knowing that its self-pity is a joke, since world without end it has the laugh of everything. So, watching the tears flow down her face and refusing them that final luxurious surrender which would have been dis-figuring, she decided to forgive her silly husband and be gracious about his tantrums for this once.

As she accorded this decision to her shadow in the mirror, smiling a little at the shining of that shadow's eyes, and the touching wetness of its cheeks, her husband entered the room, and stood behind her, to look with her into the glass. She saw him there, very white and tired, and smiled without moving. He smiled, too, or moved his mouth in outline of a smile. Then turning away before he saw a friendly backward movement of her hand to him, he said:

"I wish to God I couldn't read your thoughts."

She bit her lip.

"But perhaps you can't, Vin."

"Perhaps not. I suppose you weren't thinking just now that you are so lovely that really it's a great comfort and a source of strength to you, and that that being so, and you, as a lovely woman being invincible, you might as well be noble for this once about *my* disgusting behaviour——"

He paused for an answer and looked into the mirror at her again. But her eyes were shut, her mouth was composed in a hard line.

"Were those your thoughts, Marie-Rose?"

"Since you know, why bother to ask?"

She went on brushing her hair.

Vincent O'Regan was intelligent and did not much more than other men fool himself about his own conduct. When, as now, he made unprovoked attacks of malice on his wife he was as much aware as any eavesdropper might be that he was offending against all the laws of decency. But this knowledge worked on his nervous system to irritate rather than to quiet it. He was intelligent, but he was also young and restive. In the first year or more of his marriage, their delicate marital situation had been nicely balanced between his wife and him. One day it would be her turn for injustice and insolence, and a week later he would have his head. But in between and all about

their chill islands of self-assertion had been then a rich
and marvellous sea of passion. For a while it seemed
as if that tide would never ebb; her imperious womanhood left little space in which to mourn the quiet
company of one's own mind, her beauties so furnished
day and night that their lost spaciousness was very
rarely hankered for. Life with Marie-Rose, irritating,
cruel, amusing, unexpected, was the life love brought,
and must be understood, he reasoned with himself, to
be worth its exactions. Mostly he had conceded this—
and she would have agreed with him. And when
either had not been in this acceptant mood, they had
quarrelled, had found a stony island, until the sea
proved irresistible again.

But now for him all that was changed. He had seen
that the life they led was not a love life. And he had
come to this by no more clever means than by falling
in love elsewhere. A process which proves nothing,
and carries no conviction. Nevertheless, he was con-
vinced that in the arms of this new love that could be
found which he had never believed in and for which
happiness was by no means the term, nor knowledge
either; he knew that he would find an answer there—
that seemed to him the nearest word—and an acceptance. No fatuous understanding, but a living give
and take, from hands that would claim no feminine
or motherly prerogative, but would be simply his to
stretch to, as his would be forever hers.

And because he knew of this, and could not go and

take it, he was becoming the most insolent and unreasonable of boors; because he knew this and could not even boast of it, but had to play the husband game, he took his vengeance, without desiring to, but yet unmercifully, upon a wife who did not see, and never could be told, what really ailed him.

Still drunk, he was dead tired now as well—had felt so tired climbing the stairs as to be uncertain whether he might not already be asleep. And that state of doubt had given him courage to enter his wife's bedroom. No devilish stupidity would escape from him in such mood. He was too tired even to plague her. And yet he had done so. Oh well—he was an ass, and tethered to asinine arrangements, ordaining this for instance, that no matter how a day had been for husband and wife, there was nothing for them to do at the end of it but lie down together for sleep. A curious intimacy which the world called natural.

Pondering it in the garden he had grown hot, remembering ecstasies given and taken by Marie-Rose, frenzies of neither love nor hate, but furnishing rather an escape from those questionable terms, minutes in which, staring into each other's eyes, they had known themselves, but with a knowledge not to be sustained or extended into the routine of days, a knowledge as unhelpful and static as it was pure. It had been real, nevertheless, that passion, but they had not known how to use it. And it was gone though their bodies remained together. But now he did not so much resent as despise their condition of marital intimacy. In spite of the spurting venom of his attack on Marie-Rose, he was in real pain of spirit, really tired, so tired that at this moment, reacting from his ill-tempered moment of vigour, he felt more like a man recalling bitter experience than one deep wading in it. He had even the illusion that he had done with married life. This comforted and clouded him. He would sleep. Married life was over. Hugging the thought he got into the vast double bed and closed his eyes.

Married life was over. The life of fantasy was in the bud. Life of love—probably in dream was the only way to live it. Dreams of sin, dreams without hope. His wife's sister. There was no place in time where she could love him, where he could have her in honour or dishonour. She had said "Never again" as he had known she would. But the echo it made in his head had been unbearable, and he had got drunk, thinking that might ease it. And there had been peace for a few minutes with someone singing. "'. . . Mein Himmel du, darin ich lebe. . . .'" He sang the line softly now, but it was like a knife turning in him. He buried his face in the pillow and gave in to an agony of imagination.

Marie-Rose, still seated at her dressing-table, was uncertain what to do—whether, since he was asking for it, to vent her exasperation on him, or to control herself. But she remembered her mother. If I quarrel with him I won't be fit to go to Communion in the morning, she thought, and she knelt down and tried to pray.

She was surprised to hear him singing while she prayed—the song she had sung to-night. She was touched. Poor old Vin! Was this his way of saying he was sorry? It was rather like him. He had a proud knack of indirect surrender. So he had liked her singing then?

She took off her dressing-gown, and glancing at herself as she lowered the lamps, was made happy again by the little white-robed wraith she saw, so slim and golden-haired.

She slipped into bed. In a bar of moonlight she could see her husband who was lying flat on his face. He's pretending to be asleep, she thought amusedly. This reconciliation scene was familiar—they staged it, with variations, from time to time.

She laid a hand on his shoulder.

"Sound asleep, Vin?"

There was no response or movement, but she was feeling very kind and tolerant.

He really is the most conceited creature, she thought amusedly, and moved quite close to him, letting her hand caress the back of his head.

"Wake up a minute, Vin."

He moved his head slowly until his eyes stared into hers.

"What do you want?" he asked.

Marie-Rose hesitated. This was a new version of the well-known scene.

"But—Vin——"

"Go away," he said, like a man in a trance, softly and deliberately. "Please go away."

His inexpressible desire was heavy on him. He hardly knew to whom he spoke—except that it was not Agnes.

"Go away?"

"Yes, please. Just go away and leave me in peace."

She sprang from the bed as if he had leprosy.

"I should think I will," she cried. "Oh Heaven, I'll be glad to!"

She stumbled about the room, searching for slippers, for a dressing-gown. She was shaking with misery and shame. Fully conscious of her now, he understood what he had done. He lay and considered, with hopelessness, how he might remedy it. He could not drive her out of her own bed.

He sat up.

"Be quiet a minute, Marie-Rose," he said. "Let's think a minute."

But she was at the other end of the room and paying no heed to him.

Nag, she was saying to herself unconsciously, oh Nag, what will I do?

Wrapped in her white robe, she melted from the room like a ghost.

For a long time Vincent seemed to hear her sobbing, Oh Nag, what will I do? He let his thoughts go with her, down the stairs and along the first-floor corridor—to sanctuary. She would be made warm and welcome there, in the bed that had been hers so long. She knew where peace was—he'd say that for her; she knew where to scamper ahead of everyone else. And no cruelty would be allowed to touch her there. She would be safe all night in the only arms that could ever safeguard him; she would sleep in peace for once where his heart always slept.

He composed himself rigidly on his pillows. The pain that crept upon him was so vile and sickening that he wondered if it was anything like the approach of death. Death and hell—perhaps this was all that they were in fact—a sickening pain, a sweat. Agnes, he groaned—oh Agnes, my dear love—and then, remembering that her attention was now deflected to his wife, he burst out laughing.

BOOK II

THE FEAST OF ALL SAINTS

The First Chapter

THE dressing-room which opened from Teresa
Mulqueen's bedroom and in which for years her
husband had kept his wardrobe and boot-rack and the
unnecessary desk that he liked to fuss at, had lately
been turned into a sort of nurse's pantry and surgical
store. For All Saints' Day it was to suffer another and
much larger change. It was to be a chapel for an hour,
the sanctuary of a chapel—and to hold the mystery of
transubstantiation. The table which was chosen to
carry the consecrated altar-stone which only Canon
Considine might touch, was placed in relation to the
open dressing-room door so that Teresa from her bed
might hear and see every word and movement of the
sacrifice.

With murmured apologies to her mistress, old Bessie
came to the bedroom with brushes and dusters at seven
o'clock. But Teresa was glad to hear the curtains
drawn back, and the comforting movements of day
about her. Light was good and put things in their
places. The fears and pains of night did not thrive
as well in the sun. Blessed be God in His Goodness,
it was a lovely fine day for the feast of all His Saints.

Teresa began her morning offering. Through the
dressing-room door she could see her brother Tom,

in alb and stole, come in and place the consecrated stone in the exact centre of the altar table. Then Agnes, careful amateur sacristan, unrolled the altar cloth. Teresa recognised this approvingly as the most perfect piece of linen in her possession. Six lordly silver candlesticks with candles of pure wax in them; four vases of Waterford glass filled with red chrysanthemums; the tall silver crucifix with the figure of Christ in ivory, which she had brought back from Rome in jubilee year, just about the time this pain had started at her—a heavy thing to carry, but Agnes put it down with care, exactly where it should be, behind the consecrated stone. A lovely altar. Teresa thought of the great mystery about to take place under her roof, thought stormily and passionately of God's goodness, and lifted all her pain and her great trouble once more into His sight. "Reggie, my son—I'll go to you, Lord, and gladly, and to whatever judgment and punishment may wait for me, if you'll show me just what is to become of him. It's not so much his worldly comfort that I'm praying for, or his health or happiness either—but his poor soul, that I've kept near to you—and kept from wronging any other of your creatures. Tell me how that will be done when I am gone. Tell me who is to protect my helpless child. Oh God, hear my prayer—and then do with me as Thou wilt."

Figures whispered and tiptoed in the room. By the draught screen Teresa saw Nurse Cunningham's white capped head confabulating with Sister Emmanuel's blue veil. Agnes came to her side.

"Good morning, Mother darling."

"What are you looking so tired for, child?" Teresa asked.

"Early rising."

"This was a late hour when I was young."

"Here's your veil, Mother. Let me fix it."

She held a black lace mantilla in her hand, and bent over Teresa to slip it between her hair and the pillow.

"I'd better see to that, Miss Mulqueen."

Nurse Cunningham, smiling affectionately at her patient, took hold of the veil, which Agnes dropped as if it burnt her. As her daughter moved away Teresa looked after her regretfully, but admitting to herself the while that she was mighty touchy and that there was no harm at all in Nurse.

"Now you look very nice and holy," said the latter. "Like a Spanish lady."

And indeed the black lace drooping on her forehead and across her neck took something of its deathly misery from Teresa's face.

Her husband came to peep at her, a missal in his hand and an immediate worry in his eyes.

"What is it?" said Teresa with a flicker of amusement. "What's on your mind?"

"Nothing, my dear, nothing in this world, except to know how you feel this morning."

But, in fact, he had acute stage fright. The

gardener's son was to be acolyte for Mass, but did
not know the Latin responses yet and Danny had to say
them for him. He left his wife's bedside muttering uneasily: "Ad Deum qui laetificat juventutem meam."

A gong sounded in the hall to warn the household
that Mass would soon begin. Danny spread a silk
handkerchief on the carpet and, kneeling on it, laid
his Mass book open ready on the seat of a chair. Sister
Emmanuel dropped to her knees also and fastened
her eyes on the ivory figure on the Cross. Agnes,
having lighted the six candles, came and knelt against
a chair near her mother's bed where she was joined
by Marie-Rose. Both were tired this morning, and
much aware of the world and its impingements, but
as they knelt side by side in their demure, dark dresses,
and adjusted the black lace veils which they had worn
in chapel at school, and had dug out of oblivion this
morning, as, finding the old knack of wearing them,
they smiled at each other in soft reminiscence,
they looked very young and innocent—or so Teresa
thought, observing them.

Eight o'clock struck, and hard on its second chime
the gong resounded. Reggie came in and, smiling at
his mother, knelt down a little way from her. With
a respectful scuffle old Bessie and Maggie the cook
and the young parlourmaid Delia came round the
screen and took their modest places. Scanlan the
gardener pushed his wife on to her knees beside Mrs.
O'Keeffe, the washerwoman, and took up his stand

near the screen with O'Keeffe, the enormous, wheezing coachman, who had driven Teresa as a bride and since. The room was well-filled and very quiet when Vincent made his way through the phalanx of servants, and stood alone in a distant window. Marie-Rose glanced across the room at him in cold surprise. When she went upstairs to dress he had seemed profoundly and insolently asleep and she had not bothered to call him. Oh well—she opened her prayer-book and shut him from her mind, anxious to keep herself from angry thoughts, and in any case at this early, fasting hour having no vitality for them. Agnes looked at him too, more slowly than Marie-Rose, but as un-emotionally, she noted to herself, as at any other member of the congregation. (She also forgot that at eight o'clock on a cold morning it is easy to feel neutral and dispassionate.) But she did concede a gentle blessing to him for having troubled to be present at Mass. Her mother would be pleased to see him there, and Agnes knew that he knew that.

Canon Considine stood before the velvet prie-dieu that was to be his altar steps. He wore the glorious white vestment of the day; the morning sun struck on his silvered head.

"Introibo ad altare Dei."

Danny cleared his throat and took a rush at the response, and as naturally as if this bedroom were a monastery chapel Mass began.

At first Agnes was distracted though not at once

by thoughts of Vincent or Marie-Rose. Their names
had pounded in her brain last night long after the
little visiting ghost of a sister had scolded and sobbed
into sleep beside her—and now for the moment she
was weary of them. She would pray for their peace
this morning as she always did, but she would not
think about them. A more immediate and simple
irritation, a question that she found disgusting, was
in the front of her mind.

Parting from Marie-Rose on the first-floor landing
the night before she had turned into her own wing of
the house in time to see Reggie, moving furtively with
a smile on his face, emerge from Nurse Cunningham's
sitting-room. Not seeing Agnes, he had paused a
second outside the door, paused as a man does to
think on a private satisfaction. Then he had shuffled
to his own room.

There was nothing in this perhaps—but to Agnes
it constituted an embarrassing and unclean worry. As
keeper of her mother's house she felt obliged to be
watchdog also of her anxieties, and she could not be
blind to the extraordinary fact that Nurse Cunningham was encouraging Reggie's attentions. Agnes had
to ignore the curious coarseness that could beckon the
gallantries of such a man, and keep her mind fixed
on the question of a grown woman's irresponsibility.
If she knew his state, and the problem he presented
to his family, how could she play so careless a game,
rousing him—abortively, of course, in regard to herself

—but enough to leave the impression in him that he was, after all, a dog, and still well enough and young enough for conquests. Once really in that condition of mind, he was more dangerous than pitiful. And if, incredibly, she didn't know—but Agnes shuddered now, and turned to her prayer-book with a savage half-thought that a woman who can ogle anyone for ogling's sake, deserves whatever disaster such spiritual incontinence may bring. But she suppressed that relentlessness, and mused instead on the absurdity of innocence in a grown-up woman, and on the unexpectedness of such demonstration of it in the shrewd-looking nurse. An innocent meditation.

Teresa was distracted too. She had seen the glance of greeting that passed between Reggie and Nurse Cunningham when he entered the room. She knew her son's face, and recognised now, not without a pang, that in this intercepted look of his there was a hint, a faraway rumour, of the way in which through all the years of hopelessness his eyes had turned to her. But the pang was easily lost in the ideas that crowded on it. These, hovering within sight for some days, came near now in a swoop and made Teresa's heart leap painfully.

She looked at the nurse, demure and dutiful beside her. Nonsense, she told herself—the creature is very young and pretty. But after all, her boy, her son—he had once been a splendid man, God bless him, and he was kind, he was good-hearted, he was pitiful.

And there was something in the way she said "Mr. Mulqueen" sometimes, something friendly and gentle——

Teresa groaned and tried to move. Her heart was hurting her. She hoped this wasn't going to be one of her bad days. Oh, God must help her, give her patience! Nurse Cunningham was at her side now, very gentle, helping her with great skill to be more comfortable. She was kind, she was understanding.

The gospel of the day made Agnes sorrowful. It was the opening of the Sermon on the Mount: "Blessed are the poor in spirit. . . ." It turned her thoughts from her brother, and into a more dangerous, more habitual groove.

If this writ ran, she pondered as she read it, there was little hope for Vincent here or hereafter. If these were the *sine qua non* of the soul's happiness, it was difficult to see how, when or where he might blunder on repose. He was not meek, he was not poor in spirit; he would sulk rather than mourn; neither justice nor mercy was especially his affair, he would say, and he would not be sure of what was meant by clean of heart; as for the peacemakers and those that suffered persecution, he would honestly be unable to understand them. He was a walking negation of beatitude. Supposing then that one were free to love him, what good would it be?

She looked at him. He was standing very straight and staring at the altar. He had no prayer-book and his arms were folded. The morning sun made an aura for him, made him look glorious. Her heart contracted. These were devilish distractions for one who was about to receive the Body and Blood of God. She bowed her head and recollected herself.

After the offertory, the room, the chapel, became profoundly quiet. A stillness which seemed of vast but undefined significance and as if exacted by some unknown, external will, which unified while it subjugated this assemblage of isolated hearts. In each of these personal thoughts, if they rose up at all, were now no more than a drift of vague impressions, without hurt in them, or urgency; in each, unconscious of it as he might be, the ritual of the eternal church was preparing the soul against all the odds of individual fret and sin for the tremendous canon of the Mass— so that, deeply stilled in their spirits by the quiet, well-known prayers and movements of the priest, they were able when he cried out: "Sursum Corda", to answer voicelessly but honestly with stumbling Danny —"Habemus ad Dominum." Thus through a brief din of "Holy, Holy, Holy!" they reached the quietest moment of their faith, a moment so still that bells must ring and sometimes guns must sound to make it humanly bearable. This morning only one bell rang, a little silver dining-room bell, tinkled by a gardener's boy. There was no other sound, save an unheeded birdsong from the garden.

Canon Considine bent over his altar-stone. Thirty-five years of priesthood, years as imperfect as they were virtuous, years in which his vocation had as often truly failed as conventionally upheld him and in which his period-philosophy had revealed confusing differences from his eternal one; years in which the fanatic in him had learnt to keep step with the bourgeois, but which had also given curious moments of self-distrust and wistfulness; years in which he had unconsciously trained vanity to reward more than to wound him, thirty-five years in which he had been at least as faithful to his own idea of himself as to the eternal idea of God—had yet not taken from him a central wonder before this recurring moment of his priesthood. He was no contemplative and only a mystic in the sense in which every Catholic is, yet it had happened to him that in thirty-five years he had learnt how to keep the minute of Consecration pure. No personal thought came to him then, no plea, no anxiety, no human preoccupation. There was not even the mystic's pain or ecstasy. There was only in him as he spoke his Latin, an entirely cold and calm understanding that God was in his hands. He never petitioned at that moment—not even to-day when the need of his sister was tearing his affectionate heart— he never made a personal sign towards his descending Christ. He only said the words the Church ordained to him, and was aware without cloud, pang or question of the everlasting miracle. "Mysterium fidei . . . pro multis effundetur."

Silence relaxed into quietude. God was present; the room and the morning were full of peace. The Latin ·murmuring of the priest, the holy sighs of old Bessie, the prayerful sibilations of Sister Emmanuel, softly relaxing tension, brought back its human reality to each consciousness, though keeping it mercifully illumined still by the miracle in which it was participant. It was the time of intercession now, and so of remembering misery and fear, but only of remembering, not yet of feeling them again. It was the hour in which these souls understood that the easy-sounding phrase "God's Will," was not a mere cloud with which to soften inconsistencies, but the name of an aged principle out of which a million million patterns and formulas could rise, but which spans and covers all. The hour when the most stupid felt, rather than saw, the point of view of God. Then He became in Communion the mystic visitant of each one in the room, save only one. Prayer deepened and searched and every breast had to bear Heaven's light on its darkness.

Vincent, who had not received the Host, contemplated Agnes's bowed head and was glad no duty of adoration need recall his eyes from her.

Canon Considine, gathering up all the faith and restlessness and longing that his sensitiveness felt in this well-filled chapel of a day, lifted it and his own brotherly pity once more into Heaven's sight—and suddenly felt at peace. "Ite missa est," he said out of a lightened heart.

Teresa was disappointed that she should be in such pain all through this blessed Mass in her room, and now when Our Lord Himself was in her heart. If only she could pray, if only she could think to pray properly! . . . He's a good boy, and I don't know, but the way she says "Mr. Mulqueen" sometimes—oh, Thy most Holy and Blessed Will be done, on earth as it is in Heaven——

The Second Chapter

THE morning was busy for Agnes. At breakfast news
came that Dr. Coyle, as was his custom, would arrive
at Roseholm before dinner that evening accompanied
by the English specialist, Sir Godfrey Bartlett-Crowe.
That meant much deliberation and surmise between
her father and her uncle at breakfast, with her for
necessary chorus. It also meant conferences in the
kitchen and linen-room, as well as the giving of some
tranquillising advice to her father on the subject of
wines and cigars.

She was grateful for the activity because in its
pauses she realised that in spite of confession, in spite
of communion, she was intensely worried and unhappy. And looking at Marie-Rose, who followed her
about like a tamed and sad gazelle and sought in vain
for occupation, looking at Vincent, looming proudly,
silently in and out of the garden, his face a sulky mask,
she felt that her advantage over them, in being in her
own house, amounted to an insult. At last, to her
relief, Marie-Rose, making herself look delicious in
sables, got into the carriage and drove away to make
a round of calls on aunts and uncles. She would enjoy
that—she always liked to play comedy in Mellick as
the luxurious and spoilt young matron from the

capital. On an impulse of great affection Agnes, as she tucked her up in the carriage, bent and kissed her with a little laugh.

"It's absurd," she said, "you're far too sweet not to be divinely happy."

But she was sorry she said it when tears flashed into her sister's eyes.

"Oh Nag, you darling!"

Agnes stood on the steps and watched the carriage roll away in the cold sunshine. She reflected that what was essential to Marie-Rose in intimate relationship was an exaggerated gentleness, an acute preoccupation with what might be called the inessentials of her personality. This might seem desirable to anyone, but to her sister was as necessary as air. Unfortunately she had married a man whose similar need differed only in being stronger and less easy to placate. He, too, must have from his lover an unjust, exhaustive gentleness, a fierce preoccupation of intelligence and nerves. Were he given such fantastic measure, he might or might not prove worth the bargain—not that the bargainer would care, passion cried in her unguardedly —but if Marie-Rose got back from love her easier demand, there was no question of how generous and adorable she could be.

The day was exquisite, and held Agnes idle a minute in spits of its cold. Her mother had loved the panorama from these steps so deeply that her children had the habit of relating it to her. "Mother's view," and nowadays had to marvel sadly that it could never again be that. South-east, beyond the embanked azalea bushes, beyond the laburnums and weeping ash trees of the drive the outlines of Mellick made a grave mass of permanence. Below the lawns and shrubbery the high wall hid the road but revealed further off the marshy river-field and the wide cold stream itself. Westward a thicket of firs and cypresses cut off her mother's small beloved rose garden and the old rustic garden house, but did not hide the sweeping nobility of the seaward-forging river, or the dim hills and ruins and isolated homesteads of its further bank. Under the cold sky the winter-coloured scene was desolately noble.

Vincent came out of the house and stood beside her.

"Let's get pneumonia," he said.

This shoddy for despair offended her.

"I was thinking of how we used to call this 'Mother's view,' " she said.

"I know. Is there any hope in all this fuss?"

"No medical hope, Dr. Curran says."

"He has a brain, I suppose?"

She was nettled.

"Haven't you noticed?"

"Not specially."

Ah! the misery and youth of his face as he stared ahead, comforting himself with his sneer! He turned and caught her gentle glance.

"You don't expect me to be on the look-out for *his*

good qualities?" he asked.

"Or anyone's," she answered, smiling. "It's not your habit."

"You think me cruel—a cruel husband?"

"Oh, Vincent, please don't drag me in as judge!"

He shrugged. And then, looking westward across the garden, "Those dark trees are glorious," he said. " 'Mother's view' is looking its best."

"Ah! It has so many bests."

"Agnes," he spoke softly and solemnly, in a manner that startled her.

"I must go in," she answered, but without moving.

"And what am I to do?"

"Oh, how can I say?"

He did not scowl at her snapping manner, but turned and spoke in matter-of-fact tones, his blue eyes holding hers.

"When I'm in Dublin, I manage most of the time to live a fantasy life," he said, "but here, when I see you, how real you are, with activities and plans that have nothing to do with me—that goes. And then there is nothing."

Many virtuous or wise retorts occurred to Agnes, but each seemed as perfect an insult to her sister as to him. What he was saying might be wicked or unfortunate or silly—but it did not seem to be untrue. He had in his eyes the look of a man who has nothing. The more fool he, the world would say, or the more unscrupulous or self-indulgent. But she was not the world. She was one of two women who had put him in this plight, and having no remedy, must make no comment. He saw her dilemma and came to her assistance.

"What do you suggest?" he asked, self-mocking, with a lift of his brows.

"A walk on the hills," she waved a hand towards the north-west, "or if you took the dog-cart up to Falvey's, perhaps they'd beat up snipe for you."

"Will you come?"

The idea of a day in the lonely mountains with him dazzled her. She closed her eyes, then opened them to mock him gently.

"I saw that look on your face," he said, and she was near enough to him to feel a new vibration in his body. "It's something to go on with! Where are the guns?"

"Where you last left them, I suppose," she said. "In the garden house." She waved her hand towards the fir trees.

"I'll have a look at them and order the trap," he said, and went down the steps, smiling back at her boyishly.

But as she went upstairs she was heavy-hearted.

Dr. Curran was with her mother, but she knew that she might enter the dressing-room from the window without disturbing them. She wished to see that the little room had been restored to its hospital order and aspect.

She turned its door handle quietly and entered. Her brother was shuffling towards her with a smile on his face, while Nurse Cunningham, smiling too, held in her hands a few late roses, sweet and frosty from the garden. Reggie slid past Agnes and departed. The door closed.

"Lovely, aren't they, Miss Mulqueen?"

The nurse held the flowers towards her.

Agnes, to her own surprise, felt a sudden pity for this self-possessed young woman. She touched the roses shyly, and murmured something about their beauty. Then, moving across the room, she put up a defence of examining it carefully.

"I see they have put the place to rights for you, Nurse," she said.

Nurse Cunningham had poured water from a carafe into a glass vase, and was arranging her roses.

"Oh yes, Miss Mulqueen. The servants are perfect here—a credit to you."

Agnes winced. The other woman was watching her out of the corner of an eye.

"Do you dislike me, Miss Mulqueen?" she asked.

"What a curious question!"

"Perhaps—to as cold a person as you."

Agnes moved towards the door, but the other woman, gracefully and as if playfully, barred her way. "No, no. Do answer. Do you disapprove of me?"

Agnes had an amused, wild thought of how Marie-Rose would giggle about this scene. To her "standoffish" spirit, as to Agnes's, it would seem both hideous and very funny.

"But—why should I?" she asked, at bay. "I don't know you."

"I've been nearly three weeks in the house."

There was ruthlessness in the pretty, smiling face, Agnes thought.

"I understand," she said, rising to what seemed to be a fight, "that you are an excellent nurse, and make Mother as comfortable as possible."

Her voice was icy. Nurse Cunningham's face flushed. Her eyes ceased to smile. They glittered now.

"Oh yes, all that. But I'm not made of stone, Miss Mulqueen," she said. "I'm not like you, you know—a dutiful machine!"

Agnes could not resist the opening.

"I had observed that," she said.

Nurse Cunningham assumed a professional manner.

"Then you wish to find fault with me?"

Agnes again felt a pity that surprised her.

"Oh no," she said. "Professionally not at all. Indeed 'fault-finding' isn't the word. But—well, about my brother——" The colour rose in her white cheeks. Her eyes were averted so that she could not see the interested expression in the nurse's eyes.

"I see. Your brother is kind to me, and friendly. And you desire me to be incivil."

"I only desire him not to misunderstand your

civility, nurse—which he may easily do."

"Would you be so good as to explain?"

"Ten years ago he caught an illness which it has not been found possible to cure beyond suspicion. The doctors think that he is probably cured now, but they will not guarantee that. Meantime the persistent doctoring and his own self-indulgence have ruined his health, as you can see. He is invalided and incapable. Mother devoted herself to keeping him fairly happy here and out of mischief. After her death— Heaven knows how he will bear his life. He can never marry, of course, but he is inclined to think the doctors over-fussy, and loneliness could easily lead him into trouble. He will misunderstand your kindness, and will become troublesome—perhaps not to you, but to himself and other people—if he gets the idea that people still find him attractive—I should have thought you might have guessed——"

It was a long speech—but it was over. No need to worry any more. The woman knew the situation now. Agnes flashed a quick glance at her. She was demurely arranging bottles on a shelf.

"Thank you, Miss Mulqueen," she said. The neutrality of her tone was curious; Agnes told herself that it probably covered embarrassment.

There was nothing more to be said. Dr. Curran would now be waiting to instruct the nurse. She moved in the direction of her duty, and Agnes, as she went downstairs, informed herself that she was in no

mood at all for the routine interview with her alert
medical admirer. Nevertheless it did not please her
to discover when she joined him in the dining-room
five minutes later that he was apparently in no mood
for her.

He frowned as he took her hand in a clasp which
was intended for hail and farewell.

"I must fly," he said. "I'm very late on my round.
Everyone a bit worse than they should be, and taking
that much extra time. Including your mother.
Weaker and in more pain than she need be this morning. What's exciting her nerves? These specialist
gentlemen?"

"I think Mass in her room exhausted her."

"A bit, perhaps. But holy things help her as a rule—
in themselves. She's agitated over something—not
unhappily—but whatever it is it's too stimulating. I've
left instructions about drugs. She needs a great deal
of help if she's to get through to-morrow reasonably
well. These know-alls!"

How vain he is! thought Agnes.

True enough he was vain. But he also hated
pomposity and waste of money, and he considered this
visit of two specialists an example of both. In any
case he was in an extremely bad mood this morning.
He had lost his head completely the night before, when
confronted with full knowledge of her heart. Long
after he had forced himself home from the cold river-
side, long after he had flung himself into bed, he had

writhed in a sickening pain of loss and jealousy. Inviting her ghost, inviting all his recent most conceited hopes, he let them make a pitiful, romantic havoc of the night. And when the sun returned and he got up, he laughed into the mirror at his own unrecognisably exhausted face. But the hysteria which he heard in this laugh had horrified him and brought about a savage onslaught of reaction so that he descended to his work in deadliest mood of rationalism, a creature of flat prose, a Victorian bourgeois in a temper, an overworked man in need of sleep.

On his breakfast-plate amid bills and circulars there had been a patronising note from Dr. Coyle to announce the morrow's consultation with the great Bartlett-Crowe.

"Caw! Caw!" he had snarled, tearing the letter into shreds. Afterwards in his study he held his aching head in his hands a minute and calmed himself with resolutions. There was to be no more schoolboy nonsense about Agnes Mulqueen. She loved what she couldn't have—she was as silly as that. She would get over the absurdity, and really it was a schoolgirl notion. Meantime, she was only a woman like any other, and there was no need to make midnight scenes about her. She was not going to vanish just because she cared for this—this Dublin fellow. She would be there, and he could wait, and meantime, maybe if he trained himself to be more reasonable about her, to look at her less and think of her less—maybe if she did marry him in the end, it would be more like the kind of quiet marriage he had always wanted. *Femme fatale,* indeed! He looked up again at the familiar furnishings of his solid, ugly study, and he laughed. This was 1880, and he was a small-town doctor. Where had his sense of humour gone?

It had gone at least this far that it did not reveal to him that even now, in this cold hour of discipline, he could not hint to himself that he might never win her.

He jumped to his feet and in movement was again aware with fury of his state of physical exhaustion. The savage voice in which he commanded his gig astonished servants grown used to his inattentive courtesy.

His calls, as luck would have it, had been worrying, and a touchy conscience was fretted by awareness that he was too tired to be a match for their exactions. It was the last straw to find Mrs. Mulqueen less well than she should be. So he had reached the dining-room disgusted with himself and with the inefficiency which love, as he had always known, put on a man. The thing to do, however, was to keep it in its place. Be brisk and busy, and avoid considering it. Let its satisfactions come or not, as might be. Meantime a man had work and responsibilities and no time to waste. He wished, by the way, she'd be more punctual. He really hadn't a minute, and only wanted to tell her the hour of to-morrow's appointment.

And then she had entered the room, and frowning and as inattentive to her as good manners allowed—conscious that he was managing the inattention extremely well, he had shaken her hand and grumbled about her mother's condition.

And it was easy! See how calm he was as she crossed the room to him! See how he could frown indifferently into the glance of her grey eyes! And how clear they were, those eyes, how blue-white and young the whites of them, how innocent the sweet curve of their lashes! Oh yes, she was beautiful, only a fool would deny it—but she was a woman, too. There were millions of her.

He turned away to the window, feeling deadly tired again. A horse and trap flashed by outside, throwing a long shadow into the room.

"Who was that?"

"Vincent. Going out after snipe."

As she pronounced the name William Curran's eyes flashed on to her. She felt their sharpness and stirred uneasily.

"Rather a peculiar fellow, isn't he?"

The tone of the inquiry was cold and tolerant.

"Yes, I suppose so."

"Do you like him?"

The movement which she made, the quick turn of her face away from him was involuntary, even unconscious—but it was, he knew, a shameless cry for mercy. He would have said that he was in no mood to hear it.

But moods in her hands were, it seemed, no more than snowflakes. Yesterday he had been her suitor, last night her sobbing clown, a minute ago her affectionate and patient critic—and now, in a flash, in the time in which it took her to turn her head away, he was her very heart, he saw, herself, the foolish and impossible desire she carried in her. He could not say why. She had done nothing noteworthy since entering the room. Rather she was more depressed than usual, more like the rest of worried and distrait humanity. Often talking with her here he had been consciously ravished by the grace with which she could be gay, or the soft malice of her gossip; often uplifted by betrayals of the anguish which she bore in her heart for her mother. Frequently he had seen her look more brilliant, either for comedy or for distress. Last night, for instance, she had worn the glory of a star—but just now it had helped, relieved him, to see her a little toneless, a little dull. He had felt safe and irresponsive, even while he appraised the beauty of her eyes. Now, with nothing said and not twenty seconds passed, the chain was on his neck again. The blaze of all the months was in his heart, new-fuelled with pity and knowledge. She was his fate. It was better so, easier. And if it wasn't—she was still his fate.

He did not wonder or smile at himself. He was conscious only of the foolish mania that was eating up her happiness, he was looking at it with her eyes, it was his. And this gymnastic of his spirit, which was no more than a pang of the absolute sympathy which she could always rouse in him, carried him back, without resistance or regret, to his state of yesterday, of unconditional love for her which was to be the state of all his life.

He smiled.

"It seems as if we are more or less in the same boat," he said gently, but her face betrayed no understanding and did not even harden.

"Father wondered," she said, "if you would like to dine here to-night, to meet your friends the specialists?"

"A macabre celebration. And when am I to read up the developments of my profession?"

"All right, I'll explain to Father."

Her eyes were faintly mischievous.

"You'll do nothing of the sort. Who told you to deal with my invitations? Most certainly I'm coming to dinner to-night."

"We'll all be very pleased to see you." She smiled at him.

"You see," he said, "I'm such a fool that the grimmest excuse is good enough."

"Oh—I'm sorry."

"No, you aren't—and there's no need to be. You've changed the world, love. You've given me new eyes."

He picked up her hand and kissed it. Then with quick steps, almost as if he were happy, he left the room.

The Third Chapter

AGNES went to four o'clock Benediction at the Dominican Church and found the sabled Marie-Rose there, under the escort of a pious cousin. On the drive home it was explained that, having lunched with the parents of this cousin in Finlay Square, Mrs. de Courcy O'Regan had been trapped into devoutness—"Not, indeed, that I oughtn't to be ashamed to talk like this— the way you and Uncle Tom and everyone are praying these days for Mother—but—oh, being holy seems to force one back to realities—and, Nag, I hate realities!"

When they came in and went up softly, arm-in-arm, to Agnes's room, they put a match to the fire and rang for tea. Agnes took her sister's wraps from her and pulled out the old repp sofa.

"Sit there and watch the fire," she said. "I'll go and take a look at Mother."

"Can't I come?"

"Well, I imagine she's—asleep."

Teresa's room was darker than usual. Agnes, growing used to the shadows, bent above her bed. Nurse Cunningham was at the other side, smiling and patting the patient's hand.

"Like Reggie, did you say? Oh, then he'll be nice—

the flower of them all. Like Reggie—well, God bless him."

The sick eyes had the bright glaze of delirium.

"Oh, Mother, Mother darling!"

"She thinks she's had another baby," Nurse Cunningham said. "She asked me which of you it was like."

Agnes inclined her head and tiptoed away.

Marie-Rose hated "realities," Vincent lived "a fantasy life," and William Curran had to pretend that she altered the world. Her father kept pseudo-cheerful behind a haze of prayers and mottoes. Her brother lived from hour to hour on bits of Chopin and bits of false gaiety compelled, for his sanity, from his exhausted mother. And that mother was kept this side of agony by dreams, in death, that she relived her long-gone hours of strength and life-giving. What, then, was her own delusion, Agnes wondered? Like her father's—that God heard prayers? Like her confessor's —that human love can die? Or was her present foolery the pharisaical one that she had, by one confession, one repentance, killed desire?

She stood still in the corridor, where last night she had listened a moment to his love. She searched her conscience. Yes, she had listened—but not willingly, and not for as long as a full minute. She must not listen again. "A fantasy life." Oh, she knew what he meant. He thought it was an escape, apparently, but it had been her prison. To her it had lately seemed, in its sweetness, its uncertainty, its truthfulness, to be taking on the very bulk and texture of reality. It had made fantasy of every day and of what she saw and touched. Had been as real to her as this morphia-delusion was real to her mother. And so she had scotched it last night, and returned to the things it had made dream-like.

She came to her own fire.

"What are 'realities'?" she asked Marie-Rose.

"Oh—anything that makes you cross or uncomfortable."

Agnes smiled.

"Yes," she said. "That's what everyone means by them, I suppose. Except Reggie. But he doesn't see them."

"Poor Reggie."

"What's to become of him without Mother?"

Marie-Rose poked the fire.

"She's—she's really dying, Nag?"

The voice was soft and frightened.

"I—I think so."

"Will it—have to be terrible for her—before the end?"

Agnes put a hand wearily across her forehead, and kept it there. She seemed to ponder the question, but she did not reply.

Marie-Rose, on her knees by the fender, fidgeted with the poker.

"There's a reality if you like," she mused—"and I

can't, I simply can't keep it in mind. There's Mother dying. Mother. She bore us. We wouldn't be here without her. She brought us up and looked after us and knocked us into shape. She was extravagant about us, and saw that we had everything we wanted. She used to be very severe and prudish sometimes, and often—it was maddening—she seemed to be reading our thoughts. Did you ever notice that?"

Agnes didn't move.

"And now she's dying," Marie-Rose went on. "She's always been as natural to existence as the ground you walk on—and soon it will be over. The whole thing will be changed. I wish I could realise it—but I'm only saying it, Nag. I'm not feeling it. Isn't that terrible? When one's mother is dying it ought to be as if some part of oneself were shrivelling off——"

"It is, in a way."

"I keep wanting to tell her, Nag, every time I go into her room—I keep wanting to say that all this keeping up appearances is nonsense, and these other things that are always in my head are nothing compared to the fact that she'll soon be gone——"

"Would that be true if you said it?"

"No. But I think it ought to be—oh, it's confusing, Nag—this deadly matter-of-factness about her, and such absurd preoccupation with oneself!"

"Darling, it's natural."

Marie-Rose crouched back a little from the fire and leant her head against her sister's knee. It was dark in the room, and through the two big windows Agnes could see night advancing as occasional stars broke up the pallid coldness of the sky. She thought of him descending from the hills alone.

"The First of November," said Marie-Rose. "Funny to think there are schoolgirls everywhere this minute feeling about this holiday just as we used to! I remember all the excitements so well, don't you, Nag? I can really and truly feel them all over again."

Her head was turned away from Agnes, her arm lay, young and slender, across Agnes's knee. In spite of her modish chignon of gold hair, she looked very babyish.

"It's this room does it to you," Agnes said; "whenever you're in it for five minutes you don't just grow reminiscent—you go straight back to the past—even in your looks."

"I'm not so sure I like that idea, Nag. I must have been a sight at school."

"I always thought you the belle of the place."

"Ah, you were a darling of a little sister. Is Vincent still out shooting?"

"I believe so."

"Heaven help the birds!"

"It'll soon be time to change—there are those two doctors arriving to-night, you know."

"Yes."

Neither of them moved.

"Mother's in delirium," Agnes said. "She was

dreaming just now she'd had another baby."

"Ah, Heaven!"

"Somehow, I think that's—unbearable."

Agnes's voice broke down.

"Oh, Nag, don't cry. Sweet Nag—oh, my pet, don't cry!"

Marie-Rose caught hold of Agnes's hand and pressed it to her face.

"There, there," she murmured, "there, there, my Nag."

They grew quiet again, as quiet as the room, as the world.

"I wonder if you're in love with him——" said Marie-Rose.

Agnes's thoughts had been astray and the sound of these words frightened her. The room seemed to drop from dusk to darkness.

"In love with whom?"

"With Dr. Curran."

"No."

"That's a pity."

"Yes. I think so."

Marie-Rose laughed.

"What do you mean by that?" she asked, and glancing back at Agnes: "What are you listening to?"

"I thought I heard the trap in the drive——"

"Oh. Did Vin take it?"

"Yes. Are you uneasy when he's out like that?"

Agnes marvelled at herself for this idiotic question.

"Uneasy? Good Lord, no! And I never thought you were that sort of female, Nag!"

"I'm not, really."

"Vincent's eccentric, the Lord knows, but he always turns up when he's expected, and so on. He believes in decorum, you know."

Agnes was thinking, some devil in her insisted on thinking: Suppose I had gone with him to-day when he said, 'Will you come?' suppose up on the hills I had persuaded him to disappear with me, to behave impossibly and forsake all this, to forsake even her, my sister. And the same devil said aloud, consumed with curiosity:

"Yes, but supposing once he *didn't* turn up?"

She heard Marie-Rose take in a slow and careful breath, she felt her body stiffen—not violently, but as if with reluctance.

"Would it matter?"

Agnes felt ashamed of these questions in the manner in which one suffers shame for an embarrassing relative. It could not be she herself who was behaving thus. But she must hear the answer.

It came after a pause.

"It would." Marie-Rose spoke softly. "I know the things I've said about him; I've meant them. I mean them this minute. It's difficult to explain. But, Nag, if I could wipe out having known him, if I could go back to where I was the day before I met him, and begin from there and marry some kinder and more normal man—oh—I'd be glad of that, if I'd never known him, if he were just swept out of my mind. But'"—she laughed without comfort—"he's one of these realities we were talking about, you see, and—I've been married to him—and I—I don't want anyone else! That's the terrible thing! That's what makes me hate him!"

Her voice dropped away into a whisper, and she shuddered a little. Agnes sat very still. The devil of curiosity had been well answered. She was not sorry, she told herself, that she had permitted the intensive questioning. The air was cleared and her own folly, falseness, disloyalty, and impurity of heart once and for all revealed to her. The last barrier, in human terms the strongest, was in position now. Good. Splendid.

She stroked her sister's silky head. Under the cold tranquillity which Marie-Rose's words had laid on her, she was aware, or half aware, of a curious emotion, half envy, half elation. "I've been married to him, and I don't want anyone else!" Naturally. But she, without being married to him, had known that it must be like that. She, from merely seeing him, knew every other man to be impossible. Oh, devilish thoughts! When, when would she have finally cleared her mind of him?

"Lovely hair! What are you going to wear to-night?"

"I don't know. I've brought so little. I'd no idea there'd be all these dinner-parties."

"There aren't any dinner-parties—but I like showing you off."

"Dear Nag! I'll do my best. Must we move now?"

"*I* must, pet. I've got to have a few last words with Maggie, and I must receive the gentlemen when they arrive from the train."

She got up, assembling duties with which to re-establish her self-confidence. She went to the dressing-table and lighted candles. She combed her hair.

Marie-Rose fidgeted about her.

"What is it, pet?"

"Nothing, Nag."

"I hope they've lighted the fire in your room."

"Oh, sure to have. Old Bessie's a marvel."

Silence.

"Nag?"

"Yes, little Rose?"

"May I—sleep here to-night?"

"But of course." They did not look at each other.

"You see, there's no dressing-room to that room——"

"But I can have the one next door arranged for——"

"Oh, the servants——"

"But, surely if you choose to ask your husband to sleep elsewhere sometimes——"

"I know. But I don't want to ask. I don't want any sort of discussion with him, Nag——"

"All right, darling. Come and sleep here."

Still their eyes avoided a meeting. Marie-Rose

moved towards the door, then paused again and spoke more softly, but in a different, colder tone.

"As a matter of fact, I won't. Why should he turn me out? It's my room, after all."

Agnes, not knowing what to say, said nothing. She wondered mockingly what the finding of the law would be in such a case, and then reflected that it would need to have the facts, which she had not. How sordid a private love became, and how extremely embarrassing! ". . . whereas in the idea of God there is matter for eternity." Yes, holy Jesuit, that's all very fine. But we aren't made in the most convenient form in which to pursue ideas, and we have no notion at all of how to front eternity.

The door closed softly. Marie-Rose was gone.

The Fourth Chapter

AGNES, eating grapes, thought of the irrelevancy of visible life.

Dinner had gone without a hitch. Food, wines and conversation were suave and reassuring. Marie-Rose, looking lovely, had been deftly complementary to her sister in the tasks of hospitality. The six men, each in character, had talked as if with pleasure—even Reggie doing his part, even her father bracing himself super-stitiously to make Dr. Coyle enjoy his evening, as though such enjoyment might influence to-morrow's fate.

It was a grim dinner-party, Agnes thought—and quite a pleasant one.

For none so pleasant as for Sir Godfrey Bartlett-Crowe. When his friend Coyle, whom he had known as long ago as in Vienna, had asked him to make this journey into the dark interior of Ireland, he had been, to put it mildly, astonished. Dublin, though in many ways a deplorable and dangerous place, was at least a capital, and had, if one knew where to look for them, some of the airs and amenities of a capital. It had lurking wealth, too, and a few good cellars. This was not the first time Sir Godfrey had condescended to travel his eminent opinion as far as Dublin. And, of course, were he asked to attend at any of the great historic houses scattered about the district called The Pale, he would not hesitate to pursue his guineas even there. But to plunge right into the murderous and stormy south, to stay in the home of a real Irishman, a Catholic, to attend the wife of a small-town merchant, and waste twenty-four hours, and perhaps encounter danger in so doing—that at first blush had seemed an absurd suggestion.

But Coyle was truly anxious about this case, and Sir Godfrey was, even if he himself was acutely aware of it, a very gifted and conscientious doctor. Further, his engagement book was by chance quite empty of important events for the next few days, and, after all, the thing with its disadvantages would be an adventure.

The carriage and pair outside Mellick station had been the first reassurance to his timidity. The spaciousness and warmth of Roseholm was an even better surprise. Certainly his host was quite as vulgar-looking as he had expected, but amusingly mild. There had been a brief impression of a slim girl with dark hair, a welcoming murmur in a very feminine and gracious voice—and: "This is my daughter," the fat little man had said. "Impossible," Sir Godfrey had almost answered, but "my son," a too easily diagnosed wreck of a man, had borne him off at that moment with Coyle to have a drink. He had not liked, until Coyle, who obviously knew the fellow and his history, had done so, to take a drink from those puffy hands. But this one unpleasant impression had been shrugged off in the comfort of his bedroom, where a great fire, a mighty bed and the hospitable and deferential fussings in and out with hot water of a venerable housemaid had most consolingly adjusted his notions of native Irish life.

Descending then to the drawing-room, Sir Godfrey was at his most urbane, though still on the look-out for indigenous drolleries. He advanced in his very best manner towards the graceful young creature who was his hostess, and she, bewildering enough in her beauty, presented him at once to a lovely blonde flower at her side, her sister, Mrs. de Courcy O'Regan.

Sir Godfrey was a connoisseur of women up and down the social scale, but he had never met a colleen. Amusedly in the train he had wondered about the species. Shy and wild, no doubt—perhaps even barefoot—and in need of masterly coaxing. He had an idea his technique would serve. Perhaps a little teasing—a playful reproduction of their quaint brogue——

These ladies were not shy and wild, and though they had a brogue, Sir Godfrey felt that its movements were too subtle for immediate imitation. In any case—that obviously would not be in the way to please, or to be understood. He bowed in rather excited courtesy over Marie-Rose's beautiful and mondaine hand.

The rest of the party was presented to him, the local doctor, to whom he condescended pleasantly, and then the husband of the lovely blonde, who strode belatedly

into the room. An odd young man, Sir Godfrey
thought. When their two names were murmured by
Mr. Mulqueen, he had stared for quite a second out
of cold blue eyes which, the doctor knew, were absolutely inattentive to what they focused. A remarkable
and insolent face, very white, very aristocratically
boned. A face made into a mask by sensitiveness; perhaps the face of someone a little mad. And this was
the husband of that exquisite blonde lady! Sir Godfrey glanced towards her, wondering somewhat, both
as man and as doctor.

He began to perceive that, contrary to his expecta-
tions, he would need skill if he was to get the true
essence of this company in which he found himself—
and that even then it very likely would elude him.
Surprising! In this painfully old-fashioned drawing-
room, and among people who did not dress—that is to
say, really dress for dinner! He had been irritated
when Coyle told him not to. He hated dining without
the ritualistic exposure of a starched white breast-
plate. But, indeed, the black suitings and white linen
of all these men were perfectly presentable, and the
ladies, though, of course, their décolletages were not
ceremonial, were exquisite in silks and jewels. Though
the tall one—he looked again—was not in silk, but in
velvet, black velvet as smooth and undulating as the
sea on a dark, calm night. Sir Godfrey smiled. And
the little one, in her chic white frills, a dress of frills
it seemed, was perhaps the foam, suddenly gleaming

on the edge of that sea. He laughed, and moved towards sea and foam. So this was Ireland! Surprise was still naïvely in his face, and still there was the nervous desire to make a joke of his surprise, and yet again the uneasy feeling that he had better not do that.

In the dining-room he sat at the right hand of his hostess, with the little white-frilled blonde, the foam of the sea, on his own right. Very much pleased at his position, he smiled at Coyle, diagonally opposite him, at the right side of their chubby little host. The table appointments were good, he noted, the parlour-maid immaculate, the ladies young and glorious; he certainly ran an excellent chance of enjoying dinner. He sipped his sherry, tasted his soup—then almost wriggled in his chair for satisfaction.

Vincent, sitting directly opposite, smiled at the stranger. And how very blue his eyes are, Sir Godfrey thought. As if made of ice.

"You look like a wise man," Vincent said.

Sir Godfrey indicated his wine-glass, his surroundings, and the beautiful young women to left and right of him.

"I almost begin to think I am one," he said. "But why do *you* think it?"

"I only said you *look* like one."

"It seems to me," said Agnes, "that you'd have to be very wise not to resent being told you look it."

"And you suspect, Miss Mulqueen, that I may not be quite wise enough for that?"

"But in five minutes does one dare to suspect anything?"

"How wise! But women are born that way."

"I don't think so. More's the pity."

She smiled.

"My sister is, as you see, Sir Godfrey, a disillusioned woman. A new type!" Marie-Rose's eyes mocked Agnes tenderly.

The Englishman turned with delight from dark to fair.

"But I thought that Ireland suffered no new types. I thought it was the sanctuary of the old ideal feminine!"

"That is very exacting of you," said Marie-Rose. Sir Godfrey gave himself up awhile to the delight of flattering her.

"He doesn't talk like a wise man, though," said Vincent to Agnes.

"Are you looking for such a creature?"

"No. I've more sense than that."

His voice was contented and brotherly. She hoped hers rang with as steady a note.

From the time when he parted with Agnes on the house steps until now, when he likened the stranger to a wise man, Vincent had spoken to no one save briefly to a stableman and to a farmer and his son up in the hills. The interlude was spacious, as if unpursued by time; indeed, did anyone tell him that he had been six days rather than six hours away, he would not have marvelled. The period had been cool and dreamy, what careless men might call "unreal," and during it he had wandered through many caverns of himself. Not earnestly or with a purpose, any more than there was purpose in his snipe-shooting, which he soon abandoned to walk in peace along the mountain ridges. In peace—that was it, and it was very curious—in peace, with her ghost lightly and intermittently evoked for company.

The day was cold, gracious and imperturbable—but he wondered why he also should be like that. "I'm almost happy," he had said aloud to Agnes, as if she walked with him. "Coldly happy, you know, like a man who has had things taken out of his hands and settled for him. What does it mean?" But meanings never stayed him long, who had learnt defensively to savour moods for what they in themselves were worth and to leave prophetic souls to nursery maids. This peace was a beneficence dropped surprisingly into the clean, unrelenting day, and no doubt to die with it.

But no, or not exactly. He harnessed his horse in the farm stable as the first stars sprang into the unready sky, and he was still serene then, and knew it, wondering. He drove back to Mellick slowly, letting darkness reach the town ahead of him. There he paced the garden until the lowering of lights in certain windows told him that his wife had descended from their room, and he might go up without encountering her. And even as he timed this mundane matter, and smiled appreciatively at the skill with which he and Marie-Rose played Box and Cox, his sense of being outside the dust of life remained. Washing, changing his clothes, brushing his hair, he sang: "Mein Himmel du, darin ich lebe . . ." Before he went downstairs he stared at himself in the glass. "My God!" he said in a queer, uneasy way. "My God! I believe I'm feeling happy! Why? What is it?"

And now here was dinner with its ritual. This was the long day's point of definition, where dream and actuality could a little fuse, the hour of wine and lamplight when visible beauty made nonsense of remembering, and established poor reality's full triumph over fantasy. This was the hour when he could see and adore her, when she was compelled to look again and again into his face.

"It was a lovely day," he said to her. "Your notion that you couldn't come made no difference."

She knew what he meant, and it saddened her. Heaven! let them be done with the soft food of dreaming. If she couldn't have him in his flesh and life—and she couldn't—she was not going to live in half sin with his ghost.

"I'm glad," she said, nevertheless, and scrutinised his face. "The wind has done you good. Is that all you found up there?"

"Oh, a few snipe, too, and—and——"

"And wisdom?"

"No. Expectancy."

"Ah! What is that like?"

"Agnes, my dear," her father was piping, "here's something that you'll like to hear about. Dr. Coyle has met Mr. Parnell, if you please——"

Everyone looked towards Dr. Coyle, Vincent with great eagerness.

"I'd like to meet him," he said.

"Well, Mr. O'Regan," Dr. Coyle was pleased to be the focal point, and took his moment slowly, "I can tell you in advance you'll be disappointed."

"Very likely. He looks too good to be true."

"Or too true to be good—in politics," said William Curran, who was seated far from Agnes, at the left hand of her father.

Sir Godfrey Bartlett-Crowe shook Mrs. de Courcy O'Regan from the forefront of his attention for a second.

"What does he look like?" he asked amiably.

Everyone contributed. Tall, pale, serious, very handsome, very enigmatic——

Vincent smiled at Sir Godfrey.

"Your beard and your forehead remind me of him," he said. "That's why you look like a wise man."

"Sir Godfrey looks gayer than Mr. Parnell," said Marie-Rose.

"I wouldn't call Mr. Parnell a wise man, if you were asking me," said Danny.

"Neither would I," said Vincent.

"Actually, I would," said Dr. Curran. "He's the kind that reaches wisdom, I imagine."

"Well, now," said Dr. Coyle, "there's for and against, there's for and against."

"True for you, indeed, Doctor," said Danny, who delighted in such pronouncements.

"Why don't you think Parnell looks wise?" William Curran inquired, with faint sarcasm, of Vincent.

"Because I think he looks something quite different. A demigod, if you like."

"Ah," said Curran, as if condescending to hysteria, "you're that kind of worshipper?"

"No. If I insulted him with an emotion it would be pity."

"But he's not pitiable, you know."

" 'Tis we'll be to be pitied soon at his hands," said Reggie.

Agnes was watchful while Vincent and William Curran sparred.

"Mr. Parnell doesn't look like a demigod," she said at random, to distract them.

"What does he look like then?"

"Well—a god perhaps. One of the fierce ones."

"What's that, Agnes?" said Danny. "What's that you're saying, my dear?"

"High time you interfered, Father," said Marie-Rose. "She's breaking the first commandment."

Sir Godfrey laughed delightedly.

"If she ever does that, Mrs. O'Regan," he said,

"don't you think it ought to be for a better man than your present political leader?"

Expectancy. Agnes, puzzled by Vincent's uncharacteristic declaration of it, thought that, sad as this occasion of hospitality was, perhaps it was its infusion of some of that quality into the hour that made it easier and its antics less irrelevant than she had thought. She tried to voice the idea.

"Father has found a little expectancy, too, I think," she said softly to Vincent.

He glanced at the other end of the table and then at her.

"In the coming of the wise men?"

How kind he could make his voice for matters that were remote from him!

"Yes; he can't help having a little hope, you see—and, oh, if he were right!"

Vincent shook his head.

"Don't think that way," he said gently.

"I don't, really," she said.

"Always you need the truth to live with. It's your kind of thing."

"If I do," Agnes asked him, "if anyone does, what is the point of this pseudo-pleasure we are taking, say, here at this table? And why isn't it completely pseudo?" She spoke as if to herself and softly, slowly —while her eyes travelled up and down the room.

Sir Godfrey—she knew nothing of him, but it was safe to assume that the truth of his life was not in-

volved by the amusing story he was relating to Marie-
Rose. And assuredly there was no more than a tenth
of her real sister in the laughing, pretty creature now
listening to that story. William Curran—ah, perhaps
he, nodding with bare politeness at the pronouncements of Dr. Coyle, and keeping his profile markedly
still—did he feel her eyes on him, and was she right
in thinking that he sulked because Vincent sat beside
her?—perhaps he, by some rigidity he had, some stiff
integrity, underlined the unreality of their sociable
exchanges, and did wear if not his heart then at least
his sensibility on his sleeve? He was not forgetting her
mother upstairs, and the desperate ignorance of his
profession. He was not unhurt by her father's pitiful
optimism. Nor, perhaps, were the good wines making
love seem easier. But even he sat still, and did not cry
out against the masquerade. Her father, however—her
eyes rested miserably on him—her father, conducting
with Dr. Coyle the kind of politics-and-state-of-the-
country talk which he enjoyed, full of wise saws, but
virgin of modern instances, her father actually was
then letting himself think that God, through the hands
of these famous men, was going to grant a miracle,
was going to make old age worth living through? No;
in his heart, behind those desolate little eyes, a more
permanent knowledge stayed to plague him, Agnes
thought. And Dr. Coyle—surely his manner, of vague
and kindly compromise, was the crutch of one whom
realities had long ago disabled? Then there was her

brother, seated between Dr. Coyle and Vincent—not fidgeting much, but drinking steadily. Behaving well and listening to what people said, making remarks about wine and weather and Land Leaguers—all the while in an irrational agony he did not dare examine. And even he, Agnes thought, sits still, and seems to enjoy this dinner-party. Lastly, there was herself and there was Vincent.

She looked at him, and turning from his consideration of the table, he smiled at her.

"I can't answer for them," he said, with a gay, dismissing movement of his hand. "But I'm not feeling any 'pseudo-pleasure.' "

"What then?"

"What I told you—expectancy." He looked about him. "To-day is an ante-room," he said dreamily. "It's only this moment struck me, but that's what it is. That's what I feel."

"It's an obvious enough comparison—for everyone's state of mind, Father's and everyone's."

"Perhaps. I wasn't thinking of them."

"A mystical experience?" Her voice was ironical.

"It may be, but it doesn't require a name. It doesn't even need to be anything but an illusion."

She was irritated—she could not say why.

"And yet you recommend other people 'to live with the truth,' " she said. "Is it not 'your kind of thing,' then?"

"Not specially," he said, and almost eagerly—"don't

try to trap me. Not you. There's no need. I talk—because it's a way of communication—and there is no other."

She dropped her eyes because she knew that tears had risen to them. Unexplainable tears. But through this burning glaze the whole of life, its deepest loves and loyalties, appeared, save one of them, irrelevant as dinner-party chatter. She stared at her plate, then closed her eyes to retain the burning tears. The moment would pass—since it could not be borne.

He watched her. Head bent unhappily, tears spangling her lashes, little teeth biting distressfully on her lower lip—she looked almost a child, he thought. Black velvet sweeping royally to the floor might give to her, unjewelled as she was to-night, the air of a queen led into execution. But the bent head made nonsense of all that—the head of a girl who wanted to be happy, and was hurt at the elusiveness of happiness.

He did not quite know what he meant by all this talk—nor did he greatly care. The important thing was this curious stretch of peace which remained even here among the symbols of his predicament. If she must argue with him, and lift her brows and be a sceptic—then bow her head and fight with baby tears—such phases only decorated the felicitous hour. How still it had been in those mountains. He could listen to the stillness now. He had brought it back with him.

He would like to tell her that. That would be natural and good, to hold her in his arms and talk about these things. That would be rest. Experimentally, not without fear, for his thoughts were steering now into regions that always skirted hell, but still deliberately, to test his day of quietude, he let himself think of her in his embrace, against his breast. "Softly," his spirit warned, but blackness did not come. Keeping his eyes on her where she sat and talked now with the stranger and with Marie-Rose, he found that instead of blindly and vainly striving to conjure up her physical love for him, he was to-night, as it were, remembering it. Oh, Heaven, what sweet madness! To be persuaded that no other mouth had ever kissed him, so accurately could he feel the unknown touch of hers! To know the coolness of her eyelids and exactly the warmth of her breast! To be so naturally possessed by memory of what had never happened that it drove out all recorded life and became his sole experience! And still to be happy! Still to have this quiet, this expectancy within! He wondered with detachment whether any of these doctors, could they see the immediate curvetting of his ideas, would certify him as sane. But, he pondered amusedly, if I'm insane just now, I am much more tenderly disposed to life than when I see things in the sequences that are called normal—I mean, I'm far less dangerous now. It's very dangerous to be sane. But if I'm hers and she's mine—if that's settled, do I become ridiculous at once—more of a smiler even than

I feel? If hell stops, do we turn silly? In other words, does hell win, anyway?

He did not care. Through half-shut eyes he watched her. Too pure perhaps, too translucent for velvet. She should wear clothes of diamond or of ice. Prima donnas wear velvet—but how she dismisses its voluptuousness. And yet he knew her own. He closed his eyes and knew it all again. Dear love, that love should be like this! Dear love.

Sir Godfrey, something of a naturalist, had heard of his day after snipe. The Scolopax Gallenago, he presumed, the bécassine of France?

But Vincent smiled at the formidable words for which he cared nothing and randomly summoned William Curran to his aid.

Yes—Dr. Curran thought it could only be the bécassine, which was very plentiful along these lake-studded hills, which harboured *scolopax rusticola* too, the woodcock—and Reggie even said that if Sir Godfrey thought he'd like some sport, he was sure— what did Vincent think?—that among those guns of his brothers'——

Vincent said that all the guns were in need of cleaning, but Sir Godfrey regretted—no one but he, who had been studying Marie-Rose with passion, knew how much—that his hours in Ireland must be numbered.

And Agnes, seeing all the males well swung into conversation, ate grapes and pondered.

The Fifth Chapter

THE ladies, his sisters, had hardly left the dining-room when Reggie departed from it too. But he did not cross the hall to the drawing-room. He climbed upstairs and knocked at the door of Nurse Cunningham's sitting-room.

"Come in," her bright voice said.

She was sitting by a fire, crocheting. She looked fair and gentle—a familiar, almost a homely figure.

"What is it?" She was coy, taken unawares by his visit. That pleased him.

"Oh, nothing. Only—are you coming downstairs to-night?"

She shook her head amusedly.

"Ladies wait till they're asked," she said.

"Oh—as to that——" but she laughed contentedly.

"I'm tired."

"May I sit here a while?"

Again a coy look that pleased him.

"Well, you mustn't stay long, you know."

He mopped his forehead and stared into the fire. He had no idea why he had come into this room. He had turned to it as an animal to cover.

"Mother's had a bad day?" he asked.

She nodded.

Reggie, trained by Teresa into absolute dependence on her, never felt fear, but only panic and the menaces of fear. He brought these always to his mother to be dissolved before they grew to the true thing. To-day at Mass he had actually tried to look at her as a doctor might and had found the courage to ask himself if her death was really near. But he could not see her face save with his own self-protecting eyes —the strong mocking face that from his babyhood and through all the shock and sorrow he had brought her had been the same to him, the unchanging face of love. Wish as he might for true vision, he could not see death in her eyes. Because that was to see his own decaying life bereft of her—a hideous, hopeless sight which he could not examine. She had looked at him as usual at the end of Mass, out of those eyes that did not change— and against all the panoply of special praying, and medical visitations, his heart had leapt.

And then Curran had come later and been gloomy —and there had been morphia. So that she raved and did not know him. In the very hour when those unbearable doctor fellows were arriving, and when he had to, *had* to hear her voice making little of them— she was still away from him—still drugged and out of reach. And now he had had to eat and drink with them, and try to behave as if their faces were endurable, as if to-morrow only mattered as much to him as it might to any normal son—oh, God!

He groaned aloud. The menaces had turned to

fear, and she was not there to help him.

" 'Sh," said Nurse Cunningham. " 'Sh—'Sh."

"But I'm afraid!"

"Of what?"

"Of these—these doctors."

"They won't do anything terrible to her."

"They'll talk, though! They'll say she's going to die!"

He covered his sweating face with his hands.

Nurse Cunningham considered his dead and dusty hair, and how the sweat shone along his shining cranium.

"They may not—this time," she said slowly.

He looked up. She was startled by the foolish eagerness in his face.

"You think so?"

"Oh, don't look like that. They'll have to say it soon."

"God! God!"

"But it's—unkind of you to go on like this. Life will be nothing but torture to her now until it's over."

He stared into the fire, a mulish look on his face.

"She says that isn't true. She says you all make it out to be worse than it is."

"She is the bravest patient I have ever nursed."

"I know she's brave. But still—look at her, how gay she can be still, and the way she sees a joke—and——"

"She adores you——"

He did not see her point. The reminder of this

love he was to lose distracted him.

"What will I do? Oh, tell me what I am to do?"

"Help her to die in peace. Don't make this claim on her that keeps her fighting and fretting for life. Let her rest now."

"I see."

He was very quiet. The nurse went on talking.

"After all," she said, "it would be sheer brutality not to. And you are a man and young and have your own life to live, and will certainly have to get used to living it without her. That's natural. That's the way life has to go. . . ."

She strung out the consoling platitudes with a convincing sincerity, paraphrasing them, repeating them, to make a long and supposedly sedative speech. She said all the things which a woman unaware of his circumstances might be expected to say to a youngish man whose mother was dying. But there was a watchful, professional look in her eye.

He exploded at last into the hysteria she had expected. Bending forward in his chair and rocking back again, cramming his silk handkerchief against his mouth, against his streaming eyes, he sobbed and spluttered.

"But you don't know, oh, you can't understand——" he wailed. "All that you're saying has nothing to do with me! I'm not like other people, and I have no life to live—I can't trust myself, I'm no good and I'm sick, and no one has any pity on me, no one cares except

her—oh, you don't know and I can't explain—but if
she dies—I'm finished—there's nothing! Nothing, do
you hear? Life! Live my life! With nothing to do!
And no one to bother about me! People are afraid
of me, I tell you—people hate me! But she doesn't—
she's all I have—she understands me——"

He went on and on. His voice ripped up into high
sobs, and gurgled down again. Tears streamed about
his face. He got up and shuffled round the room, then
dropped, breathing hard, into another chair. He made
a hideous scene, not knowing that this was what instinct had driven him here to do, not knowing that he
was almost happy.

Nurse Cunningham watched him. Among her
qualities was a self-control which the exercise of her
profession had not yet hardened into callousness—for
she was still young. She possessed this virtue, but she
also admired, would once have said exacted it in
others. Its absence always seemed to her very disgusting, and she reflected now, not for the first time, that
this man must have been born without a vestige of it.
But he had been born lazy, too, and that should have
kept him from the mischiefs of the first defect. However, he had not had that much luck. Her realist's eye,
helped by professional training, took in all the details
of his appearance. Disease, mercury, tippling, idleness,
over-eating, hopelessness, and a lascivious mind—all
these had made this ruin, and he was the second son.
But his elder brother was a priest. He would own this

house, he would be wealthy. His name stood well in the town. He might be lascivious, but he had no real sensuality left. He was an invalid and manageable. He was also pitiable, and she was not unkind. She could keep a bargain. She was a nurse and could look after people.

She watched him, and was very quiet. No shudder escaped her. But she was pretty, she had feeling, she had sensuality. Still, she would be rich. She would be unencumbered. It would be a fair return for a life of difficult good humour, difficult flattery, difficult nursing. Such comfort and prosperity as she found in this house were not offered by normal men to women in her circumstances. It would be fair—a fair bargain.

She shuddered.

He dried his eyes; he wheezed distressfully. He was exhausted. And there was a creeping comfort in his nerves. All day he had wanted to cry out and make a scene—and there had been no one to accept it. Now strangely and yet naturally there was this quiet, pretty woman——

"—She's all I have. I'll never have anyone else. I—I can't. You see——"

"Why can't you?"

He had not expected an interruption. He was embarrassed.

"Well—I——"

"Why can't you?"

"Oh, I've been ill—a long time ago——"

"I thought perhaps—that might have been so."

In spite of the measured hesitation, there was something level and simple in her voice that to Reggie sounded like heavenly music. Like the peace that his mother's reassurance could bring, only more amazing.

"You did? And still you—you didn't hate me?"

Nurse Cunningham felt panic. What was it his sister, stuck-up creature, had said: "He will misunderstand your kindness, and become troublesome. . . ." She would have to be careful.

"One mustn't hate anyone," she said primly.

His face lost its liveliness.

"Oh—I know. Only, you've been so very nice to me, so cheery——"

She was sorry for him again.

"Yes. I thought you needed cheeriness. You see—I—half-guessed about your ill-health, and now from what you tell me, I see I was right. But—you take an exaggerated view, I think."

"How do you mean?"

"There are more things in life than—than all you've lost by your illness."

"Mother says that. That's what she always hammered into my head. And while she's there—there are more things—that's right—but——"

"But other people might—take her place."

"Who?"

She took a careful breath.

"A wife, Mr. Mulqueen."

"But—I can't marry."

"You could marry a wife who understood that."

"There's no one I could ask. Everyone knows. Everyone's afraid of me."

"I'm sure that isn't true!"

"Who'd marry me? What's there to marry?"

"You're young and you're kind; you're nice to look at." She paused uneasily, for he was leaning towards her, and his bloodshot eyes were bright. "You play the piano nicely, you have very good manners, you live in a lovely house——" She caught her breath again. There was a hardness of terror in her eyes.

"Oh, Nurse, what do you mean? Oh, if it were possible—oh, Nurse!"

She stood up. She could not go on.

"But what right have I to advise you in this way—a stranger in your house? Do please forgive me."

"You're not a stranger. No one's ever been so kind to me."

She bent to poke the fire.

"What an exaggeration! Now, please, Mr. Mulqueen, go downstairs to your guests."

"But—I thought——" He seemed bewildered, but she was merciless.

"No, no. Run along. They'll wonder where you've got to."

Reggie was at sea. He trundled obediently to the door, grumbling in his mind but, in spite of confusion, happier than he could understand.

Nurse Cunningham watched him go, and remembered the poverty of life outside these walls, remembered the bleak years and her defencelessness.

He turned at the door—looking big and almost impressive now that the full lamplight was not on him. He was smiling very simply.

"I'd rather stay up here," he pleaded.

"Another time," she said, with kindness, "I promise you—another time. But not just now."

He went out, still smiling.

The Sixth Chapter

WHEN the hall clock finished striking nine, Agnes put down her embroidery-frame and, as was her custom, left the drawing-room to pay her last visit of the day to her mother.

It was dark and quiet to-night where Teresa lay. Sister Emmanuel sat in firelight. Agnes, tiptoeing to the bed, saw that her father knelt beside it in the shadows. She had noticed his absence from the drawing-room, and guessed that he was either here or praying, or sobbing, in his own room. She stood behind him now and made no sign. He was unaware of her.

In this light, which was no light at all but only an irregular lifting here and there of darkness, Teresa seemed a stranger, and was by that the easier to observe. A dying stranger. The agonies of the unknown are not very hurtful to consider—and if she only were the alien she seems, cried Agnes's heart! A corpse, a shadow of a corpse, breathing in heaviness and fear, a corpse made dreadful to the senses, and groaning in its half-dream, half-pang—a corpse, unrecognisable, were it not for the little sobbing familiar man who knelt beside it, and whose woe identified its story. These people made us, Agnes thought with weary detachment—Reggie and Marie-Rose and all the others, and so all the life and complications of this house and minute. They mean all that to us—they mean the point of feeling we are at just now. And here they are like this—for ever divided from each other, and from us. Oh, Mother! If I could do something more useful than just marvel at this misery!

Teresa was talking in a voice that dragged and stumbled.

"That's a good boy," was that what she said? "Big boys don't cry, Reggie. You're seven now, you know."

Danny lifted his head.

"Oh, Tessie!" he sobbed. "Oh, Tessie, speak to *me!*"

Agnes crept away from the room. She was shaking with pity. Her teeth chattered. In all her life she had never heard her father call her mother anything but "Mother." In all her life she had never heard him make a directly personal claim on her. So now this cry revealed a desolation that she had not counted on, and could not face. Her cheeks burnt—she had eavesdropped upon their past, the past which love so savagely and incongruously makes everlasting.

She paused by the landing window and drew aside the curtain to look at the sky. She had just realised in time that tears were streaming down her face, and that she could not re-enter the drawing-room.

The night was full of stars. She blinked at them.

William Curran came into the hall and saw her,

knew by her shoulders she was in distress. He sprang up the flight of steps.

"What is it?" he said.

She turned her head further away.

"What is it?"

"Hysterics, I suppose."

"You shouldn't go into your mother's room during her bad spells. I'm always telling you that."

"Oh, how can I stay out? I'm not made of iron——"

"That's it exactly. You're not made of iron."

She leant her arms on the window-sash and pressed her head against them.

"Too much misery," she said. "All this politeness and pretending—but it's all misery. And yet we keep on talking about God's mercy!"

"All the same, He has some," said William Curran softly. He was looking at her white neck, considering its childishness, its pure beauty—and in that mood of quiet believed a little in the mercy of God. The fall of his voice, as once or twice before it had done, stirred Agnes. She turned to look at him.

"Queer of *you* to say that," she said.

"Love, He's given me eyes to see you."

He took her in his arms. He kissed her. He felt her tears against his face. He held her gently, but without relinquishing. Agnes thought confusedly about the mercy of God and about her father.

"My darling," this man was saying, his mouth against her mouth, "my dear, my darling." That was wrong, she thought dreamily, that was a confusing implication. But how peaceful it was in this embrace, how dark and deep this oblivion! But it must end— and then?

"Peace," she said to some ghost that jostled her. "Dear love—it's only a little peace."

But the ghost would not have the plea. She felt it drive her, startled, docile from the dark embrace. She stood erect, embarrassed. The man's arms fell from her gently.

"I am sorry," she was saying——

"Oh, Agnes, please." She noticed how his eyes shone as he bent to kiss her hands.

There were footsteps in the hall. They both looked down at Vincent. His face was drawn to attentuate the skin across the bones. His eyes were coldly lighted.

"They are wanting you in the drawing-room, Dr. Curran," he said.

"Thank you."

Vincent looked with attention at the joined hands of the two above him, and then lifted his eyes in cold inquiry to William Curran's face. But the doctor did not seem to observe his pantomime.

Agnes had only one desire—to run down the steps with undignified and desperate explanations, to stamp with shameless cruelty upon sane love, and soothe this insolent sneerer.

But William Curran's composure was an immense reproof.

"I suppose I must go and see what they want," he said, smiling at her as reluctantly he yielded up her hands. So that she remembered she had rested, even if faithlessly, in his embrace, she had taken and been glad of its peace—and therefore now, for no matter what spoilt and posturing god, could not fling his trifling gift in the giver's face. There were mad and misleading rules, it seemed, to the game.

She smiled at William Curran.

"Yes, we'll both go," she said, and went down the flight of steps with him. Vincent stood aside to let her pass.

In the drawing-room the habitual sorrow of the house had begun to prevail a little over that "pseudo-pleasure" upon which Agnes had meditated during dinner. Dr. Coyle, sincerely fond of the Mulqueens, found as he grew tired that it was difficult to keep his thoughts on national matters and away from his true business here. And Sir Godfrey, increasingly enchanted by Marie-Rose, who, saddish now, alternately drooped and was petulant, Sir Godfrey, uncomfortably troubled, was the more so by awareness of the double impropriety of such preoccupation and, above all, by its bitter hopelessness. He hovered at her side and yet was distracted from her by self-reproach.

"And why won't you sing?" he asked.

"I sang last night, and that was enough," she said irritably.

"I wasn't here last night. I'll never be here again."

"Oh, well—even so——"

He had hoped for a vague contradiction of finality, but guessed that he was on her nerves.

Vincent, watching him, felt a vague sympathy. The same mistake, he reflected wearily. Agnes, watching him, was amused. Another scalp for Marie-Rose.

The Englishman spoke with grave courtesy to Reggie.

"It is very kind of your father, of all of you," he said, "to receive us with such hospitality at a time when you must be heavy-hearted——"

Reggie fiddled with the keyboard.

"Oh, not at all, Sir Godfrey——"

"But, yes. One does not like to talk in this way to emphasise sadness——"

Agnes noticed with admiration that her brother, whose eyes were red, stood up with more courage than could have been expected to this attack on what he usually could not suffer to be touched.

"Yes," he mumbled. "It's not cheerful here. But while there's life there's hope—while there's life——"

The automatic words made William Curran wince. He never could bear the tag, which the desperate used so often, coaxingly.

But it was time now for the preliminary conference which the doctors must hold. To-morrow's consultation was to be at 10 o'clock, and that meant they must talk together to-night. They looked at their watches.

Agnes led them to a little-used sitting-room which

was to be at their disposal. Fire and cigars and tray of drinks—all was well and she left them.

Marie-Rose watched for her return to the drawing-room fire.

"There are tear-marks on your face, Nag. Why were you crying?"

"Oh—this state of things."

"I'd like to cry for the coldness I feel in my heart."

"If you feel it, I don't think it's coldness."

Reggie was at the piano; his uncertain music was a veil under which the sisters might talk.

"I was amused at dinner, Nag."

"So were we all, a bit. You can't help that."

Vincent was standing far off in the bay-window, perfectly still; Agnes had her back to him, but she could see him, she thought, with as much exactitude as if her eyes were turned his way. If he had seen that embrace, that infidelity!

She turned her mind resolutely upon her mother.

"But to flirt, Nag! To be flirtatious to-night with that total stranger!" Marie-Rose's voice was very unhappy.

Agnes tried to coax her.

"My pet, you have the bad habit of making conquests—you really can't help it."

But a mood of disconsolateness was taking toll of the house. Marie-Rose put both hands to her face and shivered.

"This feeling," she said. "I know it means nothing!

It's only self-indulgence—conscience-money! I wish I
were different, Nag—steady and level and good—like
you!"

Agnes smiled.

"You would be all these things if you were happy,"
she said, "and some day you'll be that."

"Happy?" It was Vincent's voice which answered.
He came across the room and stood beside them. He
seemed very calm as he had been at dinner, and the
cold glitter of a few minutes ago had left his eyes. He
looked down at Marie-Rose who stared at him. She
had forgotten that he was in the room.

"Yes, you'll be happy," he said to his wife, in a very
soft, reassuring tone—as if he were hypnotising her,
Agnes thought. Marie-Rose's eyes searched his face
with a puzzled, childish look.

Reggie was playing "Widmung."

"Sing it again, Rosie?" he asked.

She turned towards her brother in a startled movement and shook her head violently, but could not
answer him. Vincent turned away and Agnes put her
arms about her sister. "Du bist die Ruh," the piano
murmured, "Du bist der Friede."

The Seventh Chapter

VINCENT sat on the wooden step of the garden-house. It was not yet midnight, but the immediate world was very still. Nor was there much of it to be seen. In the foreground his mother-in-law's rose-garden sloped down, prim and simple, to the gloom of trees and a high wall. East and west of the little rustic house dark fir-trees curved thickly along the slope, so thickly that at night it was difficult to find the tunnels through them which gave access to and from the roses.

From where Vincent sat there was no reminder of the house which stood a hundred yards to the east, but he supposed that it was silent now, and dark. Night prayers had been said early, and they were long and sad, Danny adding to the usual rosary not only the Litany of the Saints to-night, but also "Veni Creator Spiritus," to invoke wisdom for to-morrow on the doctors then conferring. But the hymn to the Holy Spirit had been beyond his rendering, and he had handed the book to Agnes.

Afterwards, sitting alone in Reggie's little smoke-room, Vincent heard Dr. Curran depart and his colleagues mount the staircase with their host. And perhaps a long time afterwards he had grown tired of the heat and staleness of indoors, and had come out into the frosty night. He would probably spend the night in this little hut, he thought, turning back and looking into it with sudden satisfaction. There were rugs and old garden cushions piled on the bench against the wall. It would be easier than looking for a bed in a house he did not know very well—easier than talking to a wife.

The easy way. That was what he always looked for. Well, why not? Since it was more likely than any other to be the true way.

Agnes reading the "Veni Creator." "Hostem repellas longius, Pacemque dones. . . ." He smiled. The accidents of beauty that were always striking about her like lighting shafts were ominous. A man would have to become senseless to be saved. And he would never be that, he thought contentedly.

It was cold sitting on the wooden step; but he could not yet be bothered to move. He stared at the rose-garden. It was not nobly planned, but the night, careless and royal, had beauty enough to override smallness. He remembered the first time he walked here—with Teresa on the day when he was accepted as a son-in-law. She had looked plain and sallow in the sunlight—not a very promising relation. But he had grown to like her, and nowadays profoundly to respect and pity her. Savagery, he thought, a savagery which it seemed no Christian could help, to keep her living—but the eternal Church, making so little of visible woe to the flesh, and so much of the soul's elected stay within that woe, did ring a harsh peal which imagination answered. The horrible death-bed had its point then, would he say?

He leapt to his feet. How easy to assent to what only touches pity! But what about another harsh imperative which refused him not only possession of his love, but even that cold delight in her which he insistently preserved?

Poseur, he said to himself. You are here in the cold because desire has made her father's house a menace. And your coldness of all this day, your careful outward mood of faraway and gentleness, was perhaps no more than a sensualist's game of skill. You have yourself in hand, and want no kisses snatched on stairways—he paused in his striding and snorted a laugh to the stars —as if love were a scuffle at a children's party! You have yourself in hand, but at dinner you condescended to instruct yourself, not her, when you spoke of expectancy. "To-day is an ante-room," you said. Admit your meaning. Or are you trapped now by the inex-orability of time? What was your meaning then?

An ante-room—well, perhaps to truth, or fate, or any of these useful abstracts. And she was all of them, entangled in their moonshine, making both sense and nonsense of their echoes.

He stood and shivered. Midnight was striking in the town. A jumble of reminder—there were so many spires—but at last it was no longer midnight. It was

All Saints' Day, he thought irrelevantly. And as he savoured again the quiet which the subsided clocks enhanced, he heard footsteps coming from the east, from beyond the fir-trees.

After night prayers Agnes had seen Marie-Rose to bed.

"I'd better sleep in the usual room, Nag," the latter had said with embarrassment. "I don't want a fuss here at home, and I can't discuss things with him at present. Besides, he seemed quite kind—funny but kind, didn't you think?—in the drawing-room just now."

"The room next door has been got ready anyhow," Agnes answered hastily.

Marie-Rose was not a weeper, and her struggle with tears by the drawing-room fire had exhausted and surprised her. Going to bed therefore she was too tired for anything more searching than a wry-mouthed optimism. "Men have no sense," Agnes generalised contemptuously to herself as, brushing the golden hair, she mused over her sister's lovely, delicate face in the mirror; it should be easy to live in peace with this charming creature.

But as she thought so, Marie-Rose said sleepily, "Vin never brushes my hair."

Agnes was jarred. The brush fell. What was the good of generalising?

She fussed her sister into bed.

"What's the hurry?"

The room with its emblems had become intolerable. Growing used to the candlelight, Agnes had begun to see his brushes, his bottles, his dressing-gown—absurd, lifeless things, that leapt about to make ridiculous charades for her. Charades of married life.

"Be quick, little Rose."

"Have you a pain or something?"

"Oh, a little pain. Nothing."

"Poor Nag!"

Rose slithered, white and silky, into bed, into one side of a mighty bed arranged for two. Agnes, watching, wanted to slap herself.

"You're looking very angry. Come and sit here a minute, darling Nag." She patted the eiderdown. "Tell me about your pain."

How pretty she was! Agnes sat down.

"It's gone. Are you feeling all right now?"

"Yes. I'm sorry I was so silly in the drawing-room. It's this feeling about mother, I think."

"This isn't a reassuring house to come to when you're unhappy!"

Marie-Rose sighed softly.

"Anyhow, as long as you're in it, I'll always be turning up with my misfortunes on my back!"

"I wonder why."

"But, Nag! Don't you want me to?"

Agnes took the end of her sister's plait and scuffled it over its owner's face as if it were a shaving-brush.

"Ah! That's a sign your pain has gone. Though I don't believe you had one!"

"Why?"

"You're looking too nice. You've turned out a tremendous beauty, Nag." She yawned a little. "In the poetic style, you know—like those—those legendary sorts of women——"

Agnes smiled. It was curious, she thought, that the flatteries laid before her were always good, and always quite unsatisfactory.

"You're sleepy now, little Rose. Sleep well."

"Oh—don't go yet."

"I must, darling. You really have to sleep to-night."

"But if I start thinking when you've gone?"

Agnes, standing up now, spoke with gentle entreaty.

"Don't think. Not to-night. The house is too full of strain—it's not a good time for thinking."

"It never is. There's nothing to think about— ever."

Agnes stroked the fair head.

"Well, perhaps that's best. Good night to you."

"Is the window open?"

Agnes went to see that it was. And paused there a second. Far off among frozen trees she could see him wandering.

"There! Is that enough?"

Marie-Rose made a tired sound of assent. Agnes bent and kissed her.

"Forget everything now, him and—and everything

—just sleep well. And come to eight o'clock Mass with me to-morrow—for mother."

"Oh yes. Poor mother. You're an angel to me, Nag."

Agnes blew out the candle.

"God bless you, silly."

There was no audible answer. She went downstairs to her own room.

There, without undressing, she said her private night prayers, and reminding herself of a spiritual victoriousness and pride which were not much more than twenty-four hours sped from her, she put a vigour of shame and contrition into her words. Indeed, she told herself, the spirit might or might not be willing, but it got no assistance whatever from the wily flesh. In spite of yesterday's confession and its rewarding courage, in spite of the rein she had struggled to keep on herself last night, in spite, above all, of this morning's reassurance in Communion, the day had been —her conscience would not hide it from her—the day had been one long assault, one long desire.

What was to be done?

She stood up and paced her room. Here were Christian and social duty combining with sisterly love to make one foolish craving of hers impossible. And she with brains and blood and training found them justified and her desire insane. It followed it must die. It would die—but how quickly? If not at once—if only through the dragging of years, the beating down by inch and inch of dreams, if only by a slattern petering out—that, though conscience might be somehow tranquillised, though purity might be preserved and a technical loyalty of sisterhood remain—that death of love would be at an immorally high price. For even if she was prepared to sacrifice her early womanhood to the strains and sillinesses of an unexpressed infatuation, even if she was prepared to pray herself resolutely into an enfeebled spinsterhood, the careful process would react on others, and be too slow to give them a fair chance to recapture life. No—it came to her suddenly and made her pause in her pacing—violence must drive out violence. A desperate remedy must be found for a disease that smeared so many lives. No point in long, enfeebling treatment. Let her be quick, and him also. Let them face each other and decide on the cleanliness of a complete good-bye.

She would go to him now—they could fight it out there in the frost. There would be no other time—no better.

She pulled on a velvet jacket over her velvet dress. And then the devil jogged her elbow: Aren't you fooling yourself perhaps? he said. This running out into the moonlight with a message of purity! He that loveth the danger shall perish in it.

She paused. If there was a line of Scripture that could always lay the whip of stimulation to her spirit it was that one. And now again it thrilled her. But she threw back her head and challenged heaven gallantly. I have only what wits and strength you give me to fight this battle that you have imposed, she said. Whatever I do, I am in your hands, and you can punish me if I am in fact a hypocrite. She fastened her jacket tightly round her neck and made the sign of the Cross. "Remember, oh most gracious Virgin Mary, that never was it known that anyone. . . ." Saint Bernard's prayer would be her shield.

She sped along the corridor and down the stairs. As she went, she was vaguely conscious that a door opened and shut—Nurse Cunningham's door, she thought, and then forgot it, ". . . Oh Mother of the Word Incarnate, . . ."

On the threshold of the house she hesitated. The bells and clocks of Mellick were withdrawing one by one from their discussion of midnight. The stars were clear. The freezing air had danger in it.

BOOK III

THE FEAST OF ALL SOULS

The First Chapter

VINCENT waited for her near the tunnel of fir-trees, and as he saw the moonlight assault their darkness to reveal her, he thought that if ever the stage was set for the barn-stormer's play, it was now; if ever two characters were correctly placed to exemplify to an excited gallery that love is the lord of all, it was he and she.

She was before him, halted—her eyes more incandescent that the stars, her breath a frosty garland.

He trembled.

"It's cold," he said.

"I'm burning."

She laid a hand on his to prove it, and her fire was not to be endured. He took her in his arms.

"Warm me," he cried.

Line for line, bone for bone, they seemed to fit together as if by heaven grooved to take each other, as if the platonic split was mended here, and a completed creature stood united to itself at last. "He that loveth the danger——" a desperate angel cried again to Agnes, but a voice from heaven was not the one most likely at this minute to attain to her. And she might have answered that indeed this danger merited love.

"It's cold, Agnes; I'm cold."

She was not astonished or shocked at herself. One plane of her mind was certainly thinking: He and I are Catholics, and he is married and his wife is my sister—but against the fantastic proclamation of his mouth on her hair, on her neck, such prose was still as thin as the angel's voice. And yet she knew that she was cheating heaven and him. For what was happening was impossible, and yet it was impossible to deny it.

She turned her face that he might look in it—and his, by some new light which was too brilliant to be happiness, was changed so that it startled her.

But he spoke in a happy tone.

"You're too little," he said, "too slim and little to warm a man."

She put her hand against his face, and marvelled at how natural it was to touch him.

"My darling," she said. But then a stupid violence of trembling shook her. She closed her eyes and wondered at the space that lay between one second and the next.

She felt herself being lifted, being carried. She opened her eyes as he set her down on the floor of the garden-house. She opened her eyes, and looking round her at the shadowy, familiar little room, full of memories, full of croquet hoops and guns and rusty garden treasures, full of impedimenta of scattered brothers, vanished childhood, she remembered with integrity, as with a violent blow, who she was and what she had come out to do. She moved away from Vincent, far, far away across the little room. He sprang to catch her, but she flung up a hand of absolute denial, and he paused, becoming statue-quiet in a strip of light that fell about him. She sought the shadows.

"I came to ask a favour of you," she said. Then, looking at him, reconsidered the word "favour." "Oh no, not a favour."

"Don't ask it!"

"Can *you* endure things, then?"

He hesitated.

"I must."

"I can't! But even if I could—must *she?*"

"What has *she* to bear?"

"Ah, Vincent!"

"She was disillusioned before my mind was filled with you."

"Now she's unhappy."

"If that were true, her way back couldn't be through me."

"You're hard."

"When two people lose the knack of being at peace, it's gone. And she and I never really had it."

"But what's to happen?"

"There's a fantasy-life——"

"No use to Marie-Rose."

"Oh, it's no *use* to anyone! But it *is* one's servant, and it decorates some hours."

"It's waste!"

"It's nothing of the kind. It's sheer starvation."

"But is *she* to wither at your pleasure?"

"She won't wither. I told her to-night—you heard me—that she'd be happy. She thought I was making a magic prophecy, but I was only talking common sense. She said to you that she wanted to weep for the coldness of her heart. She often says that. You see, she knows she's not vulnerable. I've done things to her that I hope she's never told you. I've sneered at her and humiliated her. I've thwarted her feelings when my own were stone-dead, and the next day I've despised her for coldness. I've treated her vanity as if it were a loathsome thing—oh, there isn't a mental humiliation or torture that some devil in me hasn't tried on her at one time or another—but, heaven be praised, she hasn't understood! She hasn't imagination, you see, and so I've really never done anything more serious than enrage her——"

Agnes pressed her hand against her breast as though she were wounded.

"But if you had?" she whispered in horror. "If one of your shots had hit the little thing?"

"Then there might have been a hope," he said.

"Vincent! She loves you! Why, even to-day she told me——"

"Believe me, she'll be happy. 'Her heart is in the right place,' as the saying goes."

"And is that a crime?"

"No. Only an advantage."

"You gave her no peace till she accepted you. I remember that. I was about."

"Yes. You were about." He laughed. "Oh heavens, heavens, don't say that!"

"You're very unscrupulous."

"Well, if I can't speak of things as they are, to *you*——!"

She moved towards him and then drew back.

"I have no love for my wife. Right or wrong—that is true."

Agnes sank to the low bench that ran against the wall, and covered her face with her hands. In a stride he came and was on his knees before her. His arms went round her, he laid his forehead against her breast.

She held him to her and let him be. Staring beyond him to the garden, she thought about the ease of love. To her cool mind it had sometimes seemed that the initial expressions of tenderness to someone who was—however adored—a stranger, would be difficult to the point of impossibility. It had never occurred to her that the danger of passion might lie not in its novelty but in its naturalness. And now it was the latter which paralysed her. She reflected that it had not been so earlier in the night when Dr. Curran kissed her, and she smiled above Vincent's head. This was her day, apparently. But in William Curran's arms she had not felt natural; she was sure of that because of the sensation of anxiety she experienced as to how the embrace should end. Her hand moved over the quiet head on her breast, as she thought triumphantly that with this lover she could end or begin a million caresses without taking half a thought. William Curran's kiss had had the vast, dark comfort of a mystery, a strangeness hiding weary life a second, an anæsthetic—that was it.

Here was no anæsthetic, but only a wound unalleviated. There was no hope for this septic wound.

"I came out here," she said, "to ask your help in arranging something."

He moved and looked up at her. Keeping his arm about her he turned sideways to see her better, squatting on his heels. She took courage.

"We mustn't see each other again," she said.

He threw back his head.

"That at least can't happen to us, love!"

"Ah, but I beg of you!"

"I told you *not* to ask your favour!"

"You talk as if you were a god!"

He sprang to his feet and strode about the little room.

"Even if I'm not, where could you hide from me?"

"Here, for a while, if you'd do as I ask—because my duty is here just now—some of it."

"All of it!"

"Oh no! My real duty is to God, and Marie-Rose,

and should take me miles from here."

"Your duty to God?"

She sighed wearily.

"Don't pretend this isn't a sin."

His tradition, as Catholic as hers, allowed him no protest. She went on, speaking very softly:

"If you say it isn't, you have to say a great many other things. In fact you have to say you don't believe in the Church. But I do believe in it."

"So do I," he said, "though I wonder why!"

"I don't believe there's a 'why', a reasonable one, anyway." She paused and looked away to the stars. "At school I always suspected that there are no real reasons for belief."

"But they gave you some."

"I never needed them."

"Still—all the childishnesses, and all the cruelties and lapses——"

"They matter humanly—but, if the story was fifty times worse, they wouldn't really matter anything to my belief. Because that's a natural thing, that it's just silly to bludgeon with facts. I feel that in the end the Church is right, only we can't see it except in our own terms—we can't see it, well, transfigured. And I think we will, when we're dead. So all the wrong things——"

"Don't matter? Sins don't matter?"

"Oh—they do!"

"But they are committed."

"Yes, that's different. You can be honest, and choose to commit a sin."

"Oh, love, you're so judicial!"

She laughed. If this was how a judge had to flog himself to justice!

"Yesterday, before you came—how long ago it seems! —I went to confession," she said. "I hadn't been for ten weeks——"

"You didn't know I was coming?"

"Oh, I knew. I was sick with thinking of you; I was ashamed and exhausted. It was a shock to know I would have to see you again while I was so—out of hand. And then Uncle Tom came and suggested special prayers for mother—and I couldn't go to communion for her unless I cleaned my heart of you— and so I did, just before you came. And I was full of self-confidence then—oh, I was happy, Vincent!"

"I saw you."

"Ever since, I swear I've tried to hold on to the courage confession gave me! But your being here, and your audacity this time—and the unhappiness of everyone—oh, it's all too much! I'm going to end it."

"How?"

"I want your promise that you won't come to Mellick for a year. I promise not to go to Dublin."

"Even if I promised—what's a year?"

"At the end of it, if—if mother is no longer here— I—I'll marry Dr. Curran, if he'll have me."

He wheeled about. His hand struck violently

against the table, rattling the guns that lay there.

"You'll marry Dr. Curran. And then ask me and my wife on a congratulatory visit?"

"No."

"You called me unscrupulous just now!"

"He would know about this—and he needn't have me."

"Oh no, he needn't! Most men, as you know, would look you over and pass you by."

"One did."

"Oh, love—don't *you* get angry, too."

"I *am* angry! Vincent, Vincent—can't you see? Because of one silly mistake the feelings of four people must be lacerated!—and if they're not, or even if, letting them take their chance, any shot is made at least to save the decencies, to save understanding, and peace and pride and responsibility and usefulness, to save the innocent—you look at me as if I were obscene!"

He came and took her up into his arms.

"Ah, my heart! my darling!" he cried, his whole frame shaking——

"Oh, stop it! Stop, I say!" She pressed her hands on to his breast to escape, but he would not let her go.

"You used the word 'obscene'," he said. "Then let me tell you there is only one obscenity for me—and that is, to imagine he might have you!"

"Ah, but you're mad!"

"What does that alter? I have no hopes, but if you take away the fantasies that keep me quiet——"

"Who could do that?"

"He could. The man who—had you. I'd never see
you as you are again. He kissed you to-night—I saw
him. For a second it was as if— as if someone had said
you were dead."

She grew limp in his arms. She seemed to lose the
argument.

Dead? she pondered. I wonder what I'd feel if I
had to die now?

There was a deathly weariness upon her face. He
drew her down on to the bench and sat in silence
by her.

"I was thinking about death to-day," he said. "No,
not so much about death really as about mother."

"What was your mother like?"

He hesitated.

"A bit like me--I think—in her face. She was small,
of course." He laughed. "As little as you."

"I'm tall."

"She used to say that too." He bent forward and
clasped his hands together between his knees. "The
only way I can explain mother to you," he said, "is
this. She used to make me feel something that you do
too—a kind of finality of appreciation—a stillness, as
if her mere being alive justified everything. It's a
lovely, cool sensation, and although it's love, I suppose,
it has nothing to do with the other feeling, of wanting
to touch you. Perhaps it's the sort of thing some
absolutely perfect work of art should cause—but, still,

it's warmer than that, and it's surer. It's that you *see* perfection, in your own image, alive and walking—and it's a comfort somehow. . . ."

Agnes said nothing. His voice had a vibration in it that she dared not answer.

"One day I said to mother—'I hope I'll think of you when I'm dying.' She asked me why I said that, and I couldn't explain. But *you* see what I mean, don't you? The best thing that there was, the most superb—the most complete apology for life—that'd be a good idea to hold on to then. Now, I suppose it's you I'd see——"

"No, no—you'd think of her——"

"I don't know. When I'm tired the two of you get mixed in my head. But she wasn't ever, I should think, as beautiful as you. Only she had the trick you have—of somehow being perfection!"

She took his hands and kissed them.

"It seems to me," she said, "that she passed on that trick to you! Oh, I love you so much, so much!"

He knelt again to gather her against him. She felt him trembling violently, and that his face was wet against her throat.

"If you're ever the mother of a son," he sobbed, "oh, don't die until he's hardened to the idea!"

"I'd be afraid to have a child! There's too much in this business of attachment!"

"Oh Agnes, Agnes!"

"I shall love you all my life, I imagine," she said, "I

cannot think that any number of years or centuries could change the thing I feel when I remember you or look at you. Of course, they say that years change everything, but I don't believe it. I shall love you always—and there are only two things possible to me. Either I keep you out of sight and mind, and marry someone else—oh Vincent, let me speak!—or, if you refuse me that, I'll give you my vow of chastity, and go away at once, right, right away, a thousand miles from Ireland, and live an old maid devoted to good works, and never come home again!"

"You can't do that."

"If I have to, I can. I can invent an illness. I can make some arrangement for mother and the household."

"You'd die of grief."

"Not die."

"I'd find you."

"I'd think of a way to make that impossible."

"You're talking madly."

"I expect I am."

"And if you stay—and marry, what is the advantage then?"

"Oh, there are many. I would spare myself and Marie-Rose a separation which might never end. I would gratify and even make happy a man who's worth that trouble, the only man, except you, whom I have felt I could be a good wife to. I would have occupations and responsibilities, and things to fill the days and make me tired at night. Companionship, too, instead of exile. Oh, sturdy facts to keep me sane, and build a barrier between us! Am I asking too much? Am I being shrewd and vulgar?"

"Perhaps. I don't know."

He got up, and walked to the door. He leant against its frame, his hands in his pockets, his head in the air.

"There is another alternative, my darling."

"What is it? Tell me."

"You said just now that people can be honest, and choose to commit a sin."

"Ah——!"

"You did say that?"

"But I only meant you could be honest, or insolent if you like—with *God*."

"Of course. But I hadn't thought of cheating the world. I meant that you need not be alone in exile. We could go together."

He shut his eyes, and dropped and slowed his voice on the last sentence. He was speaking a fantasy out loud at last, he was suggesting that it might take shape. He saw the ancient, sunlit world of the further Mediterranean, white-shored islands and blue waters, broken temples, red-sailed ships. He saw his love amid these things that she thought strange to her, while muleteers and fishermen and beggars marked her rare grace with smiles of atavistic reminiscence. He heard the music of a flute. He saw a sickle moon beyond an open window. The voice of the sea, like an old god counselling, would guide them through their passion into sleep.

"We would go together, dear love."

They would stay far away for ever, so that no mud flung by the righteous should disfigure them. They would stay among the simple, ancient peoples who, whether thinking Christianly or paganly, take their courtesy from the sweet morning of their world and are disinclined to make astonishment about forbidden love. Her beauty would be their fatal explanation everywhere on those shores where men have eyes, and in any case he would love her so much that it would be obvious he had no right to her. He smiled, and turned to look upon her face. For all her fears of too much caring, she must give him children. Children playing their first games on the Ægean hills and Adriatic rocks, children with her for mother, would be so lucky already that namelessness would be a joke. And she would grow old with a divine, noncombatant reluctance, a rueful grace like that which was his mother's. She would grow old and he with her, and then there would be death and for their sin whatever theologians meant by hell. And it would have to be hell indeed to make its cause regrettable. For if it left a man his human memories——

Agnes wondered why this alternative had never once occurred to her. She had, she saw now, allowed for every issue of their situation except this—that she should take and keep him. She had sought escape from love by many means, by plans of absolute evasion or of compromise on the one hand, and on the other by surrender to such dreams and hungers as she had the day before confessed. And the latter device by its very revelation of herself to her was perhaps, she thought, as true a barrier between her and him as flight from his living presence might be. For fantasy had taught her that once to surrender to the reality it shadowed would be for ever to surrender—and that was simply never to be done. So even to-night, however close he held her, however exquisite the game of "just this once", and "this last minute", she knew all the time that she was cheating him and having it both ways—because she burnt to be his lover, and that was rapture, but she knew, some inexorable censor in her knew that it would never happen, and that the wildest danger was not danger.

Was she ignoble then? Was all her struggle falsity, and she content to lose her spirit's virginity while saving her ridiculous, mortal body? Did she love this man at all?

She leant forward on the bench. Her elbows were on her knees, her chin in her hands. She stared at him and tenderness overflowed in all her nerves and senses, flooding the problem of her hardness. Indeed, indeed she loved him—and her spirit by its own roads fled to meet him in that far country of their mutual peace where she knew he wandered dreaming now. She could not have named the places that he saw them in, or told whether there would be snow or sand or cobblestones beneath their feet; she only knew that she was with him in his paradise and that it was hers because he was there. Ah, yes—she could at least assure herself she loved him, for would she not grow old delightedly like this, just sitting here to satisfy her eyes on his relaxed and gentle beauty, content, though blindfold from the images of his thought, to follow its mood which his dreamer's face evoked?

If she loved him then, and if only sin and her immortal soul prevented—ah, but how vast a barricade! Yes, yes, but still her own affair? Her own and God's. But God could surely take some fraction of responsibility for the needs He planted in His helpless creatures? He gave you grace and the moral law and the True Church. And put *Him* in my path, she retorted softly and gladly, thrust Him down into my life and gave me eyes to see Him! Who had said that before to-day? Ah, William Curran! And he had thought it was a sign of heaven's mercy? Vincent—I can't help it. I do love you. Come back from far away, my darling—come back and take me with you——

He turned to her again and moved his hands in lazy gesture, as if to say how simple everything was.

"We'll never be parted then," he said.

Never be parted. What was the good of denying so natural a plan?

She lifted her head from the indolent cupping of

her hands. Sighing a little she felt, without moving at all, that she had crossed the small space between them and was in his heart, in safety.

He was turned full round towards her, not dreaming now, but speculative. He was thinking of the chances and crudities, the necessities and indignities which were this girl's unalterable human part as surely as another's; he thought of the savagery and lasciviousness of passion, and the surprising isolation from each other of participants in its zenith; he thought of the fatuous egotism of love; of the wounds that malice gives, and the stupidity of good intentions; of the final impenetrability of one mind by another, however in need, however caring; he thought of the world's burden and tale of disillusionment, of how all things tarnish into a regret; into disease and age. He thought of the encroaching worm, and at last of her white bones, clean, dissociated, nameless in the dark. Against it all he had only the unwise mania of his worship; for treading the terrible pattern he had no more than his illicit, unreliable hand to give her.

But there was *her* hand for him; there was her magnitude. And passion, which held together as many as it destroyed. They might come through. Against the story of the world.

He smiled at her beauty and the tender fall of moonlight on her.

She said: "We'll never be together."

She spoke softly, yet to both the words were a hard

ripple of pistol-shots. But Agnes, as she heard them issue from her astonished lips, understood their truth. For a ghost passed before her eyes then, and had no doubt selected them.

Marie-Rose was the ghost, and she had chosen well. They were the only possible words.

Vincent did not move, but it seemed to Agnes that his eyes drew back into black, alien caverns, gathering a wild blaze, so that they were not blue eyes, but burning coals.

She looked up into them and felt lost, stupid, impotent, indifferent. She could never explain this withering blast of fact, this discovery of the residuum of herself.

Silence swelled hideously, but she had to let it be. She marvelled that it held so vast a shock, so much sense of bitterness and grievance. Two minutes ago— was it?—there had been no question that they could ever be together. What, then, did this plain denial murder? An unreality? Had they dreamt so deeply in that little space of time? Had they so nimbly taken for granted the romantic fate of lovers for ever banished to the sun? So that the pricking of a second's myth seemed the taking of a life?

For him, the dreamer, it was so. He had travelled so far into illusion since presenting her with *his* alternative that her words had somewhat the same effect on his body and mind as if, after years of love, she had betrayed him. The pain was breath-taking.

"What did you say?" he asked, using his voice delicately lest it should whimper.

But she still had no energy.

"You heard," she said.

"Yes." He put a hand to his forehead, then let it fall. What was the matter? There was a confusion somewhere, a hiatus. He had misunderstood something. But as a bull will unawares gather his own rage while feeling stunned, he became himself before he knew it.

"What game is this?" he snarled. "See-saw?"

"It was, I suppose. But the see-saw's down now—finished."

"Why?"

"Marie-Rose."

He drew himself up, and when he spoke she could feel his lips sneering.

"And she is *my* responsibility," he said, "the burden on *my* conscience."

Agnes felt inclined to laugh.

"Conventionally, yes."

"The whole trouble is in that convention—that I have a wife."

"No. I see now, after to-night, that however I might boast and pray and fight, I would never be *safe* from sin just because you're married——"

"Oh, sweet——"

"And whatever the law is, it doesn't matter a scrap to me that I'm your wife's sister——"

"Well then?"

"But your wife is Marie-Rose."

"I'm not so ruthless as I sound, my darling. I whirled her into marriage, and adored her for a while. I'll reckon with the remorse and misery of that. But leave it to me, since it *is* mine! Don't pry!"

"I'm not prying. I'm not thinking about you at all."

"What *do* you mean, then?"

"You talked just now about her not being vulnerable and how your worst unkindness never did more than enrage her. That frightened me, but for a few minutes it seemed that you must be right, that she isn't vulnerable. You see, I'm so much in love with you that it was easy to think that anyone whom you couldn't really hurt must be—rather hard. And perhaps she is. But she isn't completely—I could hurt her. Perhaps I'm the only person who could——"

"Oh, as children you adored each other——"

"If your mother were alive you'd never ask me to run away with you."

He winced. "She *isn't* alive."

"Marie-Rose and I adored each other, as you say. And I didn't marry, and she didn't marry happily. So the devotion was not brushed aside. I think that now I'm the only living soul she feels safe with—and look at me!"

She flung out her hands in comment on them both.

"Supposing what you say is true," he cried, "why should she be spared? Why should the lucky person with only one tender spot be saved at the expense of those who're raw all over?"

"Or supposing that you're so little exacting that you only ask one fellow-creature for a real relationship——"

"You'd let her drag on in misery with a man who drives her mad?"

"Since she still wants you, and you can't set her free. Let her at least have the kind of life she decorates so well, and the certainty of me. It isn't much."

"She'd be happier if I went—in the end."

"Perhaps. But not if I did."

"You're very sure of her blind faith in you."

"I'd have the same in her. Vincent, my darling— understand. It's so long ago since I began to relate everything in life to Marie-Rose. I was a baby when I first discovered how pretty and gay she was. And she was kind to me always! Once someone told me I was the plainest girl in the school, and Marie-Rose gave me no peace until I told her what had upset me. The revenge she took! The way she lampooned that plain little girl before the Junior School! I think I'd have died for her that night!"

"And she has long ago forgotten it."

"The only point is that *I* haven't. Or a million other things. She made a kind of revelation of growing up! She was such fun!"

"And now, for that—I am to do without you."

"Her eyes—they'd be bewildered! Oh, they'd haunt me, Vincent!"

"Why didn't you say this an hour ago?"

"I didn't understand it then—I came out here quite honestly to try and find a solution. Oh, I was tempted, too, by the thought of being alone with you. But all the time something I couldn't quite get at kept insisting that I was a cheat to talk to you of love. Still, when you said we could go away together——"

"Yes?"

"Then for a minute—oh, my darling!"

"God!"

"But this other thing would have been there all the same."

"You love her more than me."

"I've never thought about how I love her."

He made no answer, no movement. He continued to lean wearily against the frame of the door. She crossed the little room suddenly, as if to touch or comfort him, but then swerved and leant against the opposite doorpost. Moonlight made a dividing stream between them.

He considered her desperately. She was the one thing he asked of life. He was in the habit of having what he wanted. She loved him with passion, each contact proclaimed their aching physical sympathy. But she was virgin and could not foresee the real claims of her senses. If they were once revealed to her——

"If I were to take you now," he said, "if I were to make you my mistress to-night——"

She closed her eyes.

"Are you afraid?"

"Not of you," she said.

"Listen. I could take you now; I could rape you, ruin you—there are heaps of words. You'd be hurt and bruised and miserable and a great deal disillusioned—but still, if you loved me, you would begin perhaps to see what I mean, what I'm asking for. You might begin to understand that there's one thing in the world which may be worth regrets and dishonours——"

"Yes, of course—*we'd* have our *quid pro quo.* There's only one person who'd get nothing out of the bargain."

"And you would *never* forget that? There's *nothing* I could do?"

"Nothing. If there were, I'd hate you for doing it."

"Hate me?"

"It would be as if you'd killed her. I can't explain. I suppose the things we've always known are the last we understand. Probably the whole affair was settled that night in Junior Recreation."

He understood. Violence and passion could have their tortured minute if he insisted, but they could not retrace, unplait, unravel the long slow weaving of childhood. It was the sort of fact he grasped with fatalism, which told him also that it was the child of that inexorable making whom he loved in the woman now before him. Had she been differently woven, by happy accident, he might have won and would not have wanted her.

All the cards were on the table then—and the game was over. There seemed to be nothing to say.

"I don't seem to have done much good by coming out here to talk," said Agnes.

"But surely, yes. Isn't everything settled now?"

"Not for me."

He looked at her resentfully. See-saw again?

"We've settled that there's no use in loving each other. But we haven't decided how to stop it."

"I'm not going to."

"I am. I can't face turning into a crazy old maid."

"So you want me to face the spectacle of your marriage to Curran?"

"Or let me go away as soon as I can, and promise not to follow me."

"How about Marie-Rose?"

"She could come to where I was sometimes. We could write. Some day I'd come back."

"With your love for me well scotched?"

"I suppose so."

"I am to take my choice?"

"Vincent—don't talk in that hateful voice——"

"I'm sorry you find it 'hateful.' "

"Well, I do."

Two o'clock struck. The bells of Mellick had their usual tussle in announcing the small hour. When silence came back Vincent and Agnes were still motionless against their doorposts.

"I believe we're quarrelling," she said.

"Oh, let's not bother! We're too tired."

"Yes. We must go in. Won't you help me at all about the future?"

He looked across the stream of moonlight and studied her with attention. Her face was turned to him in direct appeal. It was—he informed himself coldly, for he was very tired—a divine triumph of a face, to be learnt and re-learnt in many lives; a boy's face and a woman's, the face of an archangel and of a lost little girl.

"If I never see you again, I shall be, when I have got used to it, quite dead and bored. If I am occasionally permitted to see you under his smug patronage I shall live in hell. Either way will be hard on Marie-Rose. Which would *you* choose?"

"The first."

"And exact your vow to be a crazy old maid?"

"Not crazy, perhaps."

"Give me time. Give me until to-morrow!"

"I wanted to have no excuse for discussing it again."

"Why this mania for tidiness?"

"I'm sick of the mess of things. Father, Mother, Reggie, Dr. Curran, you, Marie-Rose—myself—it seems as if someone ought to try to tidy something!"

"Oh, I agree. Life has no shape."

"How tired your voice is!"

"Not hateful?"

"Oh!"

With a young, wild sob she came to him.

"Not hateful ever! The dearest, dearest, dearest voice! Ah, you! My heart, my darling!"

They clung together.

"And it is love that has beaten us," he whispered.

"I wonder—I don't know."

"She's very lucky—Marie-Rose."

"I thought that three years ago," said Agnes, with bitter tenderness.

He looked down hungrily into her lifted face.

"Ah, you're so sweet to me," he said, "so sweet and generous, and I am a selfish, sulky fool who's made a mess of life for you!"

She ran her hand along his face.

"Yes, you're selfish and sulky," she said, with a tenderness that set his heart pounding.

"My love! My foolish love! How can I make sure that you'll be happy sometime?"

She put a hand on his mouth. Her eyes filled with tears.

"'Ssh. There's no way. But I'll grow middlingly content and so will you, and we'll be middle-aged eventually."

"That's no good; you'll be glorious then."

"And so will you."

She turned her face against his shoulder a minute, then lifted it again.

"I'm going in now," she said, "but before I go I'll kiss you—your darling mouth." She trailed her fingers over it.

She thought that they might part in tenderness; her idea was to reach him in a gentle expression of love, a caress of resignation. That would explain and pacify, and somehow set them free. It seemed that his eyes resisted her, and were afraid, but she drew his head down unrelentingly till their mouths met.

Then she understood her sentimental mistake. There was no pacification here, or freedom. There was no such thing—she ought to have known—as kissing him good-bye and saying "God bless you." Love had been painful in fantasy, but here in its clumsy truth it was anguish, with the worst of it that its moment must pass, that there must be an end of the pang of insatiability.

Open-eyed they kissed, she hardly recognising his brilliant eyes, yet very sure that they were his. As more and more he forced her body to the hard slant of his embrace, as the storms of their breasts became one and their mouths gave only thirst for thirst, she understood her own innocence.

He also saw that this kiss was a trap. Long ago he had grown sick of the kisses of flippancy, and afterwards in married life had come to hate those of anger and remorse. He had imagined every aspect of love with Agnes, but because he had to keep a show of decorum had never in the centre of his heart allowed that the intermittent high moments of any earthly passion could be to the last edge of imaginability worth while. He had managed, that is to say, to keep a film of incredulity between himself and the final absurdities of his romanticism. An inner, consoling doctrine of his was that he could visualise what life could not supply.

Now that was gone. From her mouth he was drawing in a poisonous vitality, an irrational knowledge of happiness which made it as clear as light to him that life, contrary to his comforting idea, could justify a dreamer. Could, but would not. From her mouth he was drinking credulity, conviction. In her kiss he was able to measure the finality of his desire for her and its cruel rightness. It was as he had alternately dreamt and denied it—heaven, and the gateway to a further heaven. Useless now and henceforward to drag up the old argument, that in embrace the beloved being too near for focusing, and the sensations of the body too violent for sensitive analysis, she might be any-one, her uniqueness having done its work and been lost in the darkness of desire. That was not so. The world was sick of perpetual kissing and yearning, of which far too much fuss was made—but once in a while a man might know his fate. And here was his, denied him.

He folded her against him.

"I cannot live without you," he said.

Her arms were round his neck.

"Or I without you."

"This is love—it hardly ever happens."

She drooped, drew back from him.

"You mean—it never happens."

Her face had a look of death. Looking into his, drained and weary. "I'm sorry," she said, "I—I thought it would be no harm to kiss you—once."

He put his hand under her chin and smiled at her. "You little love," he whispered, "it was no harm."

"Will you forgive me?" she asked him. "Will you forgive me for everything?"

"What is everything?"

She paused and looked about her perplexedly.

"Marie-Rose."

"You were my fate," he said. "It is something to have seen that, even now."

"She is our fate. Ah, little Rose!" She withdrew from his arms. "I must go in," she said wearily. "I must go in."

They looked at each other, and understood that there was not another word to say.

Agnes passed under the fir-trees and through the cold garden slowly, not as she had come. She shivered a little. That coming had been a fool's errand; it had done no more than prove to her, in one silly kiss, that she could not do without what she must never have.

There was no hope or courage anywhere now. Only starvation. Only disgust with everything that was not he, and that for that reason might be hers.

Vincent, still leaning against the doorpost, also thought of her kiss and its lesson—that he could not do without what he could never have.

The Second Chapter

It was exactly a quarter of noon when Delia came into the drawing-room and said that the doctors would like to speak to the master, please.

Agnes, who, with Marie-Rose and Uncle Tom, had been helping her father to await this summons, would have given much to be allowed to take it for him now, but as he stood up she saw with admiration that outwardly he was, as usual, the little fat ineffectual figure whose sufferings, if any, the world must assume to be ineffectual and secondary. He crossed the room and left it, muttering fussily: "Very good, Delia; very good." He was quite unaware of the passion of protectiveness that strained after him from Agnes. But had he known of it that would only have added another darkness to the stupefaction of fear and pity which he was enduring.

As the door closed on him, Marie-Rose's hard-held quietude forsook her. She moved with violence about the room.

"Oh, Nag—what are they going to say to him? Oh, poor Mother! Darling Mother!"

The priest turned from the fire. He looked grey and old.

"God's will be done," he said. "She is under the

protection of His Infinite Wisdom."

Agnes could say nothing. Her heart was arid. What was there to wait for after all? A short reprieve or none? The point of the former was, she supposed, that hopeless and little as it might seem, it had the hope of the indefinable—whereas the latter was a simple sentence of death. A pronouncement which, she was beginning to guess, might be paradoxically harder for the elderly to hear than for the young. For though her uncle was grey-headed and her father bald and feeble, these were as much signs of the deep grooves life had made in them as of its nearing dissolution. And if life had proved real and hard, how much the harder, she thought compassionately, to be stripped of one of its major alleviations when just about to face the years which must be supposed to offer none? Her father and her uncle were waiting this morning to be told how much longer an everyday love and a long routine would be allowed to them; they were waiting to hear how much longer they might possess a wife, a sister. Sheer agony, she thought, and saw what the simplest affection might become in thirty, forty years of habit—love for a sister, love for a wife. No wonder her uncle looked grey and old, for all the sonority with which he forestalled the possibilities of God's will; and for the unprotesting, fussing, courageous miracle of her father as he trotted from the room, where was there a true measure of praise?

She folded her hands, amazed to the point of weariness by the irresponsibility, in human terms, of a God who claimed human sensibilities and had, in fact, become man. In any case, she was weary in body and mind to-day. Weary and neutral, seeing recent events from a confusing perspective of remoteness. For instance, it seemed about a month, at this moment, since she had run into the starlit garden to talk with Vincent. But the clock told her it was not yet twelve hours.

At seven o'clock she had got up, and meeting Marie-Rose in the hall, a white and weary Marie-Rose—for neither of these sisters found early Mass an easy undertaking—had walked at her side, with hardly a word said, to Saint Anthony's. Walked, because their mother had brought them up to practise that "little mortification," as she called it, and to be considerate of the coachman at that hour of the day. A consideration which in normal times Marie-Rose always fumed against with stridency, protesting that O'Keeffe was ten million times stronger than she would ever be, and that early Mass was hard enough, anyhow. However to-day the effort was "for Mother's intention," and they made it without comment. But during Mass Agnes was far too tired to pray; her spirit was too leaden in neutrality. Instead she held a cold, slow colloquy with her conscience; she also set out perfunctorily before Heaven the griefs and troubles of her house and did her best to feel united with the celebrant in offering the renewed sacrifice of Calvary for their alleviation, and in entreaty of forgiveness for her own sins and the sins of the world. Marie-Rose received Holy Communion, and Agnes, observing the gold head bowed in thanksgiving, so young, so chic a head, wondered with guilt, as if such wonder were a prying indecency, what her sister said in those strange, still minutes to the Divine Visitant.

They had walked home in absolute silence, too cold and exhausted now for the least conversational effort. When they entered the dining-room there was no one else there as yet, but someone had breakfasted. Agnes raised her brows at the used cover, and Delia, removing it, said that: "Mr. Vincent had just this minute had his breakfast, miss, and gone out for a walk." When the maid left the room, Marie-Rose, having drunk some tea, found energy to say: "I don't know where he slept last night, but he was in my room, and changed his clothes, while we were at Mass. When I went up now to take off my things, that was obvious."

Breakfast, with attention to her father and guests, and after breakfast the manifold exactions of her household had kept Agnes too busy to indulge her sense of deadness and fatigue. But when the three doctors had descended the stairs and withdrawn to their sitting-room, having seen the look of almost terror behind the calm and holy mask which her priest uncle, just arrived at the house, presented to her, she knew that in mercy he must be allowed to endure the next half-hour in some degree of selfishness, must not be asked to expend himself in supporting others through it. So she had gone with him to the drawing-room where her father was trying to behave as if his distress was no one's business and of no importance. Marie-Rose, uneasily shadowing her, had come, too, and Reggie, red-eyed and in visible anxiety, but mercifully not abandoned to hysterics as Agnes had half expected him to be, had come shuffling into the unhappy family tent for shelter.

Then in that half-hour, which stretched to be an hour, of sitting still and talking gently, of patting her father's hand and making indeterminate sympathetic signs, of being filial with every jaded nerve, she saw life telescoping back from her into a new perspective of remoteness. So that what she was experiencing now, of compassion and helplessness, seemed remembered rather than felt, and what she remembered of last night, the long, unhappy, torturing dialogue and the kiss that ended it—was not a memory, but the narrative of some dream. And the stories she had told in that dream, of loving the man she dreamt it with, and loving a pretty sister who had been kind to her at school—these pictures within a picture were, indeed, far off this morning—as far away as nothingness. Oh, idiotic unrealities, which cannot be trusted to keep their character, but from hour to hour assume and abdicate a senseless power!

Meantime there was this family reality of her mother's ending life; contemplating that grey fact in her uncle's eyes, in Reggie's and her sister's, Agnes felt almost relieved that there was still something that did not recede from her, something that defied her relativity. If only she had a little hope, a little passion to give to this dilemma, some help to bring where it might, in fact, be help.

"Poor Reggie!" she said suddenly, stretching out a hand.

He caught it with so swift a gratitude that she had to leave it to him for a second, although the damp heat of his fingers horrified her.

"They're so slow, these fellows," he muttered.

"Poor Mother, poor darling!" Marie-Rose kept whispering.

Their uncle put a hand across his eyes. Everything, everyone was an inflaming irritant to him just now. Agnes, turning from Reggie, felt an all-but-uncontrollable desire to snarl "Be quiet" at her sister—and she reflected, in sad bewilderment, that the inclination was entirely new. She could remember no former occasion when Marie-Rose was on her nerves. But now she saw that she had been so all the morning. "The little thing!" she cried in her heart remorsefully. "The little, innocent thing! It's my own wickedness that's on my nerves. Oh, little Rose!"

The house, the world were very quiet. There was a sound of raking from the garden, and far off the occasional report of a gardener's gun. Agnes noticed that her uncle's lips were moving in prayer, and thought that a prayer was a better occupation of the mind than unprofitable musings.

Remember, oh, most gracious Virgin Mary . . . she began.

She heard a door open, and then footsteps. She crossed the room and entered the hall. William Curran came to her. He took her hand; she read the news in his face.

"Nothing to be done?" she asked.

"Nothing," he answered, and she marvelled at the power he had to convey an infinite kindness in economical statement. "Coyle is saying very sensible, right things to your father—and you'll know how to help him. Nurse will allow no one into your mother's room until I come back. I'll be here in an hour, to see her, and tell her whatever it is necessary for her to know."

"Then—her life is—over?"

"Very nearly. Oh, my dear!"

She turned away from him, made faint by sudden anguish in a heart that all this day had seemed stone-dead.

The two specialists were wanting to catch a train which left for Dublin at a quarter-past one, and therefore lunch had been arranged for noon.

It was one of those meals at which the act of swallowing seems impossible, and yet is somehow accomplished by everyone for everyone else's sake. Only the host,

whose ordinary life was made up of such placating and
self-neutralising behaviour, could not achieve it to-day,
and after a few inglorious attempts at normal, hospitable speech, suddenly broke into a sob and left the
room.

Agnes covered her face with her hand, and moved
her chair back involuntarily, as if to follow him. But a
hand was laid on her arm, and she looked up at Vincent,
standing by her side. He had just entered the room.

"No," he said to her very softly. "Let him be. It's
been choking him for months." And he sat down in
his usual place, still leaving his hand in the most
brotherly kindness on her arm.

Sir Godfrey, at her other side, assented gently.

"He will be better alone, Miss Mulqueen. Come
now, try to taste this wine."

She lifted her glass of Chablis, spilling some of it,
and trying to smile, so that Vincent had to turn away
sharply and make random conversation for his clerical
uncle-in-law.

"I've been out towards Bearnagh," he said.

Everyone leant on the helpful cue.

"Did you go shooting again?" Agnes asked, and Sir
Godfrey looked politely interested.

"No," said Vincent, taking the conversational
burden that they laid on him. "But I may go out after
duck to-morrow. I've heard of a lake up there——"

"Duck are very early birds, aren't they?" said Sir
Godfrey.

"Yes. Dawn-birds. I'm cleaning up some of the antique guns that they have here. If you were by any chance staying until to-morrow——?"

But the specialist shook his head. Strangely enough, he found he would be glad to go to-day. The visit, so sad in its purpose and results, so stimulating in its personal contacts, would be better over and done with and out of mind. The sooner an ageing, restless, conceited man, with an ageing, restless, conceited wife, forgot the soft, sweet Irish rose, the little fair fleck of sea foam that had carried him too far in foolish excitation overnight, the better. The sooner he lost sight of the worrying, tempting, irremediable, or perhaps entirely imaginary hint he caught of unhappiness between that lovely, virtuous creature and this cold and glorious-seeming god, her husband, the better for the peace of his quick but elderly mind. Yes, yes. There must be no duck-shooting. He must go to-day, and forget this sad house, which, tit-for-tat, had given him a flick of pain in payment for his helplessness before its own.

"No, alas!" he said, and could not yet forbear to turn to Marie-Rose and make her look at him. "This time to-morrow I don't exactly know where I shall be, but I certainly can't be here."

Marie-Rose took on the conversation gallantly.

"Well, I'm glad to feel sure that I'll be here," she said.

Reggie was also doing his best.

"If I had known that you were coming, Vin, I'd have got the guns put into decent condition for you——"

"I can get you some very good shooting any time," said the Canon.

So they got through the meal, and mercifully soon the carriage came round. The great medical visit which had been, as William Curran said, an immense emotional tax upon the house, was over. Dr. Coyle pressed Agnes's hand.

"I'll be down to her soon again, child. Be brave now and help her. And tell your father, tell your poor father——"

He turned and got into the carriage.

Sir Godfrey took her hand, and then the hand of Marie-Rose.

"If only——" he said, and did not seem to be clear as to his own meaning. But something of great kindness to her in his eyes struck straight on Marie-Rose's overwrought nerves. Tears flooded her eyes, and the Englishman fled from them into the dark carriage. As he was swept away from the house, he saw her husband bending, as if in gentleness, he had to admit, towards the little Irish rose.

Agnes, on the steps beside her sister and brother-in-law, watched the carriage out of sight, and heard Vincent's voice repeating quietly, hypnotically: "There'll be great sadness for a while and then it will be over. You'll see. Sadness for a while, Marie-Rose, and then no sadness. Anything that ends misery is bearable for a while. Only a little sadness—and then none."

Agnes looked at him, unconsciously taking consolation too from the gentle beating of his voice.

But what a dreamer he is, she thought, with envy and compassion.

The Third Chapter

IT was half-past one now. Time for Dr. Curran to return and see how his patient had borne the ordeal of the morning. Everything was quiet and orderly in her darkened room. Nurse Cunningham sat near the bed with her crochet, and glanced with kindness, almost with tenderness, every other minute at her charge.

Teresa lay quite still, very flat in the bed. Her eyes were shut. Her skin looked extraordinarily yellow against the white sheets, and all the clefts and caverns of her features were of a grotesque darkness. She looked like the corpse of someone who had been over-much beaten and driven into this belated peace. But the nurse knew that life was still rampant there—and even happy. She knew that tears, slow and tired, but still life's very convincing sign, were moving down the furrows of that dying face.

The nurse was not uneasy about this emotion which she had caused, in spite of the fact that the morning had already been severe. She knew that she had been skilful and considerate in timing the revelation of news which would, whenever delivered, overwhelm this hearer.

Teresa had been told in advance by Dr. Curran

that after their consultation he would for no reason whatever allow himself or his colleagues to return to her room, but that she was to rest absolutely and trust him to come back and bring her all the news and all the gossip in the early afternoon. He had had to have her as free of drug as possible for the consultation. Fortunately either her pain was particularly quiescent on this day or Teresa, her mind focused on other things, impossible hopes and prayers, was able to ignore it. But though she did not seem in pain, she was very restless about noon, and the restlessness grew, with mutterings and prayers. She asked repeatedly for Dr. Curran, complaining bitterly that she was kept so long in ignorance of the medical decision. "They must have an operation," she kept saying; "but they will, won't they, Nurse? And that'll give me a *little* more time, anyway. And maybe time would settle it—who knows? If they had a little longer thinking of it—oh, God! spare my life another while, till I see if there's any chance at all of helping him! Oh, dear and merciful Saviour! Why don't they come and tell me? Why doesn't that doctor come to me?"

Nurse Cunningham, listening, had decided that the narcotic which she could now administer was of a strength to nullify the news of "no operation" which the doctor was certain to bring. This morning, before the specialists' visit, Reggie had come to her in terror to be calmed, and she had found the courage then that had failed her overnight. He and she were now affianced. She knew, therefore, that she had real peace to offer, and decided to hold it back no longer. Very gently, very cautiously, she spoke to Teresa. And now, after a few minutes of an emotion that had alarmed her, experienced though she was, her patient had glided into an enchanted, holy peace. This woman who in middle life had seen her greatest treasure, the apple of her eye, destroy himself, and who had had to live watching the slow extension of that ruin, this woman who had borne the fluctuating tortures of three years of cancer, and now had about two months of pain and unreality to look to—at her eleventh hour, with no powers left her but those of faith and sentiment, was purely happy, entirely and childishly grateful to God, without pang or afterthought—because her ruined son would have a custodian when she was gone. God had heard her one prayer, her miserable, human and weak intercession, and where now in her almost lifeless body would she find strength to praise Him? He must wait until death released her soul from all these pains that did not matter now, but made her stupid. He must wait until in Purgatory, in Heaven, she might find the words to say: "Oh, but He was mighty and infinite of heart, the ever-merciful and omnipotent God, the King of Kings, the Son of Mary."

". . . But where is he? Won't they let him come to me until I kiss him, my boy, my darling? Oh, Reggie, Reggie—God is good. . . ."

Nurse Cunningham, listening, looking, and considerably moved by the happiness which her decision had brought, assured herself that she was giving good measure in return for what she might get. The bargain would be fair.

She heard the outer door of the dressing-room open and shut gently. Dr. Curran. She tiptoed through to him, and half-closed the communicating door.

His eyes were grave. For some reason his look of sane virility annoyed—she would not say hurt her.

"How is she feeling?" he asked softly.

"Very calm now. She was restless."

He raised his brows.

"Curious that she should be very calm. I haven't the news she was wanting, of course."

Nurse Cunningham was too well-trained to convey in her expression that she had known how it would be. The doctor leant against the window while the kettle heated on the spirit-lamp for his ritualistic hand-washing.

"You're tired," the nurse said. She had liked this man a good deal, and even now his visible preoccupation with another stung her.

"She's a brave creature," he said, "one can't quite take her in one's stride. Oh, it's been a strain, all this!"

"Yes. For more than you."

He turned. There was something that interested him in her tones.

"But of course. For her household—it's the most wearing sadness."

"You'll have to look after Miss Mulqueen. I think she'll be collapsing under things soon."

"She's very tired, I can imagine. But why do you say that?"

He knew she wanted the question from him—but he did not grudge her its gratification. He would always rise, wisely or foolishly, to talk of Agnes.

"Well, whether she's sleep-walking or what—I'm sure I don't know! But I saw her go downstairs and then across the garden just after midnight last night—in all that frost!—and it must have been getting on for three, I think, when she came back."

It occurred to him to point out that she, as a good nurse, would have recognised somnambulism, and would have gone in pursuit of the sleeper. But he did not wish to argue along such lines with her.

"Rash behaviour!" he said lightly. "But she *is* sleeping very badly, I believe." And he gave his whole attention then to washing his hands.

He found his patient, as the nurse had reported, very calm. Tiptoeing to her bedside, he stood looking down at her in silence for a few seconds before she opened her eyes to him. And, sensitive to all her phases, he felt that he was now to meet a new one, that she had changed in some immensely important way since his morning visit. He waited, wondering.

But when her eyes opened, and slowly, kindly

acknowledged him, he wondered still more.

"You're looking grand," he said gently, bending down to her.

She flickered her eyelids and her smile spread. He noticed the tears that were drying on her cheeks.

"I'm feeling grand," she whispered. "Oh, grand's the very word." She even tried to tease him. "I suppose you thought I was waiting for you anxiously?"

"Perhaps I flattered myself——"

"Well then, I wasn't. I don't want your fine operation after all." She smiled again directly at him. Her voice was very faint and croaky. "I don't want anything now—only to make my poor soul, and go in peace."

Her eyes closed. Her voice failed. He straightened his back, and let her rest. She was not dreaming. She couldn't be. She had had nothing to make her dream. Her eyes were sane and normal. And now they were open again, and as if compassionate of his surprise.

"I've nothing to trouble me now," she said, and then tried to beckon to Nurse Cunningham, who came at once and stood by her bed, facing the doctor. Teresa groped for her hand, which was given. "This child," she croaked, "this good girl says that she'll look after him for me. She—she knows everything—but she says she'll marry him. She says she's very fond of him— very fond of my poor boy——"

The happy eyes closed again. Slow tears moved once more along the furrows of the worn-out face.

Dr. Curran bent down.

"That's great news," he said, "and no wonder you're happy."

"No wonder," she answered, without opening her eyes. "She's a good girl. God will bless her."

"And now you must rest," the doctor said.

"Not until I see my boy. Not until I bless the two of them."

"All right. You may have a quiet visit from the family—to celebrate your news—and then a real, long rest, if you please."

He moved away from the bed and Nurse Cunningham followed him to the dressing-room. There, studying her closely and racking his brains for something friendly to say about this strange, grim turn in her affairs, he gave her some instructions. Her composure was absolute, and she did not seem to expect any personal conversation. Still, he felt sorry for her and wished he could choke out something. But a few minutes ago she had gone out of her way to injure Agnes in his eyes, and for that, though he pitied and marvelled, he was dumb against her now.

As he descended the last steps of the stairs, and was crossing the hall towards the dining-room, he met Vincent, and had the fantastic impression that he was being waylaid. He paused, though with reluctance, for he was in no mood for him. How haughty and pale the fellow was looking!

"You have quick wits, I believe, Dr. Curran?"

The doctor, furious at the tone and the silly question, kept calm nevertheless.

"Extremely quick," he said.

"May I borrow them?"

"Well, I'm busy——"

Vincent jerked that off impatiently.

"How long will you be in there?" he asked, and indicated the dining-room.

"Oh, ten, fifteen minutes."

"When you've finished, will you come up to the rose-garden, the garden-house?"

"If you really must see me, I will."

"I can count on you?"

"Yes." The doctor was irritated.

"And you'll bring your wits?"

"Unfortunately, I'm never able to shed them."

"I believe that," said Vincent, and turned away.

The Fourth Chapter

AGNES was not in the dining-room when the doctor entered it, but came there immediately after him. She had been with the other members of the family in the drawing-room, she said.

"They're wondering if they may see Mother, and they're afraid to see her."

"They needn't be afraid. I've told Nurse Cunningham they may pay her a quick, quiet visit now. They'll find her very happy."

"Happy?"

"Yes. Sit down—that's right. You look extremely tired."

"Happy? Is it that she doesn't know yet?"

"It's that she doesn't care now about her own fate— and no state of mind can be so happy, I should think. Listen. She had a curious piece of news for me just now—curious, but good. It seems that Nurse Cunningham is going to marry your brother."

Agnes's face became in a wave of lightning speed suffused in red, and then drained white again before a breath could be taken.

"Marry—Reggie?"

"Yes."

"But——"

"She knows about him. A formal marriage—which will give him companionship and a very competent protection and care. It's an excellent idea."

Agnes stood up.

"I think it's horrible——" she whispered.

"Nothing of the kind. It's a miraculous answer to all your prayers. She's a nurse and a woman of the world, and yet kind and livable with and human, and she wants to do it. She's made your mother absolutely happy."

"How queer!" Agnes said.

"You're being a bit sentimental," he suggested gently.

"But what motive can she possibly have?"

He smiled at the rich young woman who had never been poor and unprotected.

"Dear girl! Look round you! That hard-working creature upstairs has not known security since she was born, I imagine!"

"And she's prepared to marry—Reggie for money?"

"More admirable than to marry a better man for that reason."

Agnes fidgeted about the room. She was immensely confused, by her own horror and acknowledgment of its folly, by pity and bitter gladness for her mother, pity and distaste for her new sister-in-law—and a general, smudgy feeling of discomfort. She was not helped by the certainty that this man knew of those mixed sensations, and was resolute to tidy them up for her.

"In any case," his voice went on, "there is nothing dishonest in marrying for money."

"Oh, I'm not bothering about dishonesty!"

"Why bother about anything? There's nothing in this to bother about. It's a clear contract—as a marriage should be. In this the services which the wife will offer are not the usual ones, but they will be the more exacting for that. In return, perhaps her reward is more secure. Your brother is a rich man, and——"

"Please!"

"But you must listen to me——"

"I won't. I know you're talking sense—only I feel—dirty, somehow."

"You're cruel."

"I expect so. But be satisfied now. You've been very skilful in breaking the news and getting me to toe the line"—she smiled at him. "I promise not to be foolish and unhappy over it."

"You're beginning to know me," he said. "In any case, I was rather neatly blackmailed, as I see it now"—he smiled reminiscently—"into getting you to take the matter calmly."

She raised her delicate brows.

"Nurse Cunningham, fearful for your health, tells me that you spent most of last night in the garden. A clever move. She knows very well that I am far more human than gentlemanly. A gentleman would know that where you spend your nights is your business and not his, but an ordinary man who's in love with you won't be able to refrain from mentioning the curious news, in the hope—or fear—of an explanation. And so —because of his deplorable humanity—you know that you are in Nurse Cunningham's power up to a point, and she knows that you know, and that you won't be excessively haughty—as on occasion you can be— about her perfectly legitimate arrangement of her future."

"You sound as if you read Miss Braddon."

"Well, I do. And her heroines are always voluble in explanation of themselves."

"Oh, I'll explain. But not to-day. I can't be voluble to-day."

She dropped on to the window-seat and looked at him appealingly.

"Love, I was only joking," he cried, "or—half joking."

"It wouldn't make you happy—my explanation," she said.

"Well—if I could even think that it made you a little——"

She leant against the window-glass and kept looking out at the bare garden.

"No. It has nothing to do with happiness. I don't quite know what I mean—what I'm talking about."

"Don't try to. You're very tired."

There was silence now between them, broken only

by the whispering of the fire, and occasional soft foot-falls in the room above, her mother's room. Someone was potting at rooks again; someone was pacing a horse on the road.

"Have you ever noticed that some days are always themselves, year after year?" Agnes asked him idly. "Good Friday is like that. It's always the most exquisite, heart-breaking day, with a thrill in it that one is ashamed of. And All Souls' Day is like this—leaden and silent, and full of fear——"

"But the worst of to-day is over now, and for your mother it has turned out to be an intensely happy day."

"Yes. I wish I could feel that more."

"How do you feel?"

"Oh—All Souls' Day feeling! Cold and fright-ened——"

"I can't bear that."

"It'll pass. This news about—about Reggie is, funnily enough, a bit of a personal solution for me, I suppose."

"It will loosen your ties here, after your mother is gone."

"Yes. I could go away then—right out of his sight—without rousing suspicions or making a scene. Father and Reggie would be off my mind." She spoke idly, to herself, not to him.

"Out of his sight?"

"Yes." She turned and faced him, the truth and

its desolation in her face. "Vincent. Out of his sight."

"And what about mine?"

"Please!" The voice was small and pitiful. "I have no room in me for more trouble to-day."

He lost the sense of his own hunger for her, as so often by a mere trick of voice or attitude she could make him do. Lost it in apprehension of her hunger. Ah! the clumsiness of life to wound its best like this!

"To-day will pass, like any other day," he promised her.

"I'll be glad of that."

"Poor day!"

She laughed unsteadily. "Don't try to coax me," she said, with kindness. "That's what you're trying to do— and it's waste of time. I feel as if I had some kind of poison in me—as if I were dying here this minute— half dead."

"Ah, my dear heart!"

"Please, please! Oh, how I pity you!" She got up and gently brushed aside his begging hands. "I must go and see Mother. She'll wonder at my being so long."

She left him and went upstairs. On the corridor she met her father, who looked uneasy, worried. He paused before her and tried to read her face.

"Have you heard, my dear? Have you heard?"

"Yes, Father," she said, too weary to give him any clue to her feelings.

"It's for the best, my dear," he ventured. "It's for
the best, I think. Good news, child, good news."

She patted his hand.

"Yes," she said, "it's making her happy."

She passed on into the sick-room.

There are too many people here, she thought, with
a shock. Nurse Cunningham was crocheting beside
the fire, and Reggie stood and fidgeted in her vicinity.
His world, in wasteful fashion, had been rebuilt beneath his feet; Agnes, with a twinge of savage jealousy,
turned her eyes from him. Uncle Tom sat by her
mother's bed, and Marie-Rose, deft and quiet, stood
arranging flowers before the statue of Our Lady.

Too many people, Agnes thought again. They'll
exhaust her.

But the figure in the bed was very quiet, and the
face of her mother startled Agnes when she bent above
it. This is happiness, she thought, and wondered if
even here she did not grudge it.

"Mother darling," she said tenderly.

Teresa smiled at her.

"You know?" she croaked, and Agnes nodded.

"God is good," the broken voice went on. "Always
He is good. He never fails us."

Agnes looked at her uncle, and wondered what he
made of this answer to his intercessions. But his face
gave her no clue. His eyes were on Teresa, and his lips
moved in a prayer which he allowed to become audible.
"Tu rex gloriæ, Christe. Tu Patris sempiternus . . ."

"Du bist die Ruh," Marie-Rose sang under her breath.

Agnes thought: They are all alive, even Mother. But I'm dying. Vincent, if I could only die—oh, Vincent, darling——

The Fifth Chapter

VINCENT, walking towards the rose-garden, smiled at Dr. Curran's irritability, and had the impression of already considering it from the other side of death. But I can count on him, all the same, he thought. He has wits—that's quite true. He'll know exactly what I mean.

He entered the little dark garden-house and sat down on the bench. He looked about it with a sense of affection and familiarity, for he seemed now to have lived a long time in association with it. He felt very tired, and was glad that there was no more thinking to do. All that was over, that long soliloquy that had begun when her kiss ended—how many hours or days ago? He believed that he had slept a little, dreamt a little, during it. But that had not seemed to break the thread of thought.

The potentialities of simple things were vast, he thought. A gun—his eyes rested on several—could accomplish a number of simple and complicated things, and a rose—he looked out at the frozen bushes —could be any fool's delight or the symbol which in love and poetry and mysticism it was. People were always kissing each other—and no bones broken—and then she kissed you.

He went to the table, where three guns lay that he had been cleaning. Like a careful stage manager he appraised the table's effect, the opened oil-bottle, the scattered rags. The Snyder, with its breach open and empty. The little old Westbury Richards, which had a defective piston spring, loaded. He, a gun expert, had discovered how to control this defect, but it could be made to seem a source of accident. He touched the Spencer repeater, but then picked up the Westbury Richards again. A short, awkward weapon—its eccentricities and age attracted him. He carried it to the door of the hut, raised it and killed a hurrying rook. Reluctantly he put it back upon the table.

He took off his coat and threw it on the floor. He smeared the oil-rags on his hands and ruffled up his hair.

Everything was in order. His affairs and his will. But they always were. It would be a grief for everyone—and then it would be over, and they could live. No one but she—and her quick-witted lover—would dream that it was not an accident. For even if it crossed Marie-Rose's mind, Agnes, the cherisher, would know how to scotch the thought. But it wouldn't. Marie-Rose *knew* him, she would say, and did not know how deep was the misery of their marriage. All the better time for going. No suspicion anywhere. But in a house already so troubled—was it a very fine cruelty to add this shock of sadness? Perhaps, but Teresa was near death, and much protected by morphia; it would not really reach her heart or make much difference now. And for the others, the sooner they can flower again, with all their sorrows buried—why, the better. Now is the time, he insisted to himself, when they have given me coroner's evidence of accident with general talk of shooting and cleaning old guns. Now is the time—while I still know how to love her and the only honest way to give her up. It must be *now*. I cannot take her terms. I cannot live to torture her. If she takes another and is happy in my sight, oh, God, you see, you know! And if I drive her out of sight, and waste and spoil her! But that's impossible. She'll find this cruel, what I do. She won't know what to think at first, or where to turn. She'll cry——

He sat on the bench and shut his eyes. To his own amazement he was trembling and sobbing now. Oh, it was madness to think about her tears—it was the straight way back to sanity, the road he could not take.

He stood again—in frozen calm. His eyes were glazed as if sightless. He had done with life—for every good reason, not all of them cruel or selfish. It was his own affair if he put his own valuation on one girl. There was no explanation except in him, and he must be allowed it. His mother would listen to him and call him no hard names. And he would find her soon—in spite of the sin he was going to commit. Yes, it was a sin—but would God show him an alternative? To end things in one crime, or to live in an unending vulgar guilt? Agnes would see what he meant. Oh, surely Agnes would? He was going to hurt her almost to death, and still, in the end, she would see and understand. Hurt, or dead, or what you will, he was safe with her. And life and death didn't really matter, in a way, once you knew that.

He closed his glazed, tired eyes. Last night, last night. He would think of it for only one minute more. He laid his hands on the Richards, and remembered the stars of last night's sky, which would take their happy places again to-night. Perseus he had noticed, but not Andromeda. And Orion's sword was clear. Then she had come, her eyes defeating all the planets, and her breath had been like a white wreath. "I've come to ask a favour," she had said. Oh, Agnes, Agnes, I ask a favour now. I ask for evermore your dear forgiveness. I ask you the impossible, you gentle heart—that you won't cry or grieve for me. But understand! Oh, Agnes—understand! Don't cry! Don't cry! Be merciful, and promise not to cry! My love, forgive me!

He leant upon the gun, reflecting that the essential was to hit the brain, making it seem as if the weapon had gone off while he bent over it to adjust the inessential screw he had this morning loosened. So long as Curran took his cues up firmly—ah, he was tired. The metal was getting warm against his face. No need to press upon the muzzle. That would seem unnatural. He could stand straighter and trust his aim. Last

night. Dear love, last night—*Du bist die Ruh. Die Ruh.*
He remembered leaning on a gun in the garden at
home on a sunny day, leaning like this, and talking
to his mother. It was summer and she was sewing. She
had said: "Don't lean on it, Vin. It will mark your
face." Darling mother. He smiled. He could see
every detail of her smile. Darling mother. He pulled
the trigger, his thoughts far off in boyhood.

THE END

Limerick. January 18th, 1934.